PEOPLE of the LAKE

PEOPLE of the LAKE

NICK SCORZA

Sky Pony Press
New York

Sky Pony Press books may be purchased in bulk at special discounts for sales promotion, corporate gifts, fund-raising, or educational purposes. Special editions can also be created to specifications. For details, contact the Special Sales Department, Sky Pony Press, 307 West 36th Street, 11th Floor, New York, NY 10018 or info@skyhorsepublishing.com.

Sky Pony® is a registered trademark of Skyhorse Publishing, Inc.®, a Delaware corporation.

Visit our website at www.skyponypress.com.

10 9 8 7 6 5 4 3 2 1

This product conforms to CPSIA 2008

Library of Congress Cataloging-in-Publication Data is available on file.

Cover design by Kate Gartner
Cover photo credit iStock

Hardcover ISBN: 978-1-5107-4516-2
Ebook ISBN: 978-1-5107-4517-9

Printed in the United States of America

"What would your feelings be, seriously, if your cat or your dog began to talk to you, and to dispute with you in human accents? You would be overwhelmed with horror. I am sure of it. And if the roses in your garden sang a weird song, you would go mad. And suppose the stones in the road began to swell and grow before your eyes, and if the pebble that you noticed at night had shot out stony blossoms in the morning?"
—Arthur Machen, "The White People"

PEOPLE of the LAKE

I.

The first bus took me as far as Ithaca. It was full of college students going back for summer classes, or else just trying to get away from their families. I sunk lower in my seat, feeling too young and out of place—a stowaway in a world I couldn't wait to be part of. I just had to survive two more years at Queens Academy for Inhumanity, not to mention a summer with my dad.

As all the students left the station, they laughed about things I wished I could laugh at too—jokes I was sure would be hilarious if I were just a bit more adult. Instead, I unfolded the schedule I'd printed, frayed and deformed from hours in my pocket, and looked for the bus that would take me to my father.

When I finally found it at the other end of the station, I checked the ticket and the schedule three times to make sure I'd found the right vehicle. It looked more like an airport courtesy shuttle someone had decided to drive off into the country and commandeer for the local bus service, but it was definitely the right bus.

On board, I smelled cigarette smoke and cheap air freshener—the neon-orange pine tree kind. The only other occupant was an old man, smoking in defiance of the bright red NO SMOKING sign and muttering to himself.

We sat there for half an hour while I fretted that I had somehow mixed up the numbers or the bus lines when a sour, middle-aged woman in a gray uniform finally clambered onto the bus. She looked at each of us, as if giving us one last chance to get off, before grunting once and turning the ignition.

The bus hummed to life, rattling in a way that was less than reassuring, and for at least the fiftieth time that day, I wondered if I was making a terrible mistake. There was still time to hop out and catch the next ride back to the city. I looked at my phone, thought about calling, then put it away again. Things at home would be just the same as when I left, maybe worse. The Woodchuck had probably moved his stuff into our apartment as fast as possible so my mother couldn't change her mind, and I bet he was already sprawled across the sofa asking her what was for dinner.

Anger had taken me this far, and it seemed able to take me a little further yet. There was a new feeling, though— an anxious twist in my insides at the thought of seeing my father. Since the divorce, I'd only seen him for two birthdays and two Christmases, or more accurately on the nearest weekends before or after those days. This would be the first time I stayed with him—and I wouldn't have friends or a whole city to fall back on if I couldn't deal with the memories. Dad was quiet, and when things were quiet for too long, I couldn't keep my mind from drifting to thoughts of Zoe. This trip was exactly the kind of crazy, impulsive adventure my twin sister would have loved, which made it even harder to be doing it without her.

There was something else, too. Somehow, even before the fight with my mother, I had this feeling I was supposed to come out here, to see the place my father grew up. The place he never used to talk about but went running back to as soon as my parents' marriage fell apart.

Before I knew it, the bus had left Ithaca behind and was wending its way through one of those state roads that isn't a highway but isn't a normal street either. On either side, the trees grew taller and denser, until we were riding through a tunnel of green and gold light. Sometimes the tree-cover would suddenly clear on one side, and we'd look out over an expanse of wooded valley fading to blue in the distance before plunging back into the forest. I laughed quietly to myself. This bus was taking me farther from home than I'd ever been without my family along. It was like falling— totally free and yet only one way to go.

The bus passed through a tunnel in the hills, and for a moment, the green half-light was replaced by darkness.

When we emerged, the forest was different—the trees seemed older, knotted and bent and dense with vines. We passed a whole section of forest that had been taken over by some kind of invasive creeper, a great mass of dark and impenetrable green. Then we left the state road for an even narrower country lane. I thought that meant we were close, but there was at least an hour more to go. My anger at my mother faded a little, and I thought about how long I'd last

3

out here before I took the trip back to civilization. Then I thought about the Woodchuck making us watch the latest prescription drug commercial he was in, and I resolved to become a good country girl.

I got drowsy as the bus rattled along, half-asleep on a seat that felt like it was upholstered in stiff motel carpet. I had uneasy dreams of Zoe, and all the times she'd made me follow her down dark wooded paths in the little park by the house we grew up in. She had this way of making even a leafy New Jersey suburb seem like a grim enchanted forest. At the darkest part, she'd always look back, daring me to follow—a wicked half-smile on a face identical to mine.

"*Arala mir*," she whispered in my dreams—"Follow me," in the secret language we made up together—before she vanished down a tree-lined trail and left me scrambling after her, always hoping to catch up beyond the next bend. All my life, I'd been running after her, until the day she finally left me behind.

When I woke up, groggy and bleary-eyed, the bus was pulling in to what looked like an old New York City bus stop. It was as out of place as the lamp post in Narnia, a little bit of the city stuck way out here in the country—the town's one reminder of a wider world.

Redmarch Lake—I had been calling it Lake Podunk in my head since my father moved there (Dr. Bellamy said it was due to resentment from my parents' divorce—I said, gee, ya think?). Now that I was here, I swore myself to no urban snark, no Queens-girl attitude, for at least a few days. These people didn't need my sarcastic comments about what looked like a lovely little town, even if I couldn't guess why my father chose it over New York City where his daughter lived.

The bus dropped me in the tiny town square area, and already I saw a café and a few shops and restaurants. Down a steep little cobblestone street, I could just glimpse a strip of blue that must have been the lake. The sidewalks were lined with trees and flowers, and there was a statue of what looked like a Revolutionary War officer in the middle of the square. Everything looked like it had stayed just like this for decades. I thought of what Zoe would do if she were here with me—no doubt she'd be grabbing my hand and pulling me off to explore the lake, but I didn't have time to act on the impulse. I caught sight of my father getting out of his car and hurrying over to me.

Because I didn't see him very often, he looked older every time—aging like a flip book with a little less hair and a few more lines under the eyes each visit; but he still had the sad eyes and shy, little-boy smile my mother said first drew her to him. He gave me a big hug and a kiss, and he told me how wonderful it was to see me.

"I talked with your mother, and I know I shouldn't be happy given the circumstances, but damn it, it's good to see you. Let me show you the house."

As we drove through the town, he pointed out the café, the diner, a Chinese restaurant, and a fancy one with white tablecloths that people went to on special occasions.

"Used to be a hotel," said my dad. "This was a tourist destination for a little while, in the 1920s."

I imagined flappers and jazz bands jitterbugging all over the streets, and wished I could have seen it then. A minute later, we were out of the town center and driving along a little country road. The trees on one side parted and I caught my first glimpse of the lake. It was nowhere near the size of the Finger Lakes, which were near here, but it was beautiful: bright blue and calm as a mirror, surrounded by deep green swathes of trees and gray, rocky cliffs.

There was something eerie about how still it all was—like I wasn't looking at the real lake, just a picture of it. I almost expected to see VISIT SCENIC REDMARCH LAKE floating in the sky—a postcard come to life.

There was a little island near the far side, a rocky outcropping crowned with some kind of ruin. Behind it on the shore was an old mansion at the top of a hill surrounded by rows of grapevines.

"Wow, it's beautiful—but that's not quite the right word. It's more, I don't know, intense?"

"That's true," my father said.

His expression changed when I brought up the lake. He went pale and made a kind of nervous swallowing noise.

"You . . . well—I wanted you to come here, but you maybe shouldn't have. . . . I mean, you shouldn't fight with your mother like that."

I felt all my anger flood back. My parents barely spoke to each other, and now they tried to put up some kind of unified front, even with my mother moving in with another man? They were still ganging up on me, and without Zoe by my side, it wasn't a fair fight. Just then, absurdly, I hated her for dying and leaving me to deal with my parents' stupid divorce all alone. Then, of course, I hated myself for thinking that. I felt like I lost half of me when I lost Zoe, yet I could still manage to be selfish.

"I thought you were glad I was here," I said.

"No, I want you here, I just . . . I wish it were under different circumstances. Never mind, it's good that you came."

Already my father's need to paper over every conflict was making my blood start to boil. I hated to let things simmer unsaid. Whatever was bothering him, I wished he would tell me.

"Mom's boyfriend is moving into our home. Why are you worried about pissing her off?"

My father was silent for a long moment, as if desperately searching for a way to say something he'd never put into words before. From the look on his face, he didn't succeed.

"It's not that. I just worry you won't like it here. It gets a little odd out here on my own. I start worrying about all kinds of things."

Now it was my turn to be quiet. I'd been thinking of Mom and the Woodchuck on the whole ride down and trying not to dwell on Zoe. I hadn't given any thought to what my dad was going through out here alone. Still, no one had forced him to move back.

I took one last look at the weird, still lake as we drove along its shore. This place was doing bad things to my father.

Even though he was already driving me crazy, I was glad I was here to keep him company, if only for the summer.

Dad had a little wooden house on a leaf-shadowed street at the edge of town. I said little, but it was still bigger than Mom's two-bedroom in Forest Hills (which would feel even smaller now that it was thoroughly Chucked). It had a wide front porch and a back yard with deck chairs and a grill—all things I hadn't had since the place in Jersey when I was little. Dad's house was painted brown with white trim, and I couldn't help but think of it as gingerbread— not that my father was a witch, more like a grown-up Hansel moved back to the witch's house.

Dad showed me around without saying much of anything. He had quiet spells—once one of them came on, he just wouldn't talk for a while. He worked from home as some sort of data management consultant. To be honest, I didn't really understand what he did, but I worried that he didn't leave the house enough. He didn't even have a pet for company. After he quietly showed me the living room, the kitchen, and the room that would be mine, he seemed to forget whatever had made him regret my visit, and I tried not to let it get to me.

Against my will, I texted my mother to tell her I arrived safely. She responded *Good, we'll talk when you're ready*. I thought about adding something snarky about Chuck, but I was honestly tired of thinking about it. Avoiding that whole situation was the whole reason I was here—that and making sure Dad was okay.

My father made fish sticks and mac and cheese for dinner like I was still a little girl, but I didn't object, and we watched old movies as the sun set and the fireflies winked and danced in the back yard. So far, life in the country wasn't bad, as long as we didn't acknowledge all the family drama.

After a while, Dad started feeling talkative again, asking me about my friends and where we liked to go in the city. Questions like that always brought me back to those first horrible years after losing Zoe, and all the ways my parents had tried to monitor my moods and push me to rejoin a world I had never been part of in the first place. I gave Dad a few vague answers—he was always easier to appease than my mother. Then, to my surprise, he asked how Mom was doing. He kept his tone the same, but I could tell it was hard for him to bring up.

I thought of everything that had led me here and made a sour face.

"You already know about Chuck," I said.

My father nodded.

"He doesn't make you . . . . uncomfortable, does he?"

It took me a moment to realize what my father meant by this. When I shook my head, he visibly relaxed.

"He's never been creepy toward me, unless you count stupid jokes as creepy. He . . . I don't know, he puts his feet up on the coffee table, he sleeps way late when he's over, which I guess is all the time now. And he leaves his crap everywhere. He doesn't act like a grownup. I have no idea how he conned Mom into this."

"Clara, I think you should give him a chance. I don't know him, and I don't care to, but he makes your mother happy, and that wouldn't be the case if he weren't a good person in some way."

I couldn't believe what I was hearing. Charlie Woods had to drive my dad nuts, but here he was trying to act like he was above it all—and talking down to me on top if it.

"What the hell, Dad. You can't be this relaxed about the whole thing. Another man is moving into your home! Maybe if you'd fought back, all of this would be different!"

My father looked ready to shout something back at me, but his mouth just hung open and nothing came out. Even now, with me, he would rather be silent than deal with anything hard. I couldn't stand it. I got up and ran to the room he'd set up for me, slamming the door behind me.

Way to go, Clara, I imagined Zoe whispering to me, *off to a great start.*

"He's impossible," I muttered. "Why does he have to keep pretending everything is okay?"

He means well. I could imagine her replies as if she were right there with me—sometimes it was the only thing that kept me going. *You know how much he loves you.*

I sighed. Even my imaginary recollection of my sister was lecturing me. I shouldn't have yelled at Dad, even if I did have a right to be angry.

Imagining what Zoe would say about my life today was a defense mechanism I'd worked out with a series of therapists. Having a twin means never having to be alone—most people who don't have one can't grasp that, or what it's like to lose it. Dwelling on our memories together left me mired hopelessly in my own head, cut off from the world—but banishing her from my thoughts was too painful, too much like losing her all over again. Trying to carry her with me through my life was an uneasy compromise, but it was the only way I could go on. And of course she was usually right about things like this.

The room Dad had set up for me had everything I'd need for a long stay: a bed and a dresser and even a desk stocked with pens and pencils. It was nice, though it reminded me a bit of middle school. It made me wonder how long my father had had this room set aside in hopes I'd come visit. He could have asked sooner, or at all, if that was what he wanted.

There was a picture of me on top of the dresser, maybe six years old, in a little plaid dress with ribbons in my hair. Somehow dad had found one of the few childhood pictures of me without Zoe. Or more likely he'd cropped her out of the picture, which was just too hard to think about— my twin sister erased from my life. I guess I couldn't blame him. I tried to imagine her with me, making new memories together, but I couldn't imagine looking at her picture every day, staring straight into the face of everything we'd lost.

I wondered if Zoe and I would still look so alike if she were alive. They say twins look less and less identical as they grow. Life makes its mark on everyone. Back then, we'd been total mirror images: the same wavy, espresso-colored hair and matching eyes from our mother, the same pale Anglo-Irish skin from our father. Maybe by now she'd have grown half an inch taller than me, or dyed her hair pink for the hell of it. Maybe I'd be confident enough to do something like that, if losing her hadn't messed me up.

Neither of my parents ever talked about her. They never even mentioned her name. I had started my life with a perfect double, another me who shared everything I was, all up until that horrible day I would never forget, eight summers ago. It was like scissors cutting my life in half: Zoe and post-Zoe. Now I mostly knew her by the ache of her absence, like they say amputees felt the pain of their missing limbs, and tried to keep her with me in my thoughts, even though I knew it was just a pale reflection.

Sometimes I saw her in my dreams, just lying there still, and in those dreams I couldn't tell which of us was dead and which one was alive.

I couldn't sleep. My head was full of bad memories, and I couldn't relax in this strange bedroom. Even sleeping without her was hard, all these years later. The rhythm was off. The world was too silent.

Back then, the nights had belonged to the two of us, and we would stay up late whispering, daring each other not to laugh. We spoke in our secret language, and Zoe made up stories of the world beyond the mirror and our adventures there, dancing with the wood sprites or running from the wicked king, fooling everyone into thinking we were one girl who could be in two places at once.

She was always the more creative one, the bolder one, waking me at midnight, pulling me along by the hand. Even though we were the same in almost every way, I sometimes felt so gray and ordinary beside her. Sometimes I had even hated her for it. Now, without her, it felt like the whole world was gray. Now there was just me, alone and unable to sleep.

Quietly, I slipped out into the living room. My father was gently snoring on the couch with the TV still on. I shouldn't have yelled at him, but I wished just once he'd fight back instead of pretending to be so zen about everything. Trying not to disturb him, I shut off the TV and tiptoed out the sliding door to the back porch.

There were still a few ghostly firefly lights in the yard, and a cloud of moths battering themselves against the porch light. Further out, in the woods behind the house, I could hear what must have been an army of crickets filling the night with a cacophony of chirps.

I sat in one of the deck chairs and let the cool breeze and the sound of the crickets wash over me. I was far from home, I had no idea what would happen next, and I wouldn't let bad memories steal that from me. Up above, the night sky was full of more stars than I'd ever seen. I could make out Ursa Major, and a few others I knew must have been something, though I couldn't guess what. Instead I made up my own constellations—Damien the Duck, star-sign for procrastinators, highly compatible with Stella the Wombat, who represented sarcasm.

I wondered which one of the real constellations was Gemini. I was glad I didn't know.

Suddenly, the crickets were quiet. Everything in the forest was still but the breeze. Time seemed to hang there

13

for a tense moment, as if we were all hushed, waiting for something bad to happen, or for it to go away.

Then there was a rustle deeper in the woods, and the sound of twigs snapping. Something big was moving, getting closer. I felt a cold wave of animal panic, species memory telling me to run like hell. I didn't wait to see what it was. I ran back inside and bolted the door, pulling the curtain shut behind me.

Hours later, too exhausted for fear, I finally fell asleep.

II.

The next morning, I forgot where I was, and for a second I lay in bed transfixed by the strange sound of birdsong and the pale, clean light of a country morning, before my brain kicked in and I remembered why I was here. Sun and birdsong seemed a long way from whatever I heard moving around in the forest last night. I took a cautious peek out the window. The woods still looked dark and eerie in the morning fog, like under those dense branches the night had never really ended. I probably wouldn't be taking any morning walks through the forest, never mind a midnight ramble.

Out in the kitchen, my father had made coffee already—instant, to my poorly concealed dismay. I'd have to do something about that if I was going to last the summer. At least the cupboard was well-stocked with cereal. Good to see he remembered how much I hated hot breakfast.

Dad gave me a little wave when he saw me. I waited for him to say something about the fight last night. I'd probably have to wait all day—silence never drove him crazy like it did me and Mom.

"Dad, I'm sorry for yelling at you like that."

"It's okay, honey. I'm sorry, too."

I almost asked him just what he was sorry for, but that would start things up all over again. I rarely saw my dad angry, but that didn't mean I wanted to. I hoped my visit would make us both feel better, not worse. I changed the subject.

"Dad, I couldn't sleep last night, so I went out back to look at the stars. I think I heard something big moving in the woods."

My father's lips pursed in a nervous grimace. It took him a moment to answer.

"Probably a deer," he said, "or maybe a coyote. Those things are spreading all over the country. I heard they even make it into Manhattan sometimes."

I smiled, imagining neurotic urban coyotes hanging out in Central Park, complaining about all the tourists even though they'd just moved to the city. It seemed miles away from whatever had filled me with prey-animal fear last night.

"Clara, what you heard was probably harmless, but I want you to do me a favor and not wander in the woods around here. It can be dangerous."

"Dangerous how?"

"It stays dark in there, and it's easy to get lost. It's not a state park. There are no paths, at least not reliable ones. Plus, you know, there are lyme ticks and black widow spiders and things like that."

We're going, I imagined Zoe whispering, *he doesn't have to know.* After what I'd seen last night, I was in no hurry to listen to her.

I nodded.

"Now I'm sorry to say I have to work today, sweetheart." My dad did look genuinely sorry, though I bet he was glad I wouldn't be asking him any more questions. "Otherwise I'd take you into town. When this project is done in a day or two, though, we'll go hiking or to some of the vineyards a few towns over—they're really nice. For today, you can borrow the car if you get bored. Downtown is just a few minutes' drive."

"You don't have to worry about me. I invited myself, remember?"

He didn't know what to say to that; he just smiled, a helpless look in his eyes. He was so eager to make me happy and so afraid of failing I could punch him in the face. Anything to make him be normal, and maybe deal with everything he was going through with the divorce. Instead, I looked away, and he went back to his computer.

The living room walls were lined with bookcases— shelves and shelves of them Dad had never had room for in the city. I looked through some of the titles, hoping to find something good to read. There weren't many novels. Most of it was history from the area—the Iroquois Confederacy and the French and Indian War and American Revolution and all that stuff. There were a few volumes of local folk tales and ghost stories I'd probably come back and read later.

"Oh, that stuff's for a pet project," my dad said.

"Are you gonna write a book or something?"

"Nothing big, just a history of the town."

It was a strange moment, realizing how little I knew my own father. He never brought up this town when I was little, and if Zoe or I asked about it, he'd quickly change the subject. I had no idea he cared about history, or would ever try to write about it. Not only that, but some of his research was pretty odd—one cheaply-bound book claimed to present hard evidence that fairies were really aliens that had been living side-by-side with humans since the dawn of time. I flipped through some of the others. There were a few books on something called ley lines, and a multi-volume history of mediums and spiritualism in New York State. I quickly scanned the shelf for a tinfoil hat. My father was starting to worry me.

"Is this for real?" I said.

"Yeah, I mean no, not literally. I'm more interested in why people believe in things like that," he said, "especially around here."

I waited for him to tell me more, but he quickly turned back to his computer. When I realized that was his way of ending the conversation, I announced I was going into town, and he handed me the car keys.

I'm glad he didn't stop to think about how rarely I drove. I'd been behind the wheel maybe twice since getting my license. In the seven years since we moved to Queens, I'd become a city girl—half my friends didn't even bother with licenses. I adjusted the seats and the mirrors and did all the things you were supposed to—hands at ten and two and all that—but I still drifted in the lane, and went much, much slower than necessary. If the local police saw me, they'd probably think I was stoned. I could see the headline now—"City Girl Busted on Country Road. Is it Reefer Madness?"

Luckily, Dad was right. It didn't take me more than a few tense minutes to make it to the town center. I was glad there was plenty of street parking; I'd barely passed that part of the road test.

The first thing I did was walk down to the lake. The far side was still veiled in morning fog, and a chill wind made me wish I'd brought a cardigan. The breeze made the leaves rustle in the trees, but it never stirred the surface of the water. It was a perfect mirror. When I stared down, I saw my face staring back up, clear as glass.

I walked up and down the little waterfront promenade, which was paved with cobblestone and studded with wrought-iron lamp posts. I couldn't believe Redmarch Lake wasn't on one of those online travel lists—top 15 Unknown New York Weekend Trips. Most of the rich kids at school had summer houses in Westchester or Long Island, in quaint little towns on the Hudson or the Sound (I was guessing—I'd never been invited). I always pictured them looking just like this. It was kind of far from the city, but this town was so pretty I couldn't imagine why it didn't have summer tourists. Even the weirdness of the lake was creepy in a picturesque way.

I looked around until I found a loose stone. Something about the stillness of the surface of the lake was really bothering me. I held the stone in my hand, and held my hand out over that smooth surface. It felt wrong, like talking in church, but then I thought, *This is crazy, it's just a lake.*

I let the stone drop.

It vanished with a little splash. There was a tiny ripple, then everything was still again.

I felt absurdly like I'd just thrown a rock through a window, and I was going to regret it. I backed away from the lake.

As I hurried up the hill toward the town square, I gave it one last look—just to make sure nothing had moved. Maybe it was stupid, but I felt uneasy turning my back to the lake. The fog had rolled back a bit on the far side, and I could see the little rocky island, crowned with one broken-tooth pillar jutting into the sky.

Back in the town square, I took a closer look at the statue in the center. It was cast in dark bronze, and at first, it looked just like every other horse and rider statue, but the man's face was odd. He was smiling or grimacing in a really strange way. Even in bronze, the eyes were wide and piercing. It almost looked like the rider was laughing as he prepared to trample you with his horse. The plaque below read *Capt. Broderick Redmarch, Founder.* Beneath the name was a strange little symbol made of sinuous lines like a nest of snakes. I originally thought it was some kind of graffiti, but it was cast in bronze just like the name.

Turning away from the creepy statue, I noticed some of the shops and the café had opened. I walked into a vintage clothing store called New Again, curious to see what kinds of things they had.

"I think you want the café," a young woman, visibly pregnant, said as soon as I walked in. She squinted at me, as if trying to make sure I was really there. I noticed her hand drift down to something behind the counter. Did she think I was going to rob her?

"I just wanted to look around."

"I don't think we'll have anything you'd like."

Her disgust was evident in the curl of her lip, but her eyes almost looked frightened. Now that she could see I was real she was looking at me like I was a weird bug. Who the hell did she think she was? I was this close to letting the Queens out and casting all sorts of aspersions on the paternity of her unborn child.

I took a deep breath. I had promised to leave the snark at home. I didn't need to make enemies on my first day in town, no matter how bad they were asking for it. Instead, I just gave her a *drop dead* look and walked out.

I told myself it wasn't my fault. The town must have a shoplifting problem—the sort of thing that happens when kids my age don't have enough to do. Still, part of me kept thinking that she knew me—or knew of me—and didn't like me. Clara Morris, terror of Redmarch Lake. Public enemy numero uno. I laughed to myself, glad the street was still empty.

Let's put spiders in her clothes, I imagined Zoe whispering. Always looking for a way to cheer me up.

The café was called Clyde's Coffee Cup. The handmade sign featured a cartoon cat licking his lips over a huge caffe latte. When I walked in, I saw that Clyde was real—an old, jowly longhaired cat that looked decidedly less happy than the sign out front. He gave me a sour stare

21

when the chimes on the door rang, then went back to his pillow by the window. Apparently he was the hands-off sort of manager.

The guy behind the counter was my age, wiry and hatchet-faced but still kind of cute. His eyes widened when he saw me, like I'd just walked into his living room instead of the place he worked.

"W-what's your name?"

"Clara."

A minute later, he remembered he was on the job, and he looked at the floor while he asked me what I wanted. I ordered a cappuccino. My friend Rayna once said I was the only person our age who liked real coffee, not the chocolate and whipped cream stuff everyone else drank. I'd struck my best movie star pose and said, "That's because it's like me—hot and bitter." At the time, I was sorry Rayna was the only one around to hear that, but now I was kind of glad.

"I'm Neil," the boy said when he handed me my coffee. It was too much foam, not enough espresso, and a little burnt, but otherwise not bad. "Have I seen you somewhere before?"

I raised an eyebrow at the question. He clearly thought I looked familiar, the way he was staring at me.

"I don't think so, this is my first time here. I'm just visiting my father for the summer."

"Your father lives here?"

He was taken totally off guard, like before I said this he'd thought I was someone else entirely. He actually seemed to relax a bit.

"Yeah," I said. "Tom Morris. He grew up here too."

"No way. You're Tom's daughter? He used to come in here sometimes."

Evidently he didn't any more, which was too bad. I had to get dad out of the house somehow. It wasn't healthy for him to spend so much time at home alone.

The café was actually fairly pleasant. The walls were painted a pastel yellow, and there was a square of watery sunbeam slowly migrating across the floor from a skylight in the middle of the ceiling. One of the walls was covered with literary quotations in all different sorts of fonts—a coffee shop cliché, but I was prepared to let it slide. I could see myself becoming a regular here, if Neil would stop staring at me. He went through the motions of cleaning the espresso machine and brewing a new pot of decaf, but every so often I'd feel his eyes on me and look up to see him quickly turn away.

What was his deal? I was mostly happy with the way I looked, but I wasn't any kind of *femme fatale*. Every so often, I'd hear rumors at school that so-and-so thought I was cute, but that was always the word they used: cute, not hot. Maybe things were different in a little town like this, or maybe it was something else entirely.

Neil didn't seem like a creeper—more confused than anything else, looking at me like I was making him question his own sanity. Not exactly the effect I was going for when meeting new people.

"Everything okay over there?" I said.

"Yeah. Sorry, this place gets too quiet sometimes. The whole town does. And we don't get many new people."

I guess that was an invitation, because a minute later he came over and sat across from me.

"Sorry, I hope I'm not bothering you, it's just . . . people aren't very friendly here if they don't know you. It's like they can't handle a new face. It drives me crazy. Ranting at you about it isn't much better, I know."

Neil fidgeted when he talked, sometimes looking over at the door. I couldn't tell if he was nervous or just enthusiastic. In any case, there was something endearingly real in his awkwardness—something that stood out in this town, where so far nothing else quite felt real.

"Oh no, I already know what you mean," I said. "The lady at that New Again place basically threw me out of her store as soon as I walked in."

Neil frowned.

"That's exactly what I mean. Don't take it personally. They just don't know how to deal with new people. I hope they don't drive you off."

Well, at least there was one nice person in this town, even if he was a little odd.

"Hey Neil, could I ask you something? Why are there no summer tourists here, or rental houses on the lake, that sort of thing? Someone could probably make a killing out here; this town is really pretty."

He gave me a look that was so utterly befuddled I might as well have asked why more aliens didn't visit from outer space. Then again, maybe aliens were the sort of tourists they *did* get.

"I guess because of the Redmarch family. You've seen

the mansion on the other side of the lake? They own the bank and the quarry, and a lot of the lakefront land, and I think they like it better without tourists."

"I saw the statue in the square," I said, shuddering as I remembered the cruel expression on its face. "Is that really the same family?"

"Yeah, they go way back."

Neil looked really nervous while he said this, his eyes wandering back to the door.

"I can't say I blame them for wanting privacy, I'm just surprised. It would probably be a goldmine."

"Well, from what I hear, they have plenty of money already," Neil said.

The chime on the door rang, and Neil jumped up and ran back to serve a middle-aged couple that wandered in. He greeted them by name, and they seemed happy to see him, but they each gave me a suspicious stare. Neil turned and mouthed the word *sorry* to me while he poured their iced coffees. When I finished the last foamy sip of my cappuccino, I waved goodbye and walked out.

I had taken two steps out the door when I felt a hand on my shoulder. I whirled, ready to punch someone if I had to—city instincts—but it was just Neil.

"I'm sorry about that. People will be nicer once they know your father lives here."

"Is this whole town members-only or something?"

"It might as well be," he said. "Though I can't think why anyone would want to join. Listen, I hope you'll come back. Don't let them keep you away."

"Oh, I won't," I said, giving it more of a Queens accent than I actually had.

"I don't doubt it," he said. "See you later."

He was definitely odd, but he was nice, and that went a long way.

I walked around the rest of the town for a while. I didn't feel like heading home just yet. There wasn't much to see. A few of the other shops were still closed, and I wondered if they ever opened. Just off the square was a shop with some old maps in the window called Farley's Consignment. It was dark enough I thought it was also closed, but there was a prominent OPEN sign in the window.

Old things were piled everywhere—stacks of chairs, cupboards full of mismatched cups, display cases stuffed with little figurines of chubby kids in lederhosen. It took me a minute to notice the owner sitting behind a pile of ancient appliance parts stacked on the counter. His shoulders were stooped, and he had a baseball cap pulled low over his eyes, so it was hard to tell how old he was. He was watching a miniature TV set behind the counter. His eyes flicked up from it briefly to give me a suspicious stare when I walked in.

"Not from here."

It wasn't a question. What was wrong with people here? *Not another one*, I could imagine Zoe whispering. *I'd say we fill his store with spiders, too, but it probably already is.*

He didn't say anything else, or look up from his TV, so I started looking through the old stuff. There was a globe so old I was surprised it didn't show a flat Earth, a bunch of old medicine bottles in blue and green glass, and a lot of other old stuff. Normally I liked antiques, but so far this town was rubbing me the wrong way, and it all seemed to add up to a history I wasn't part of—even if my dad was from here.

Then I noticed an old wire birdcage with a cloth covering it near the back of the store. Did this guy have a pet bird? I knew I should probably leave it alone, but the covered cage made me curious—with everything else in the store strewn around haphazardly, this was the one thing that felt carefully placed.

The owner wasn't paying any attention to me, and what harm was a look anyway? I came closer to the cage. I couldn't hear anything moving underneath. Slowly, I lifted a corner of the cloth.

I could barely make sense of what I saw underneath. It was a statue or figurine, made of a sinuous stone that looked somehow wet or oily. Looking at it made me feel a little queasy, like it was some sort of optical illusion. I couldn't even tell if it was supposed to represent anything.

Then, suddenly, the owner was beside me, pulling down the cloth cover with a force that shocked me.

"That's not for you," he said. His eyes said the rest—*get the hell out of my store*. I was more than happy to leave on my own. My nausea went away almost instantly when he covered the statue, or whatever the hell it was, and I turned and walked out. As I opened the door, I turned around one last time to see him still watching me.

"Won't last long here if you go acting like that."

"What's that supposed to mean?"

I fixed him with a hard stare, but he didn't answer, just kept glaring back. I couldn't tell from his voice if he was actually worried about me, or hoping I'd meet some sort of bad end. Finally, I shook my head and walked out the door.

Dad was still hard at work when I got home, so I pulled a few of the folklore and history books from the shelf to entertain myself. Anything to forget my experience at that shop. I learned all sorts of interesting things about the Six Nations of the Iroquois Confederacy. They had a matrilineal system of inheritance, and a democratic government that some historians thought had inspired Jefferson and Washington—though no sense of gratitude or obligation had stopped the United States from stealing their land.

If Zoe were here, we'd probably spend all afternoon coming up with pranks to take all the rude villagers down a peg. We used to spend hours concocting brilliant schemes that would shock and humiliate anyone who dared be mean to either of us—from forged love letters to buckets of eels dropped from above, each scenario more baroque and impossible than the last. We filled entire notebooks with plots and skullduggery, but in Zoe's short life, we never got to try any of it.

I don't think Zoe would have wanted to anyway. At her heart, she was too nice. I think she only helped me plan all those pranks because she knew it made me feel better. After she was gone, plenty of people were still mean to me, worse even, but I didn't care. Nothing they said could be as bad as what I lived with every day as half of myself.

Oroco was our word for deep water. It could mean an ocean or a lake, anywhere that was dark and too deep to stand. Sometimes I still had to stop and tell myself to use the English words for things, because the words in our secret language were still the first ones that came to mind. *Oroco* came to me again last night in my sleep, as I dreamed of the still waters of Redmarch lake.

III.

The next day, I went back to the café. Neil was talking to someone when I came in, another boy our age. He was even skinnier than Neil, with a mop of jet black hair and a hint of stubble on his chin. He gave me a curt nod and a cocky smile, then looked at Neil, who looked overjoyed to see me.

"Oh, hey! Clara, this is Hector, he's from out of town, too. I can feel this place opening up already."

"I've lived here two years, man," Hector said.

"Right, of course."

Neil nodded, though he didn't seem to think it made much of a difference. Hector said he had to run and take care of some errands for his parents. He and Neil clasped hands, and he gave me another brief nod coupled with a suspicious stare before walking out the door.

"What's his deal?" I said. "I thought only the locals were unfriendly."

"Hector's not unfriendly, just . . . living here makes him a bit defensive. I can't say I blame him. Can I get you another cappuccino?"

I nodded. As much as I hated to admit it, Hector's smirk

had made me wish he'd liked me more—but I didn't want to think of that right now.

Neil still seemed afraid the rudeness of the town would make me bolt at any moment. He really needed to visit the city—he'd stop worrying about that pretty quick.

"Poor guy," said Neil. "It doesn't matter if you've lived here two years or twenty if you weren't born here."

While he made my coffee, Neil talked about how bad he wanted to get out of Redmarch Lake when he was done with high school.

"I know there's a spot for me at the quarry, but my grades are decent. I want to go to college, if I can swing the loans and stuff. My folks don't have much money."

"Come to New York," I said. "People there are still rude, but at least there you know it's nothing personal."

Midway through my coffee, Rayna texted me a picture of Leatherface from *Texas Chainsaw Massacre*, with the caption *Meet any cute guys in the country?* I chuckled, which made poor Neil jump. I finished my coffee while he helped the few locals that came in through the morning. I was happy I'd at least found this place, and I hoped it would be enough to sustain me through a long and boring summer.

"Hey, there's gonna be a party tonight, if you're interested," Neil said when I brought my cup up to the counter. "There's a spot we go to out in the woods."

My eyes narrowed. He suddenly realized how that came off.

"It's nothing weird, I swear. Just a bunch of kids from

the high school and some beer. Hector and I will both be there. Look, the easiest way to get there is to park by the church. There's a trail head and you can usually follow the music from there."

He wrote the address on a napkin for me.

"Come if you feel like it. It'll be fun, I promise."

"I'll think about it," I said.

"Oh, and one more thing. Stay on the trail. If you do decide to come, I mean."

"What?"

"Don't step off the trail. It's easy to get lost in the woods out here, but you should be fine as long as you follow it."

"I heard the woods around here are dangerous."

Neil nodded.

"They are, but it's fine as long as you stay on the path. We go to this spot all the time. Just—if you come—be sure to stay on the path."

He was deathly serious as he said this. When I nodded, his big smile was back again and he waved as I left. I didn't know what to make of the whole thing. Neil weirded me out a bit, but he seemed to be the only nice person from this town who wasn't related to me. Who knew what the other kids were like?

Just got invited to a party, I texted Rayna. *Wait till the county fair. I'll be crowned Corn Queen.*

Haha, more like Children of the Corn Queen, Rayna wrote back.

I missed the girls already: Rayna, Maddie, Amaya, and Hannah. Our little band of misfits, gathered at the edge of the school cafeteria, or meeting up at coffee shops in Astoria or Thai places in Elmhurst, laughing at stuff no one else did—pretending we were too cool for everything, mostly because everyone else ignored us anyway. I didn't care. I was convinced life was better at a meta-level—I learned a long time ago that any other way meant hurting.

Even with those girls, though, I had never felt like I belonged. I couldn't shake the feeling that by spending time with them, I was betraying Zoe. It was stupid; she was dead and I was still here, but I felt it just the same. I wished they could all meet her, or even that they'd known knew her when she was alive.

I never had friends when I was younger. With a twin sister, I never needed them. It was like having a built-in best friend who already knew you better than anyone else ever could, even your parents. The other kids at school must have thought we were so spooky—like the ghost twins from *The Shining*—but I never cared until after Zoe died, when they all avoided me like tragedy was contagious, or whispered things behind my back I was glad I couldn't hear. I might as well have been a genuine ghost—I almost was.

That year after losing Zoe was hard for me to think about, even now. I barely survived it. Moving to the city and making friends with Rayna was the only thing that helped me not feel loneliness crushing me like deep sea pressure. Even now, I caught myself wondering why I still felt cut off from everything without Zoe—half of me living in the world and the other half lost in a fog of grief. Would it be this way my whole life?

By the end of the day, I had decided to go to the party. If it was sketchy, I'd back out right away. Hell, even if all the kids in this town were weirdos, it would at least be something to do.

When dinnertime rolled around, dad suggested we go to the diner. I was glad to get him out of the house. I had been hoping for one of those old-fashioned places gleaming with chrome and neon, but the Lakeview Diner seemed even older than that—all wood paneling and once-plush booth seats now almost dangerously saggy. There were stuffed deer heads and a trophy bass on the wall. I wondered if it came from the lake—somehow I couldn't imagine it.

My burger was good, delicious even, though the waitress went out of her way to use as few words as possible when she took our order, like she couldn't wait to get away from us. Neil was definitely right about this place.

"How's school?" Dad said.

I frowned. I'd spent most of my academic career living in fear of the time it stopped being easy and I'd have to start applying myself (I always hated that phrase—like I was lip gloss or adhesive). I thought a second-tier high school like Queens Academy for Inhumanity would give me more of a grace period. Still, it turned out sophomore year was that long-awaited time of dread. My grades took a dive, which meant constant fights with Mom. It was hard to believe she and the Woodchuck were hitting it off like a goddamn rom-com at the same time.

"Let's talk about something else," I said. "Tell me about your book."

"Like I said, it's just about the history of the town. Not many people will find it as interesting as I do."

"Because you grew up here?"

Whatever had been bothering my father, he clearly enjoyed talking about the book. He lit up as soon as I mentioned it. I wondered if he had the same reaction when people asked him about his daughter.

There was something else, though—it clearly made him nervous. As soon as I spoke, he made a subtle *quiet down* gesture, and he kept looking over his shoulder. I wondered about his mood. Maybe being back in this unfriendly town was starting to turn him paranoid. Before we'd left the house, I'd used the bathroom and snuck a quick look at his medicine cabinet. He had quite a few prescriptions, including some I'd also taken in my long process of recovery after losing Zoe. Seeing them brought back a lot of bad memories.

"It's not just that I grew up here. My whole family is from here—half your roots—going back to after the Revolutionary War. There have been Morrises in Redmarch Lake for as long as it's been a town."

"I didn't know that."

I couldn't believe I was just learning this now. How had my father never brought it up when I was younger? Again, I tried to think of him telling me something about this town even once, and I couldn't think of anything. It was really starting to bother me.

"I have a complicated history with this place," he said. "The whole town has a complicated history."

"Maybe the townsfolk will be a little nicer if they know I have roots here," I said, thinking of the woman who'd thrown me out of her secondhand store the previous morning. My father frowned.

"Don't count on it. Sad to say, they're not a friendly bunch. Never have been."

Was my father writing a big book of revenge about everyone who had been a jerk to him in high school? I could see that becoming a family tradition. It still didn't explain his collection of paranormal studies tracts, though.

"So what about all the fairies and aliens and 'world of the unknown' stuff?"

My father was quiet for a moment, staring at his hamburger as if he'd just noticed it for the first time. He looked around to see if anyone was watching us, then he went on.

"There's something in the air out here," he said. "It's subtle, but it goes way back. The modern spiritualist movement began not far from here. Seances, talking boards, automatic writing, past life regression, it used to be all the rage. There were two sisters near here, in the nineteenth century, the Fox sisters, who said they could communicate with a spirit they called Mr. Splitfoot. It would answer their questions by knocking."

My father gave the table two sharp taps with his knuckles. The sound echoed through the diner. Some of the other customers turned to give us hard, disapproving stares, just like the waitress and the lady in the vintage shop. My father ignored them.

"They say both sisters had learned how to crack the bones in their feet to make the sound. They signed a confession saying they had faked the whole thing, then years later they took it back and claimed it had all been real."

I couldn't help but think of Zoe and me, up late at night daring each other to say Bloody Mary three times in the mirror and shrieking with terror and delight. I tried to change the subject to something not involving sisters, or at least something that wouldn't earn us any more evil eyes from the townsfolk. I was out of options—I asked my father about his day job and tried harder than ever to understand the world of electronic database architecture.

I'd been debating whether to tell him about the party. Finally, after an action-packed evening learning the finer points of database design, I figured I'd better ask if I really wanted to go. I waited until we were on the ride home.

"So, some of the local kids are throwing a party tonight at the church," I said. He didn't need to know it was in the woods.

"You got popular quick," he said, smiling. Then he clenched his jaw—shifting gears into father mode. "You're not going, though."

"Why not? I'll be careful. I won't stay out past eleven."

"You don't know these people," he said. "You're not going."

"What's wrong with them? You think I don't deal with weirdos in the city? I know how to take care of myself."

"This is different."

I'd never seen my father so dead set about anything, and it unnerved me. What did he know about the people here that he wasn't sharing? It was almost enough to make me want to stay home.

"Different how, Dad? I can't understand unless you tell me. I'm starting to feel like I barely know you."

My father winced like he'd been struck. I instantly felt bad. I hadn't meant to hurt him—still, I realized it was true as soon as I said it. Why else was I just hearing about our family's roots here?

"I didn't mean that. I'll stay home. I don't care about the stupid party."

That part was true; I didn't even want to go anymore.

"Be home by ten," my father said. "No drinking."

He didn't say anything else to me for the rest of the night.

IV.

The car's headlights illuminated barely ten feet ahead of me, and the road rolled on forever in the darkness beyond their reach. Distances seemed so much greater at night. As I drove through the woods, the high beams lit the trees from below, making them look like weird undersea plants. I listened for the clipped syllables of my phone's GPS telling me where to turn to reach Redmarch Lake Episcopal.

As I drove, I thought about what I had said to my father. I knew it hurt, and I wished I hadn't said it, but it was the truth—I barely knew him. Not that he hadn't always been there, and done all the stuff dads are supposed to—but I didn't know his whole family was from here until tonight. I'd never met anyone else from his side of the family. He had no brothers or sisters, and my grandparents on his side died when I was little, but I had no idea if he had cousins or anything. As I drove slowly down the outer-space-black country roads, I resolved that by the time the summer was done, I'd be able to say I knew my dad and mean it.

When I finally made it to the church, the parking lot was half full, which was a good sign. It looked like everyone was already at the party, though, so I would have to walk there alone. I felt in my purse for the little key-ring bottle of pepper spray my mom had bought me, glad it was still there.

The trail head was easy to find, a gap in the fence with a little spur of asphalt extending into the undergrowth. Only a few feet of it was paved, after that it was bare ground, growing narrower and narrower as I went further in. I was thankful for the flashlight on my phone to light the path ahead. The cricket chorus was even louder out here than at my father's house; their chirps echoed from all around me. Mosquitoes were probably eating me alive, too—every so often I felt the gossamer brush of insect wings on my legs and tried to aim a good swat, only to come up with nothing. I thought about what my father had said about lyme ticks and walked faster.

I was beginning to regret coming out when I heard music through the trees ahead—some sort of music any-way. It sounded like whistling, or high-pitched singing, and someone tapping out a strange rhythm. The problem was, it was a little ways off the trail. It had to be the party, though—where else would sounds like that be coming from?

I took a step off the trail, then another. The ground didn't open up to swallow me or anything—so far so good.

I followed the music deeper into the woods. The under-growth was thin here, making it hard to tell what was trail and what wasn't. The sound grew louder as I walked, and I saw a faint light peeking out from between the trees in a little clearing ahead. I thought I heard someone laugh, a girl's voice.

In my haste to get to the party, I didn't notice the thorn bush in my way, and I swore as my cardigan ripped and inch-long thorns scraped my arms and legs. When I fought through the bush and into the clearing, I saw it was empty. There was no music to be heard, no light but the moon shining through a gap in the branches.

I took a deep breath. Did I remember how to get back? Was there even a party out here? I could hear my heart thudding in my chest. I told myself to calm down and just go back the way I'd come. As soon as my heartbeat quieted, I realized something else that sent a chill down my spine— the crickets had stopped chirping.

I stood rooted to the spot, my back against the rough bark of a tree, hoping nothing was there. Everything was quiet for another moment. Then I heard a twig snap, horribly close. I heard another, then another—footsteps, getting closer. Something big breathed in and out—a deep, rasping snort.

I couldn't stand it anymore. I took off running, crashing though the undergrowth. It was all I could do not to scream.

I could hear it behind me—its ragged breath getting closer and closer, its footfalls crashing through the woods. I couldn't tell if it had two legs or four. I didn't dare look back.

I ran until my sides ached. A jutting root sent me sprawling, and I heard it lunge for me. I screamed as something brushed my ankle. I threw myself forward, kicking with both legs. Then I was back on my feet, running hard into the darkness.

I ran until I couldn't anymore, and when I finally collapsed against an ivy-covered tree trunk, I turned to face whatever horrible thing was coming for me.

And there was nothing there.

I stood silent for I don't know how long, catching my breath, trying to convince myself I wasn't losing my mind. There were no cuts or scrapes on my ankle, except the ones from the thorn bush. But what I heard, what I felt, had been real. I was positive.

This place was really starting to get to me.

Then I heard music, unmistakably someone's stereo this time, playing a screamy metalcore song, which is much more what I expected from the party. I laughed. Now, of course, I'd find it.

I wandered through the trees, following the sound. I came out on a large clearing, lit up by a few electric camp lanterns, with a pair of portable speakers blasting the screamo. A big knot of people clustered around the silvery bulk of a keg in a tub of ice, and a few other groups were talking or smoking. Further out, I caught glimpses of couples making out in the half-light at the far edge of the clearing. It was all so far from where I'd just been I had to laugh again.

"You made it!" Neil said, happy to see me. Then he caught sight of my torn cardigan and the scratches on my arms. "Are you okay?"

"Oh, sure. More thorn bushes than Central Park, that's all."

He handed me a red cup that was almost all foam. It was just as well since I didn't drink. Not because I was underage, but because I really didn't like not being in control of myself. No pot, no alcohol, and definitely nothing stronger—there was no telling what would come out once I lost control.

I smiled anyway, pretending to take a sip.

"Thanks. Not as easy to find this place as I'd thought."

"Sorry. I could've given you better directions, I'm not very good at that."

Neil looked sincerely crushed. I wondered if he knew anything about whatever was lurking in the woods.

"Don't beat yourself up about it. I'm a city girl, I need a grid."

"You stayed on the path, right?" he said, suddenly worried.

"Oh, yeah, not one foot outside the line."

I couldn't bring myself to tell him what I'd been through; I didn't want to believe it myself.

"Let me show you around," Neil said, making a grand gesture like he was escorting me to his country house. "Here's the keg, the smokers' corner, the uh . . . the hookup nook, and I know the casino and the shuffleboard deck must be around here somewhere . . ."

It was cute the way he blushed when he said "hookup nook."

"What, no ice sculpture?" I said.

He laughed. Then a girl a foot shorter than him walked right up to him and punched him hard in the chest.

"Oh my god, is this her?"

She had dyed black hair and black eyeliner, and she was clearly furious.

"You knew I'd be here. You just wanted to parade her in front of me, didn't you?"

"Hi, I'm Clara," I said.

The girl gave me a brief head nod. Her eyes were not friendly.

"I don't know what's going on with you two, but this isn't anything," I said. "I'm just new in town, and Neil told me about the party. We're not together."

I backed away. The girl gave me a *stay the hell out of this* glare, then she was back to yelling at Neil, who was falling all over himself trying to explain and apologize. He mouthed the word *sorry* to me just like he had in the café, then they were gone, taking their unresolved drama to the edge of the clearing where it belonged, and I was alone again with a cup of beer foam. I spilled a little of it on the ground just in case someone asked why I wasn't drinking. Not that anyone did.

I stayed in the circle around the keg for a while, feeling like a trespasser who would be discovered any minute. No one even looked at me. They were talking about other people they knew who weren't here, or things they all remembered from last year. This was probably the sort of place where you went through every grade with the same people, and whoever was the poor paste-eater in kindergarten was marked for life.

I couldn't imagine how bad my life would have been if I'd stayed at that school in New Jersey, with everything reminding me of Zoe. If I were from a town like this, I'd probably leave and never look back. The more I thought about it, the more it made me angry at my father—why would he ever want to leave the city and come back here?

I waited for some kind of entry into the conversation around the keg, something I could chime in on. One of the guys said, "Well, you know what Bone is like . . ." and everyone burst out in giggles. This was a language I didn't speak. I drifted away—no one had noticed my presence, and they definitely didn't notice my absence. It felt like the first years after Zoe's death all over. I tried hard to forget my halfhearted first attempts to connect with other people. My sister had died, but I was the one who felt like a ghost you could see right through.

I wandered back toward the edge of the clearing, looking up at the stars. I wondered how hard it would be to find my way back.

"You just tried to hang with the locals, right?"

I recognized Hector from the coffee shop. Apparently Neil had ditched him, too, for whatever drama was playing out at the edge of the woods. Hector looked up from his phone for half a second to raise an eyebrow at me.

"That obvious, huh?" I said.

"Yeah, it reminds me of a joke. So this guy goes to prison, and when he walks in, one of the inmates yells out, 'number 54!' and everyone laughs. Then later on, someone yells out 'number 16!' and everyone cracks up. Finally, he asks his cell mate what the hell is going on. 'Oh, we've all been in here forever,' says the cell mate, 'we know all the jokes, and we gave 'em all numbers to save time.' 'Wow, okay,' says the man, 'let me try—number 21!' There's like, dead silence through the whole cell block. Finally, his cell mate says, 'Man, some people just can't tell a joke.'"

I nodded.

"That was like a metaphor for this whole town."

"No, I got that," I said. "It was maybe more profound than funny."

"Yeah, well at least now that you're here, I know it's not a race thing: they just hate everyone who's not from here. Except Neil—I don't think he hates anyone. You're from the city, right? What neighborhood?"

"Forest Hills, you?"

"Uh oh, you're a Mets fan."

"I don't care about any of that."

"I thought so, it's okay. I'm from Inwood." He puffed out his chest, trying to look hard. It didn't really work. I couldn't help it, I laughed a little. Luckily, he didn't look too disappointed. "Yeah, I can't scare any of these gringos, either. They only talk to me to copy my math homework."

"Do you let them?"

"Are you kidding? I charge for that shit. It beats working at the diner."

"How'd you end up here?"

"My parents always wanted to live in the country—now my mom can have a big house and my dad can go fishing. My sister's off in college most of the year. It's just me suffering."

I waited for him to ask me about how I ended up here, trying to think of something clever, but he suddenly lowered his voice.

"Hey, you been out to the lake yet?'

I nodded. He looked around to make sure everyone was ignoring us, which of course they were.

"Creepy, right? They say no one knows how deep it actually is. No one in town will tell you this, but they used to kill people out on that island, like human sacrifice."

I remembered staring out at that eerie little island, and I suppressed a shudder.

"Yeah, right. None of the Native American tribes from here practiced human sacrifice."

"Who said I was talking about Native Americans?"

At that moment, his phone buzzed in his pocket, and he suddenly seemed to forget I existed.

"Sorry, I gotta answer this. I've been trying forever to get a signal out in this wasteland . . ." Whatever was going on with his phone was obviously more interesting than me. If I couldn't even make friends with my fellow NYC exile, what hope did I have here? This was a terrible idea. At least the Woodchuck acknowledged my existence. I would head back in a few days, if the creature in the trees didn't get me first.

Everything seemed so normal now, with the light and the music and the sound of other people around me. I looked back at the woods: the shadows deepened to impenetrable blue-black just a few feet past the lanterns' little circles of light. I wondered if whatever had chased me was still waiting out there.

"We're pretty close to the lake shore out here, but of course you can't see anything," said someone behind me.

I turned to face perhaps the best looking guy I'd ever seen outside of a magazine. He was leanly muscled, with a strong jaw and an easy smile. He looked like an actor playing a small-town boy, his dark-blond hair perfectly tousled just so. I was instantly suspicious.

"Hey, I saw you talking to Neil," he said. "We don't get too many new people around here. What's your name?"

"Clara."

"Clara, what?"

"Morris."

He perked up when he heard my last name, like he suddenly realized I was famous. My mother's last name was DiStefano. Back home, I kept wanting to use hers—less vanilla and more New York. But just now I was glad I had a local name.

"You're Tom Morris's daughter," he said. "Welcome. This town's your home, too. I'm Keith Redmarch."

"Redmarch," I said, "as in Redmarch Lake? Did your ancestors plant a flag in it or something?"

I remembered the statue in the town square and the frightening expression on its face. Keith didn't seem anything like him, I was happy to say.

"Something like that," he said. "I mean, there were already people here. The white man didn't 'discover' anything; we just stuck our names on it . . ."

"Right."

"Hey, can I get you another drink? Let me introduce you to everyone."

I'd been a bit suspicious at first, but this pushed me over the edge. I'd been the butt of too many false offers of friendship and other cruel tricks in my life, and there was no way this was legitimate. Guys like this at my high school would walk right past me like I wasn't there, unless they stopped to mutter something like "weirdo." I take that back—there weren't any guys like Keith at my high school—most of them had at least one flaw. He looked back to see me standing there with my arms crossed.

"Sorry, but is this a *Carrie* thing? Or like *Les Liaisons Dangereuses*? You're not secretly into your hot cousin, are you?"

"Ugh, no. I don't even have cousins. I'm just trying to be a good host."

"Okay, sorry. I'm from the city. I don't trust easy."

"You're family's from here," he said. "That makes you one of us. . . . I have always wanted to see the city, though."

"You should go! I think you'd do well there." He had no idea how well. He'd probably get some kind of male model contract after stepping off the bus.

Keith led me into the knot of partiers, this time as a confirmed actual person, and I tried to remember the dizzying list of new names—they were all some variation of Dave or Mike, or Jennifer or Kristen. The challenge was remembering which one was which. Keith even tried to explain one or two of the in-jokes to me. "Everyone calls him Bone because of what happened during the rope climb at gym class years ago. Yeah, immature, I know . . ."

Someone pressed a new beer into my hand, and I pretended to drink again. Then someone else passed a joint around, and I pretended to hit it. I looked for Neil and his ladyfriend. She was smoking with another group of girls by the edge of the woods, but I didn't see him. Hector was still preoccupied with his phone, caught half in shadow at the edge of the clearing. I almost felt bad until I remembered the way he ignored me. I laughed along with the in-crowd at the stories and jokes I only half appreciated, but I had an all right time after all.

The party wound down around four, and a big group of us made our way back up the path, which was so much shorter and easier than the way I'd come.

By the time I got home, there were birds singing in the trees. My father was asleep on the couch again. He probably tried to wait up for me. I felt a twinge of guilt. I'd lost track of time so easily. I went to bed knowing I'd hear about in the morning.

I was exhausted, but once again sleep did not come easy. I tossed and turned in the sheets, dreaming of the darkened woods, of fear and running, until I reached the shadowed edge of the lake, and everything went black.

1889

I have never endured such a journey as our trip to Buffalo. It was horrid at first, beset by railway delays and all manner of other inconveniences. I resolved to tell my husband he could conduct whatever business he had there alone from now on, and the children and I would await him in Manhattan, but to tell him anything I would have to reach him first.

Stevens had made all the arrangements, and I am ashamed to say I was quite cross with him, even though he could have foreseen none of the compounding misfortunes that finally culminated in our locomotive's engine dying in the middle of the journey. The damned thing would take days to repair, and we were adrift in the wilderness. Bless his heart, Stevens sent a railroad man for a horse and carriage, which conveyed us to the nearest town. I took back every intemperate word I'd hurled at him.

The town was larger than I'd expected—given I'd never heard of it before—and it was quite charming. There was a placid lake with a romantic little island at the far side, and a stately house beyond it on the hill. The inn where we roomed was modest, but not uncomfortable. The fellow who owned it, Clyburn I believe his name was, said he had plans for something more grand, a real hotel. I told him he should have to get his town on all the maps first.

Little Henrietta complained of nightmares that night, worse than before. She said there were people in the mirrors trying to come through. I told her to stop with such nonsense. It had to be that tutor of hers, telling her ghost stories again. I'd have to find a replacement when we returned to the city, but I was content to let the matter wait until then. I was quite taken with the little town.

In fact, when Stevens returned with word the train was repaired, I told him I should like to spend more time here. George could wait another day in Buffalo—no doubt he was consumed with his industrial projects—and I wanted to take a boat out to the island, and perhaps visit whomever lived in that house across the lake.

Stevens grew pale when I said this. I'd forgotten he was from this region, though not this town. He implored me to come with haste. "This is not a good place, madam," he said. "Please don't stay. Please, I beg you."

I was all set to reproach him for his superstition, but I'd never seen that look in his eye before. I told him to ready the children for the ride to the train, and he all but fell down at my feet in gratitude.

—*Memoirs of Beatrice Fallows*, 1889
From the library of Tom Morris

V.

I woke up to my father knocking on my door. He was probably agonizing about whether or not it would be appropriate to barge in. I rolled out of bed half awake, throwing my clothes on, wondering why I was so tired. Then I remembered what time I'd come home. I almost crawled right back into bed, but I knew he'd eventually get so worried he'd stop thinking of my privacy. When I opened the door, he looked relieved.

"Thank God. Don't do that to me again. I had the worst dream last night. I-I don't even want to say what it was about, but I'm so glad you're safe."

He gave me a hug. Now that the relief was over, I knew the anger would come, and I really didn't want to argue or say anything else I'd regret.

"I'm sorry, Dad. I really didn't mean to stay out so late. I got caught up in everything, and I couldn't get a phone signal. The kids out here are really nice—some of them anyway. I didn't have anything to drink—I'll even take a breathalyzer."

"What does your mother do when you do things like this?"

Funny he should ask. The morning mom had chosen to spring the news of Washed Up Chuck joining our family unit was the same morning after I stayed out all night and failed to call home. Hannah knew a bar on St. Marks that didn't card, and the girls had been planning to go for a week. We got in without a problem, but our evening of illicit fun got boring really fast, at least for me. I ended up babysitting Rayna while she puked. Then somehow we all ended up at Veselka. My mother said she found it hard to believe I'd spent the whole night looking after my drunk friends and eating pierogis, but that was the truth.

"We yell and scream at each other for a while," I said. "Then she uses it as an excuse to tell me her loser boyfriend is moving in."

I caught a glimmer of a frown on my father's face, and I thought *yes, finally*, but a moment later, he was back to self-righteous lecture mode.

"Well I'm not going to do that, but Clara, I don't want to have to worry about you. Your mother and I love you. We may show it in different ways, but we're both just concerned for your safety. I know it's not the city out here, but in its own way, it's just as dangerous."

At that moment, there was a knock on the front door. My father opened it to see a sheriff's deputy standing there in his khaki uniform.

"Good morning, Tom."

The deputy seemed friendly enough, but he didn't smile.

"Morning, Bill," my father said, "uh, what can I do for you?"

"Is that your daughter? I'm sorry, we haven't met, Miss, I'm Bill Hendricks. I know your dad from way back."

He shook my hand, again without smiling. Whatever emotion he was feeling never touched his face. I bet he made a killing on poker night.

"You remember my partner, Harry," Bill said to my father, pointing at another deputy standing out by the car. He had the same flinty expression as Bill, but on him, it seemed dour and suspicious. My father's eyes narrowed.

"What's going on, Bill? Not that I mind you dropping by."

"Well, I'm afraid we're going to have to take your daughter down to the station to answer some questions. We're talking to anyone who might have seen what happened in the woods last night."

My father mouthed the words, *the woods?* to me, the anger back in his eyes. Were they really going to bust us for a little party in the forest? Something else must have happened—something worse. I tried not to imagine all the horrible things that could happen in the woods at night.

"Is she in trouble?" my dad said.

"We just want her help clearing some things up."

"Of course," I said. "I'll help however I can."

There was no way out of this now.

"I'm coming, too," my father said.

Deputy Bill let my father drive me in while he and Deputy Harry followed in the squad car. Dad was fuming the whole time. He may not have yelled and screamed, but he did manage to channel my mother's condescending tone.

"You didn't say you were in the woods. That's a whole other story, Clara. I have to be able to trust you, and I need you to promise me that you won't go into the woods at night again."

My father didn't sound angry this time; he sounded scared.

"I'm sorry," I said. "I should have told you. It was just a stupid party. And I really didn't drink, I swear."

"No, I need you to promise me *right now* you won't go into the woods at night."

"Why?"

"Because I said so . . . Because bad things happen around here in the woods at night, and that's all I'm going to say."

"Okay, I promise."

My father went silent again after that. As we drove past the lake, he gave it a nervous glance, but I knew asking him about it would get me nowhere. What the hell was he hiding from me? The surface of the water was just as eerily still as the day before. I wished it would rain, or storm, or something, just so I could see it move again. I caught sight of the little island and thought about what Hector had said about human sacrifice.

We drove into town and then out to the other side, where the sheriffs' station was. It was tiny, just a little regional post, but the parking lot was nearly full, mostly of patrol cars.

"We only have two deputies at the Redmarch Lake station, and you just met them both," my father said. "The rest must be down from the county office. This isn't just about a party, something bad happened."

"Everything was normal when I left," I said.

They led us past the empty little waiting room toward the back of the station. I gave my father a worried look.

"Where's everyone else from last night?" I said.

"We're trying to speak to everyone in turn," said Deputy Bill.

As we walked through the hallway, another deputy was leading the girl who'd argued with Neil last night out to the exit. Her black eyeliner was streaked with tears, and she hadn't even had the chance to change from the night before. The deputy had a hand on her shoulder, as if he were trying to console her. As we walked by, I tried to give her a sympathetic look, but she fixed me with the most hateful glare I've ever received. I could only imagine her wishing my death with each passing second. I quickly looked away. I was in no state for staring contests with a possibly homicidal goth-girl. Instead I looked at the floor as she left the building. I hoped this would all be over soon.

They put us in a little room with a table and a few chairs—just like in the movies. I looked for a two-way mirror, but the walls were all cinderblock. They left us waiting there a while. My father was still stewing about the woods, but god forbid he'd actually talk about it. Did he know about whatever had chased me through the trees? I was about ready to ask him when the door opened.

A short but tough-looking Native American woman in a sheriff's uniform walked in. Her hair was tied in a tight black bun, and she looked me and my father up and down before sitting across from me. Another deputy walked in behind her.

"Clara Morris, with father Tom Morris," the deputy said, reading from a clipboard.

"Right, Mr. Morris, Clara, pleased to meet you." The woman shook hands with each of us. "I'm Deputy Chief Cross River, but you can call me Elaine."

"Hello," was all I could think to say back.

"Were you in the woods by the church last night, Clara?"

Something in her tone made me nervous. I tried hard not to stammer like an idiot.

"Yeah. I didn't have anything to drink, though. You can totally breathalyze me, or I'll take a polygraph, or-or whatever it takes."

"It's all right, we're not here to do that."

Of course they weren't. I already knew that. I told myself I had nothing to be nervous about, but it didn't help.

"Do you know a boy named Neil Patterson, and did you see him at the party?"

"I didn't know his last name, but I know Neil. I met him two days ago. He was . . . he was the first actually friendly person I met here."

It might have been my imagination, but I thought I saw Elaine give me a quick sympathetic nod before resuming her mask of professional authority.

"He was the one who invited me to the party."

"What happened at the party?"

I remembered my scramble through the woods, and what I thought had chased me. I had no proof it hadn't all been in my head. I still wasn't sure myself.

"I saw Neil there. I talked to him a little, then a girl I didn't know got really mad at him for talking to me, and they argued."

"And what's her name?"

"I-I never learned her name, but you just spoke to her. The girl in black, with the black eyeliner."

The deputy made a note on the clipboard.

"Did Neil appear intoxicated when you saw him?"

"I don't know. I'd only just met him. He had a beer when I came, but I don't know how many he had before or after."

"Who else did you talk to at the party?"

"Uh . . . a boy named Hector. And Keith."

"Keith Redmarch?"

I nodded. Elaine and the deputy exchanged looks, and he noted something else on the clipboard. My father also seemed alarmed at this, but he said nothing in front of the deputies.

"When was the last time you saw Neil?"

"I lost track of him after he got into that argument. I saw the girl he argued with later, but not him. I left with everyone else when the party wound down."

Elaine exchanged an unreadable look with the deputy before turning back to me.

"Last question—did you notice if anyone at the party was carrying a knife?"

"No . . . no, I didn't see anything like that. Is Neil okay?"

Elaine took a deep breath.

"He drowned in the lake sometime last night or early this morning. There were signs he'd been in a fight with someone beforehand."

My whole body felt numb with the news. I clenched my fingers into fists, digging my nails hard into the palms of my hands, hoping to hold back tears. I'd just met Neil. I knew nothing about who he really was, but he had been so nice to me, a total stranger. A shock of grief ran through me like an electric current, leading me all the way back to that horrible day eight years ago. All of the things I kept walled off from my present self swam back. Once again, I was on the beach where they pulled me from the sea and pushed the water from my lungs. Once again, I tried feebly to shout: *no, no, my sister is still out there. My sister is drowning . . .*

One of the deputies led us back. My father's anger had vanished for now, and he did his best to comfort me.

"I'm so sorry," he said. "It wasn't your fault. Remember that."

We walked out of the station. It was already midday and the parking lot was sweltering, the asphalt baking in direct sunlight. We were almost to the car when I heard footsteps behind us.

"Hey!"

I turned around to see the girl with the eyeliner take a final drag of her cigarette, then throw it down and crush it beneath her foot.

"I can't believe they let you walk out free."

"What?" What the hell did this girl think I'd done?

"Everything was normal that night—just like any other summer party, but he died. You were the only thing that was different. I don't know what you did, but you're the reason he's dead!"

She was coming closer as she spoke, jabbing her finger at me like it was a dagger, or a witch's curse.

"I-I didn't do anything."

"Stop lying!"

She swung her hand at me, a clumsy half-slap, half-scratch. I caught her wrist before she could connect. Then she swung with the other hand. Her arms were flailing every which way as I tried to keep her off me. Finally my father stepped between us, holding us apart.

"Ashley! Ashley calm down or I'll call your mother. This is my daughter, Clara. She's a good person, and she wouldn't do anything to hurt anyone."

Ashley took a deep breath, tears running down her cheeks.

"Don't call me Ashley," she said, gasping for breath. "It's Ash."

Of course it was.

She gave me one last, hateful glare, just to let me know this wasn't over, before she turned and walked away.

Dad was quiet on the drive back. At least he wasn't mad at me anymore, or he wasn't expressing it if he was. When I closed my eyes, I kept seeing Ash's angry stare. What could I have done for her to hate me like that? I knew what it was like to lose someone you loved—I wished I could talk to her about it.

"Dad, what did she mean back there, that I was the only thing that was different?"

Once again it took my father a while to answer. I was starting to get used to it.

"I told you people are superstitious here," he said. "It drives me crazy. One little thing is different, and they blame everything on it. This isn't your fault, sweetheart. Neil and everyone else should never have had a party in the woods."

"That sounds kind of superstitious, too," I said in a small voice.

"Well, some superstitions are true," my father said. He was silent for the rest of the drive home.

When we got to the house, Dad made eggs and bacon, which I wasn't in any mood to object to, and anyway, it was already well past morning. After we'd eaten, I could tell he was about to say something he'd been rehearsing in his head since the sheriff's office.

"I love having you here, sweetheart, but I think you should consider going back to New York."

"Dad . . ."

"I'll come back with you and stay for a while. We'll have a good time in the city. I'll come visit more often."

I thought about what he was saying, and for a moment, I actually considered it. Then I remembered there would be a third person living in our apartment. I probably couldn't avoid Chuck forever, but maybe if I could hold out a little longer, I'd get lucky and Mom would get sick of him.

There was something more, though, something about the lake, and its weird, unfriendly town, that felt like it would bother me forever if I didn't sort it out. If I could understand this place, maybe I'd understand my dad a bit better. And the more determined he seemed that I not learn about this place, the more I had to know.

"Dad, I'm not leaving."

"It's not safe here, Clara. It's . . . listen, I know you think this is just a quaint little country town, but it's dangerous."

"Dad, I hate what happened to Neil, it's awful, but he probably got really drunk, got in a fight with someone, and then fell in the lake."

As I said this, I knew it wasn't true. I couldn't see friendly, awkward Neil fighting anyone, even blackout drunk.

"Bad things happen in the woods, especially by the lake. They may all have perfectly reasonable explanations, but they happen."

Again, I wondered just what my father knew but wasn't saying. I was getting mad again. Was he trying to send me home because it was easier than telling me what was going on with him? Was there something he didn't want me to know? In any case, he was forgetting I was as stubborn as my mother.

"I'm worried about you, Dad. You're all alone in this little town, by this spooky lake, and you've got the ghost hunters' library for reading material. You need company. I'm staying, for a while longer at least."

He was quiet for a moment, and I was afraid he was going to keep arguing, but then he smiled a tight, sad smile.

"Just promise me you'll be safe."

"I promise," I said.

"I'm serious, and what I said about the woods also goes for the Redmarch boy. Stay away from that family."

"Why? He seemed nice."

"Please, Clara, just do this for me. Just trust me."

He looked so tired and worried just then, I lost my will to argue.

I meant everything I said earlier—I was really worried about Dad—but that wasn't the only thing keeping me here. Neil had invited me to a party on a whim, and now he was dead. Just like Ash had said, I was the only thing different. Maybe somehow I really had upset the equilibrium of this weird little town, and if that was true, I had to find a way to put it right.

"One more thing," my dad said. "If you're going to stay, there's something you should have."

He rummaged around in a desk drawer, pulling out random odds and ends, until he finally came up with what looked like a lump of dark metal. He handed it to me. It was iron, heavy and black. It looked like it had been, at one time, some sort of brooch or clasp, but age and rust had left it barely recognizable.

"What's this?" I said.

"Think of it as a lucky charm," my father said. "Old tradition in this area—always carry a little iron with you."

"Lucky charm?" I hadn't expected any of this from my father. Growing up, he'd always been so rational. Just a short while ago, he'd been complaining about how superstitious this town was. "Are you serious?"

"Yes," he said in a way that made it clear he had nothing else to say about it.

Dad had more work to do, and I wasn't in any kind of state to go back to town, so I sat in the back yard and read one of the Ghosts of New York books. I probably should have picked something less creepy, but it was the only thing that didn't feel like history homework. Most of the stories were pretty typical—mysterious ladies in tattered ball gowns haunting old mansions or theaters. There did seem to be a lot of fake castles in New York State, some of them brought over stone by stone, others just reproductions. Every one of them had to have a ghost or two, for the tourists' sake.

The only story that stood out was about the old Clyburn Hotel. It was just a little anecdote, not really a story, but apparently the hotel had removed all its mirrors. Ever since it opened, guests had been complaining about weird lights in the mirrors that weren't reflections of anything in their rooms. Some had even reported seeing their reflections move on their own. One man had lost his mind in the hotel, claiming the mirrors were full of shadow people looking for a way to break through. The man was committed to an asylum, but the manager had thought it best to quietly remove the mirrors anyway.

According to the guidebook, the Clyburn Hotel closed down during the Great Depression, but it had been partially renovated, and was now a restaurant "in the quaint former resort town of Redmarch Lake."

Then I heard something rustle in the undergrowth at the edge of the yard.

I jumped, afraid to look over the edge of my book. I waited, but there were no other noises. Whatever it was had been small, much different from the thing I'd heard in the woods at night; probably a chipmunk or a squirrel.

I put down the book and walked over to where I'd heard the noise. There was an old tree stump there I hadn't noticed before, standing at the edge of the forest like a warning to the other trees not to get too close to my father's yard. I came nearer, bracing myself in case I startled any little critters out of the undergrowth.

There was something wedged in a crack on the top of the stump. When I looked closer, I saw it was a piece of paper. One corner of it was just barely sticking out of the crack. I managed to grab hold and slowly pull it free. It couldn't have been in there long; it was still dry and white, freshly torn from a notebook.

Trembling a little, I unfolded it, completely unprepared for what I'd find. There were a few lines of text, written in neat cursive.

Oad af flor
Par flen shaan
Sen glof vlan
Sen sta gron

A tremor went through me, a ripple of electric grief and memory. To anyone else in the world, that note would have been pure nonsense, but I knew exactly what it meant:

Deep in the wood
Far from the town
They spilled his blood
They let him drown

I shivered again. Hot tears trickled down my cheeks. This was impossible, a sick joke, or else something I couldn't begin to comprehend.

I hadn't seen the language in that note since I was a little girl. Since Zoe and I made it up.

VI.

They call it cryptophasia, or twin talk—a sort of pre-language shared by only two people. Most twins grow out of it as soon as they learn to talk for real, but Zoe and I had kept our language alive, keeping it hidden from our parents, who would make us speak properly, and building on it as our world had grown. After I'd lost her, I still felt our words for things coming to my mind, sometimes before the real words.

I'd read every book I could find on the subject. I had to understand it to survive it. The Egyptian Pharaoh Psammetichos had ordered two babies to be raised by she-goats to see if they would emerge speaking the language of the first people. Holy Roman Emperor Frederick II tried something similar, ordering nurses to feed two children in total silence. Wise men throughout history had believed twins spoke the original tongue, the language of Babel.

Losing a twin is not just losing a sibling. I lost a way of life, a whole culture. The common tongue of the land of ClaraandZoe, with all its myth and history.

It had been a thing only the two of us shared. Not even our parents understood it. We'd never even written it down before—this note was the first time I'd seen those words written out and not spoken by my sister or me. I still used it in my head, easpecially when thinking of Zoe, but it had even felt wrong to use it in the reams of letters I'd written her after I'd lost her to help deal with her absence. Until today, I thought I would never hear or see that language outside my own head again.

Was it blind chance—nonsense words written in a way that just happened to match our secret language? Or was I losing my mind, dreaming of what was written on a blank piece of paper? I looked again. It was still there. I could feel the indentation where the pen had touched the paper. I looked frantically for some sane explanation, because the alternatives were just too much to bear. I debated showing my father, or someone else, but I didn't dare. My father would think it was some kind of traumatic grief relapse— he might think I needed treatment again. And that's assuming I could even find the words to explain.

I spent the next two days inside. I watched TV on the couch, or helped my father cook and clean. I asked him if he needed help tidying up the attic, or weeding the back yard. When I couldn't ignore it any more, I searched for news on Neil. There was a report on the local network the first night, but all they said was a boy from the area tragically drowned in a lake after a party in the woods. One of the anchors made a comment about the dangers of underage drinking, and that was that.

I knew I should have gone back to the city, or at least gotten my father to take me somewhere away from this town, but I couldn't let it go. I couldn't stand that something so awful had happened to someone I knew, even if I barely knew him, and now it seemed like the whole world was forgetting about it, just like they'd forgotten about Zoe.

After I lost my twin, I wanted the world to stop. I wanted things to match the way I felt inside—empty and changed forever—but life just went on, even for my parents. I could see the hurt in their eyes, hear them argue in hushed voices late at night, but my eight-year-old mind just couldn't understand how they still got up every day and went to work, when I couldn't even see a reason to get out of bed.

My memory of the first year without her was spotty, a blurred kaleidoscope of hurt, images flowing together. I remembered the doctors and the pills, the kids at school who'd whisper behind my back but wouldn't look me in the eye, like grief was some kind of contagious disease. I don't remember the funeral. It's a big hole in my thoughts, and probably just as well. I don't think I could stand even the memory of her body.

Most of all, I remember how it felt to see everything happening without her. People became statistics so quickly. Once someone was gone, you had to fight to keep them alive, even if it was only in your mind. That's why I still tried to talk to my sister, or write her letters. Letting go of her felt like letting go of myself.

There's a whole institute in California dedicated to studying twin loss. They say the death of an identical twin is one of the most profound losses a person can experience, like nothing else. I know for me it was like falling down a well with no bottom, just falling and falling. I couldn't get past the thought that I was also dead, and the life going on around me was a hollow fiction. Surviving twins are at a higher risk of depression, addiction, and suicide. I knew that all too well, even before I read it. My parents tried treatment, drugs, all kinds of therapy. My memory is hazy—it's hard to tell what happened when—most of it didn't help.

I stopped speaking, I barely ate. I lay awake at night and went through my days like a sleepwalker. If going on meant living without Zoe, I wanted to be numb to everything, to freeze it all in place. My parents took me out of school. I don't know how long I went on like that.

Somehow, in some small way, learning more about it made things better, like putting a name to the thing that was eating you up. At least it helped me see that if I didn't change, I would go on this way forever, or until I couldn't take it anymore. I made rules for myself—what I could think about and what I couldn't, what I had to do to keep my mind occupied. I drew pictures and made collages of my memories with Zoe. I imagined what she would say if she were still beside me, living her life. I wrote down all the things I wanted to tell her in letters I couldn't send—I wanted to have some part of our life together that would go on and would never be taken from me.

When I got better, we moved to Queens. I had to repeat fourth grade, but I was no longer in a place where everything reminded me of Zoe's absence, so I didn't care. Every night, I wrote about the things I saw and did, so that at least in my mind I could still share them with her.

I was glad for any excuse to get away from my parents, who never let me out of their sight at home, always watching me with the same brittle smiles on their faces, as if by acting cheerful they could cheer me up too—meanwhile they argued nonstop behind my back and thought I didn't notice. I forced myself to talk to people, to explore, to get to know our new neighborhood like I'd been born to it—but a part of me was still falling down that well, and probably always would be.

And now there was this matter of the note, threatening to unravel everything. Whenever I dwelled on it too much, I felt icy fingers of panic worming their way through my brain, stealing the breath from my lungs. It had taken me so long to accept that Zoe was gone, that I only carried her with me in my memory. I almost didn't want to believe it was real, because if I believed and I was wrong, it would be like losing her all over again. The note was a knife opening up all my old scars, but I couldn't let it go, I had to know more.

Why would she come back to me now, if that's really what this was? Was there some connection between her and Neil? They had both drowned, but it had to be more than that. She had also come back to me here, in this strange town our father's family was from. A place our father had all but refused to talk about. There had to be a connection.

Since I lost her, I'd fought hard to keep her a part of my life instead of someone that only lived in my past. But now here she was, or some part of her anyway, involved in things I barely understood. I had to know more. I had to get to the bottom of it. Even if it was all some misunderstanding, or a cruel joke—I couldn't leave it be. Even if this crazy town swallowed me whole. I promised myself I wouldn't leave until I knew how Zoe fit into all of this.

Three days after Neil had died, I told my father that I was borrowing the car, and I drove into town. I shivered when I passed the old hotel, remembering the story about the mirrors. The first thing I did after I parked was walk back down to the lake. I had to see it again.

It was just like the first time I came here, a perfect mirror, undisturbed by the barest ripple, bordered in the distance by slowly receding morning mist. I tried to imagine drowning in that water. I often had drowning nightmares—no surprise there, given what happened to my sister and almost happened to me. In them, I was immobile, sinking, powerless as I felt my lungs fill, all of it with an agonizing slowness, a horrible inevitability—like the universe had decided I must die, and nothing could prevent it. I shuddered imagining that happening to Neil.

Once I saw an M.C. Escher print titled *Three Worlds*. It showed fallen autumn leaves floating on the surface of a lake. Beneath this, the bare branches of the trees were reflected on the surface. And beneath this, you could just glimpse the ghostly outline of a fish in the depths. I pictured Neil lying beneath the surface of that calm mirror, cold and alone. I couldn't look at the water anymore.

I turned and walked back up the incline to the town square. Of course, the first thing I saw was the café, with the happy cat perched over his mug of coffee. There was a little HELP WANTED sign in the window, which was awful to see—life just moving on again—but it did give me an idea.

You should apply for his job, Zoe would say.

"That's crazy," I muttered to myself, glad I was alone on the square.

No, think about it—what better way to find out what happened to him.

"And what you have to do with it," I said.

And me. Besides, he was nice to you when no one else was.

Zoe's sense of justice was always far too strong for her own good, or mine. I barely knew Neil. This wasn't up to me. Still, I found myself walking toward the café door. Somewhere inside, I knew she was right. This was the right thing to do, and the only way to find out where that note came from.

I walked in. Once again, Clyde the cat looked up to give me a baleful glare before returning to his pillow. A woman about my parents' age stood behind the counter this time. Her hair was dyed a bright red and curled in ringlets, and she wore a big necklace of polished amber stones, with rings to match. On her head was an old-fashioned hat with a little black veil hanging down over her eyes. Mourning Neil, I guessed.

"What can I do for you, sweetheart?"

That wasn't the reception I'd come to expect in this town, and I was amazed and a bit embarrassed by the warm surge of relief and gratitude that came welling up in me. I didn't think I needed other people's kindness that much.

"I'm here about the job, actually," I said.

"Such a tragedy," she said. "I loved having Neil work here. I could never replace him, but I just can't be here enough myself."

"I know," I said. "I barely knew him, but he seemed like a really nice guy. I—well, I hope I can do right by the job in his memory."

"Do you have any experience working in a coffee shop?"

"No, but I can make anything someone would order."

She raised a delicately plucked eyebrow at this. I knew a challenge when I saw one.

Last year, I'd briefly dated a barista, until I caught him hooking up with Marcia Klein at a party I brought him to. In fact, I'm not even sure he'd have said we were dating if you'd asked him, but that doesn't matter now. Luckily, I'd gotten him to teach me all the tricks of the trade before he ended up with Marcia. Then my mother had bought a fancy home espresso machine, and I'd kept our mugs full of cappuccinos and caffe macchiatos through the winter.

I stepped behind the bar, taking a minute or two to familiarize myself with the hardware. I whipped up a double espresso, then a cappuccino, then a latte. As a final touch, I slowly poured the milk to make a delicate leaf pattern on the surface. I'd practiced for hours back home until I'd gotten it just right. My leaf was still a little deformed, but the woman I assumed was the owner was impressed.

"Wow, well, what's your name then, dear?"

"Clara Morris."

"Oh, are you Tom Morris's daughter? Tom showed me a picture of you the last time he was here, from quite a while ago I guess. I haven't seen him around lately."

"He stays home way too much," I said.

She nodded.

"Well, pleased to meet you, Clara Morris. I'm Lady Daphne. No need to curtsy, it's not a title. First name Lady, last name Daphne."

This town was too much. I could imagine Zoe chuckling and pretending to take a sip of tea, little finger raised in proper posh fashion. My friends back in the city would have lost it, but just now I was ready to pledge my sword to defend Lady Daphne's honor.

"We open at eight, so you have the first hour to set up and feed Mr. Clyde here. You'll have a few hours of overlap in the afternoon when the evening girl comes in. So, by any chance, could you start today? I canceled all my appointments, but some of them may still be coming in."

I nodded, and Lady Daphne breathed a theatrical sigh of relief.

"Wonderful. The café belonged to my parents, and I see it as a familial obligation. It's an obligation to the town, really—family tradition is important here, and someone's got to run the café, but I'm actually a full-time clairvoyant."

She said this like someone would say they were a medical technician.

"Mostly I see auras, not full visions. You're looking a bit dark blue today. It could mean you can't let go of something from your past, or you're afraid of acknowledging something in the here and now. That's a freebie, by the way. Once I had an actual experience of clairalience—that's extrasensory smelling, it's very rare. I smelled fire and ashes for an entire week when no one else could smell anything similar. It turned out my cousin's house up in Buffalo had burned down."

Lady laughed at this, so I guessed her cousin had come out of it all right; still, I couldn't imagine that story was a hit at family gatherings. Lady Daphne assured me she had lots more stories about her psychic abilities. She didn't seem like a fake—I think she definitely believed she had these powers. I kind of wished I believed it, too; life would be more interesting if auras and telepathy were real, but I just couldn't buy it.

If things like that really existed, I had a feeling they would be far more confusing and terrifying. Imagine if, just once, something fell up instead of down. One day you toss a pebble and, instead of falling to the ground, it shoots off into the stratosphere. It sounds like a joke, but just think if it really happened to you—you'd be terrified. I know I would be. And in a town as strange as this, it seemed to me any actual psychics would go totally bonkers.

Then again, bonkers sort of fit Lady Daphne. I was relieved when she finally took off on her errands and left me to manage the café with her sour-faced spirit animal Mr. Clyde. I found a spare apron in the back, and I cleaned the machines to keep busy. There was no morning rush, and after I'd found most of what I'd need and cleaned every piece of coffee hardware, I just watched the square of sun from the skylight slowly migrate across the floor like a ghostly glacier.

I tried to make friends with Clyde, letting him sniff my fingers to get used to my smell. He rubbed his fuzzy cheek against my hand once, then went back to sleep. At least I was all right in his book.

Around 10:30, my first customer came in. My eyes widened when I recognized Hector, and his jaw dropped when he saw me behind the counter. It looked like there were all sorts of questions running through his head, but all he could manage was to order a caffe mocha. At least it wasn't some sort of triple caramel vanilla monstrosity. I made it for him while he set up his computer. I wondered if he'd ignore me in favor of his technology this time, too.

"Here you go," I said.

"Thanks." He kept looking at me, trying to think of what to say next. His eyes were narrowed with suspicion. "Hey, can I ask you something? Are you from Queens like you said, or from here?"

"I wasn't lying to you. I'm from Forest Hills. My dad is from here."

"Is there like, a secret handshake or something? Not that anyone would believe I was a local anyway."

I suddenly felt bad—Hector had lived in Redmarch Lake a lot longer than me, and he didn't have the benefit of an old family name to open doors that didn't open for much else. And now he'd lost the only person he'd called a friend here. Still, if he hadn't ignored me, he could have had a new friend.

"To be honest, this place weirds me the hell out," I said. "They didn't look at me twice until they learned my father was from here, so don't take it personally."

"Neil was one of the few nice ones," said Hector. "Who am I kidding? He was my only friend. Hey, did they haul you down to the sheriff's office too?"

Hector's tone was suddenly anxious, unsure.

"Yeah. That wasn't fun. What did they ask you?"

"Just what happened at the party, and the last time I saw Neil."

"Me too. I saw him argue with his girlfriend, then nothing."

"You mean Ash? She's his ex. They broke up like two months ago. Then there were these rumors Neil had a new girlfriend, though he never told me, and I don't think anybody'd actually seen her. Listen to me, talking about these people like they're a stupid telenovela. That's what it feels like being here, like this is all a TV show and I can't interact with anyone because I'm the one audience member. I can't even change the channel."

"Well, now I'm watching too, and I think we changed genres to something pretty dark."

Hector looked around briefly, to make sure we were alone—the same kind of suspicious glance I'd seen my dad make. Maybe he was more a part of this town than he thought.

"I think it's always been pretty dark. Want to see something crazy?"

He walked over to the entrance, again making sure no one was loitering outside or coming down the street. A little painting of a sailboat hung on the wall above the door—the same kind I saw in a lot of motel rooms on family car trips.

Hector lifted up the painting. Underneath it, hammered into the wall, were a cluster of old iron nails. They'd only been hammered halfway in, then the heads had been twisted together to make a weird knot pattern. It reminded me of the old iron clasp my father had given me.

"All the houses here have something like this. There was one in mine when we moved in. The neighbors came by to make sure we didn't take it out. They didn't say that's what they were doing, of course, but that was like, the one and only time they came to visit."

"No one in this town will talk about what's really going on. Not even my father. Neil's just going to be remembered as a kid who got drunk and drowned unless we do something about it."

Up until now, I was feeling that spark of excitement you only get when you finally find someone thinking the same thing you are. I already forgot about Hector ignoring me at the party, which really shouldn't have bothered me that much anyway, and I was already thinking of the two of us on a mission, solving the mysteries of Redmarch Lake—just like Zoe would have wanted. That spark died abruptly when I saw the look on his face—like I'd just suggested we jump off a bridge.

"Not you too," I said.

"You're here on summer vacation," he said. "I'm stuck here for another two years."

"I won't get you in trouble," I said. "I don't even know what to do next, but I have to do something."

I could hear Zoe's voice in the back of my head, urging me to get to the bottom of things. I couldn't ignore it, not when I felt like I was the only one keeping her memory alive. And there was the matter of the note. Somehow my sister was a part of this, not just in my memory but here and now, and that thought thrilled and horrified me more than anything else.

Hector still didn't look like he was about to help me, though.

"Why don't you just ask the townsfolk? They'll talk to you, since you're in the club and all. I wouldn't know what that's like."

That stupid cocky smirk was back on his face.

"You know as well as I do no one here will talk to me," I said. "The only way we'll learn anything is if the two of us find it out ourselves."

"You have fun with that," he said. "I'm out."

He packed up his stuff, shaking his head. I couldn't believe it. Was this all because the other kids had talked to me, or was he afraid? I was about to call him a coward when two older ladies in track suits power-walked in and ordered nonfat lattes, which meant I had to get busy. Hector left as I got to work. To my surprise, he turned and looked at me one last time. I was expecting another self-satisfied smirk, but the look he gave me was almost sorry. Good, he should've been sorry. I stared daggers at him and he hurried off down the street.

The power-walk ladies were in the middle of an argument about whether the heat or the humidity was worse outside and didn't pay any attention to me, or Hector as he was leaving, though they did put a dollar in the tip jar when I gave them their lattes.

Lady Daphne had said I could have one of the café sandwiches for lunch every day—which was nice of her. They were all vegetarian but not bad. I cleaned everything until it sparkled and tried not to watch the clock as the minute hand crawled its way around. I was still furious at Hector, though I didn't know why. I could understand his reluctance; he'd been here a lot longer than me and would still be here when I left. Who knew what consequences he'd face for stepping out of line around here. Maybe that was what happened to Neil? Still, for some stupid reason, I hoped Hector would be my ally in all this. I could feel at least a part of him wanted to be.

I hope he gets a virus and his computer blows up, Zoe whispered in my head. She was never any good with technology, but the idea gave me a guilty smile.

At noon on the dot, an old man walked in. It took me a minute to realize he was the same old man I'd ridden in on the bus with, still smoking a cigarette, NO SMOKING signs be damned. He ordered a regular coffee in a voice that sounded like rocks scraping together and then added enough milk and sugar to eliminate any trace of coffee. I winced just watching. Throughout all this, he gave no indication that he knew me, but as he was leaving, he gave me a brief, conspiratorial wink.

"Watch your back out here, kid," he said.

My evening replacement was supposed to show up any minute now. I'd forgotten how boring summer jobs were. Each movement of the minute hand seemed to take a full hour. My mother once told me that the older you got, the faster time seemed to move. "Just wait," she had said, "when you're my age, it'll feel like half a year is gone before you even know what happened." I wondered if I'd ever look back on these hours of intolerable slowness with anything like longing.

Just when I was starting to think this girl was a no-show and I'd have to work a double shift, I heard the chime of the door opening. I saw a familiar tumble of long, dyed-black hair and I thought *oh no.* Judging by her expression, Ash thought the same thing at the same time.

"No," she said. "No," as if she could will me out of existence. She looked like she was about to turn around and walk right back out of the café. "You're doing this on purpose. You won't be happy until you take everything."

"Let's talk about this—"

"You show up, and Neil dies, and now here you are, in his place, standing right where he used to stand. What the hell are you doing here?"

She stood still for a moment, taking deep breaths. The more she looked at me, the less angry she seemed and the more she started to look afraid. She thought of something she hadn't considered before, and whatever it was, it made her turn two shades whiter, which I didn't think was possible.

"Who are you, really? You're not from New York. Tom Morris tells everyone he has a daughter, but I heard someone say his daughter drowned years ago. They say that's why he moved back here and he's always shut up in his house . . ."

"I'm real," I said. "I swear to god. Do you want to see my driver's license?"

"You're one of them," she said. She started backing toward the door, fumbling around in her purse for something. "You broke the rules. You can't do what you did."

I walked toward her, my hands out, trying to calm her down.

"Don't come any closer!"

She pulled out something from her purse, brandishing it like a weapon, but it was just an old iron nail.

"I'm not going to hurt you," I said. "I'm just a normal girl, I swear."

The nail wavered in her hand. I took another step toward her, praying she didn't try to stab me with it.

"Don't . . ." she said.

I reached into my pocket, pulling out the iron clasp my father had given me.

"See? I'm just like you."

Just as delusional, I thought. *What the hell was wrong with this town?*

Gently, I closed my fingers around the nail, and she let it drop into my hand. She stumbled backward, all of her fury leaving her at once. I caught her by the arm to keep her from falling into one of the tables.

When she recovered her balance, she jerked her hand out of my grasp and collapsed into one of the chairs, weeping.

VII.

I brought her a box of tissues, and she spent the next few minutes drying her eyes and blowing her nose.

"I guess you're real after all," was the first thing she said to me.

"My twin sister drowned when I was eight. That's probably where the rumor came from."

She gave me a timid glance—wary but free of hatred. I'd take that as progress.

"I'm sorry."

"It's okay. What did you think I was just now, a ghost?"

"N-never mind," said Ash. "My head hasn't been right since Neil died. I guess I was just freaking out."

There was obviously more to it than that, but it didn't look like she was going to tell me.

"So I guess we'll be working together," I said.

"For a few hours anyway."

Ash may have accepted my basic humanity, but she didn't sound thrilled to be my coworker. I tried to imagine Neil and Ash meeting at the café, seeing each other for two hours every day, falling in love little by little, until they broke up, and then Neil was dead. I felt for her, even if she thought I was undead, or possessed, or whatever that thing with the nail had been.

I could see looking at Ash that things had never been easy for her, even before Neil died. It wasn't the hair or the makeup—it was something deeper than that, in the eyes. I knew it because I saw it sometimes in my own eyes when I looked in the mirror. She'd grown up here, and who knew what that could do to a person, and what the rest of her life was like. Under different circumstances, I think we'd have been instant friends. I wasn't great at making friends, but I hoped somehow I could make things right with her.

"I know you're going through something really horrible. I barely knew Neil, but he seemed like a great guy. There's a lot I don't understand about this place. I didn't do anything to hurt anyone, and if I upset some kind of balance or broke some unwritten rule, I didn't mean to, and I'm sorry."

"I know," said Ash. "Look, I can't deal with this now. Why don't you sign out and I'll just take over."

I nodded. I didn't think I'd make things better between us by arguing with her, and I was already sick of this place. I hung up my apron, went over the totals from the register with Ash, and headed home.

As I walked out of the café, I noticed one of the sheriff's patrol cars parked nearby. The silent deputy with the hard stare—I think his name was Harry—was sitting in the driver's seat. I felt his eyes on me as I walked by, and I tried not to let it show. *It's only natural that they'd look at the café after what happened*, I thought, *it's not like they're keeping tabs on you or anything.* But the way the deputy's eyes followed me, I wasn't so sure. As I walked by, I thought I caught a glimpse of him making a call on his cell phone.

My father was working on his book when I got back, or trying to at least—he was squinting at a block of text on the screen like he was losing a staring contest to it.

"Writer's block?"

He jumped in his seat, then turned to face me. He seemed to be trying to block the screen with his head, as if what he'd written was too embarrassing to be seen.

"When do I get to read some of it?" I asked.

"Never—I mean, you wouldn't want to. . . . It's terrible."

"Come on, Dad, have a little faith in yourself. I bet it's great."

He smiled, but he still didn't volunteer to share any of it with me.

"Thanks," he said. "So where have you been all day?"

"I got a job."

He looked impressed but also worried.

"You're a lot like your mother," he said. "Once you decide you want something, you'll make it happen no matter what. I'm glad you take after her in that. So where are you working? The diner?"

"The café. I'm—well, it's Neil's old job."

Dad frowned, the worry back in his knotted brows.

"I know you love your coffee. That's why you took the job, right?"

"Right."

He probably suspected I was up to more than this, but he was willing to leave it be. With my father, there was a kind of parent-child détente; he would leave certain boundaries intact even if he suspected I was up to no good. My mother was a bloodhound—whenever she smelled something suspicious, she'd keep after it, no matter how uncomfortable it made either of us. Honestly, my father made me feel worse. I felt like I was taking advantage of his trust, even though, this time, at least I was doing it for the right reasons. I knew he wouldn't understand if I told him everything I was thinking.

"You should give your mom a call," he said.

I was so focused on everything that happened that I hadn't even thought of calling home, much less what I would say to my mother. Now I felt the familiar dread of the long, slow battle of wills that our relationship had become. The Woodchuck was just the latest fight, but it may have been the one that lost me the war. My father could sense I was trying to come up with an excuse not to call, so he handed me the handset, and it didn't look like he was leaving until I dialed.

"She's probably at work now," I said.

"I spoke to her this morning. They're finished shooting for the latest season. Your mother has some downtime before post-production."

"What if Chuck answers?"

My father made a face, just for a second, then he was back in dad mode.

"Just ask to speak to your mother, it's that easy."

My parents didn't fight often since the divorce, but that was probably because they didn't speak often. Dad must have been worried enough to fill my mother in on what was happening here, which complicated matters. My mother was an associate producer on a TV crime drama, and whenever they were filming, her head was full of worst-case-scenarios.

I dialed the number, hoping for her voicemail, but someone picked up after two rings.

"DiStefano and Woods, attorneys at law. Have you been injured on the job? We can help."

Chuck's wry tenor crackled on the other end of the line, and I could hear him chuckling at his own stupid joke. It was all I could do not to hang up then and there. He started to get nervous when there was no response, which made me a little happier.

Tell him you're the cops! Tell him that joke was criminally awful! Zoe whispered excitedly in my head, but I couldn't bring myself to interact with the Woodchuck that much. I let the awkward silence do the work.

"Uh . . . whoever this is, I'm kidding. . . . This is the DiStefano and Woods private residence, but doesn't it sound like a great law firm?"

"It's Clara."

"Clara! I'm glad you called. Your mom was worried—"

"Right, is she there?"

I could hear Chuck calling for my mother, then a shuffling noise as he handed her the phone.

"Sweetheart, your father told me what happened. I'd like you to come home."

"Mom, I'm fine. I like it here. And wouldn't you know it, all this forest but not a single woodchuck."

"I wish you wouldn't talk like that, Clara, but that's beside the point. It's not safe."

"I even found a summer job like you wanted. Listen, I know what happened sounds scary, but nothing like it's going to happen again, all right? There's no way anyone's going to have another party after that, and you know I don't drink or go swimming."

"I know," she said. "I just worry. Your father told me some stories about that town when we were first dating. It may look quaint, but it's got a bad history."

"Like what?"

"I don't remember. Just that more bad things happen there than should in a place that small. We came to visit once, when you were just a baby, and something about that whole town just felt off. I know you're careful, honey, but careful only goes so far. Listen, I had a right to be upset with you after you stayed out all night and didn't tell me, especially when you promised to get your grades up. You know I worry about you, after all you've been though, but I'm sorry for the way I yelled . . ."

This was strange. She must have really been worried. What's more, I had no idea we'd been here once when I was little.

"I'm sorry too, Mom, I should have called. And I'm upset about school and the way this year went, too. I promise to do better this fall. But I'm not coming home yet. I like it here, and I like spending some time with Dad."

"All right, Clara. But if there's anything else out of the ordinary, I want you on the next bus back, okay?"

"I understand."

I hadn't technically said yes, but I hoped my mother would let that slide. It felt good to have a normal conversation with her again, for a few minutes at least. We chatted about her work, and how tired she was of casting the murderer of the week.

"Lots of actors don't want to play serial killers," she said, "so we end up going with standup comedians. They usually get the material better anyway, plus they're more likely to have the right weird look."

I made a face when she brought that up—this was exactly how my mother had met Charlie. He wasn't a comedian, no matter how funny he seemed to find himself, just a washed up character actor my mother had cast as the Bushwick Butcher. Somehow he'd managed to talk her into a date when shooting wrapped.

"Why don't you just cast Chuck for all the killer parts? That'd make him happy."

"Clara, I need you to give Charlie a chance." My mother's voice went flat abruptly. I could picture her pinched expression on the other end of the phone. "I hope you'll see why he makes me happy. I get to be happy, don't I?"

"Of course, Mom. But did you have to bring him into our home?"

"It's my home, young lady. If I talked to my parents that way, I'd get a spanking with the belt."

"Maybe you should talk to a therapist about that, Mom. Doctor Bellamy is good."

I was over the line and I knew it. The words just slipped out, and I immediately started wishing life came with a rewind button. I was going to pay for this. Maybe when I got home, Mom would announce she married the Woodchuck, or maybe she'd just ground me for the rest of the year. The line was silent for a long time. Finally, I whispered that I was sorry into the receiver.

"Goodbye, Clara," my mother's voice was taut and brittle. "We'll talk later."

My friends all thought my mother had the coolest job, especially film-geek Rayna—at first, I thought that was the only reason she made friends with me. I guess it was cool that she worked on a TV show, but I saw how tired Mom always looked after work, how each season's taping seemed to come closer to making her snap, and I already knew I didn't want to follow in her footsteps. Especially if it meant working with guys like the Woodchuck.

"Dad?" I said when I hung up the phone. "You never told me we came here when I was a baby."

"I-I must have mentioned it sometime," he said. "It was just a short trip, so your mother could see where I grew up."

"No, you never talked about this place. . . . I didn't even know about our family history until now."

My father nodded. At least he was admitting I was right—this place was starting to make me wonder if I was imagining things.

"I thought I was done with this place, but . . . I guess you're never done with the past, are you?"

My father said this to himself as much as to me, and that was all he'd say. If he had any thoughts on my fight with Mom, he kept them to himself, and I was glad of that at least. He heated us up a frozen lasagna for dinner, but I was only hungry enough for a small piece.

"Hey Dad, can I ask you a question? Does the water we drink here come from the lake?"

My father made a disgusted face mid-chew, like his lasagna had suddenly turned into a pile of wet garbage.

"Oh no," he said, swallowing uneasily. "It tastes terrible. It's got too high a mineral content, sulphur and things like that. The same minerals that give the Redmarch marble in the quarry its color make the lake water unpalatable. It has no river access, it's fed by underground springs. Funny story, they tried to bottle the lake water and sell it as a health tonic, back in the1800s. It didn't go well."

"Why not?"

"There were rumors the makers were lacing the water with opium—which was actually legal at the time, just frowned upon. The thing is, several customers reported really vivid nightmares; sometimes so horrifying they developed insomnia or nervous disorders. Have more lasagna before it gets cold."

I was sick of everyone in this town dodging my questions, especially my father. I put my fork down with a clang on the plate and pushed it away from me, fixing him with the hardest stare I could.

"Dad, what the hell is wrong with this place? No one will talk to me, and the one boy who would is dead now. I've seen—"

My father tensed up. He seemed intensely frightened of what I would say next. I thought of the weird statue in the consignment shop, the thing I'd heard and felt in the woods. What did it all mean?

"I've seen and felt things I can't really describe, and if you don't say something, I'm going to explode."

He was quiet for a long time, staring back at me with a determination I didn't know he had. Finally he sighed. When he spoke, it was clear he'd chosen his words carefully.

"Lots of people think they want a place that never changes, but they wouldn't if they knew what it was like. It's the same here every generation—people talk about going to college, or moving away, but they stay and work in the quarry, the same shops stay open in town, folks move into their parents' houses. The Redmarches like things the way they are."

"You got out."

"And look at me, back here again . . ."

He didn't sound happy about it, and that made me want to ask him why the hell he had moved back then, but I knew that would bring on another quiet spell. It was so hard to get my dad to talk about this—I'd have to swallow my own feelings for now.

"Every year, though, we lose people in accidents, drugs, drinking, bar fights that go too far. Despite all the warnings, people still go missing in the forest. Death is one of those things that doesn't change, but everyone pretends it's normal. This town is actually a really nice place, so long . . . so long as you don't worry too much about what makes it different. I'm sorry, sweetheart, that's all I can say on the subject."

I still wanted to ask him what was so important here he couldn't stay in New York, but I didn't have it in me. Whatever reason he gave me, it wouldn't be enough.

That night, I tiptoed out to the front door after my father had gone to sleep. There was an old round clock directly above the door, in the same place where the painting had been in the café. Slowly, I stood on my tiptoes and lifted the clock. Just like Hector had said, there was another little knot of bent nails driven into the wood underneath. What were they supposed to keep out? Or in?

Feeling guilty, but also insatiably curious, I walked over to my father's computer. It was still on, but in sleep mode. I reached out and slowly moved the mouse, and watched as the screen came to life. I was about to give a guilty, silent cheer when I saw the screen-saver was password protected. I guess my father was serious about not letting anyone read what he wrote. I tried my and Zoe's birthday as a password, but it didn't work, and I felt too ashamed to keep guessing.

Just as I was about to give up, though, I saw that my father had left some handwritten notes beside the keyboard. They looked like they'd been copied from a book, but I couldn't see any books nearby. Maybe he'd traveled somewhere to do research. His handwriting was a chaotic scrawl, but with a little light I could decipher it.

. . . *following his dogs, he soon lost his companions, and he did hear the cry of other hounds, not his own, and from a different direction. And when he had come to a glade at the heart of the wood he beheld a pack of strange hounds set upon a stag. Such hounds he had never seen, with coats of white and ears of glistening red, and the white of their bodies was white as bleached bone and the red of their ears as red as blood. Seeing them he gave a cry, and drove them from the stag, and set his own dogs upon it.*

Then came a stranger from the wood, clad all in gray, with a hunting horn, saying, "Prince, I know who thou art, and I greet thee not."

"And what discourtesy have I done thee, that thou would show me such discourtesy in return?" said the prince.

"A greater discourtesy I have never seen in man, as to rob me of my rightful prey. My dogs had felled the stag, and yet you drove them off, and set thine own upon it. For that I shall be revenged upon thee for more than the value of a hundred stags."

And a great fear fell upon the prince, for he did see the gray stranger was no mortal man.

"My lord," said he, "I have done thee ill. How may I redeem thy friendship?"

"After this manner mayest thou," smiled the stranger. "I am a crowned king in my land, as thou art in thine, and I am beset by rivals who challenge my dominion, as I know thou art as well. I shall clothe thee in my features, such that none may know thou are not I, and so I shall wear thy aspect, and walk in thy realm, and thus we shall aid each other and make firm friendship."

"Gladly shall I do this," said the prince, though great fear was upon him.

97

"Come then," said the stranger, "and let me wear thy skin."

There was a note added underneath the block of text:

Believed to be a corrupted translation of the <u>Mabinogion</u>, from the collections of Lady Enid Rosegrave; translator unknown.

There was another, shorter passage copied below this in a different color ink, as if it had been added later.

He does go about in darkness with a great black book, and he will offer pretty things, and riches, and aches and pains to any as dare cross you. So many things he will offer you, if only you sign your name with blood into his black book.

Under this was written, *Testimony of Molly Goodwin, Salem Town, 1690.*

I wasn't sure what I was expecting, but it wasn't that. What could it mean? I started to look through the rest of the papers when I heard my father stirring in the other room, and I left his desk in a hurry.

When I finally fell asleep, I had the drowning dream again.

I was floating on my back in warm water. I could see the rose glow of the summer sun even through my closed eyes. The water lapped at my ears, and I felt like I could hear the echoes of the entire ocean as it moved—a deep, dull roar like a giant's breath. Sometimes the dream lingered there, and I only hung suspended on the edge of the nightmare before mercifully waking up.

This was not one of those times.

The water rose around me, filling my nose and mouth, burning my eyes. In my dream, it was slow and viscous, more like thick jelly that ocean water. I couldn't fight it, only struggle feebly as I sank and it closed over me. I coughed and gagged as I felt it fill my mouth, my throat, my lungs, until it had stolen all my breath.

On that day, Zoe had caught my hand in hers and pulled me to the surface, before the next wave crashed over us and took her from me forever.

In my dream, I waited as the water drew me down and down, but her hand never came.

1777

That morning I spied one Captain Redmarch emerge from our Quartermaster's tent, a look of murder in his eye and a hand resting uneasily on his saber. I saluted as befitted his rank and made myself scarce thereafter. I'd heard rumors of the man, and felt no urge to cross him, especially in such a fearful state. It was not until late in the day that I arranged to hear what had transpired straight from old P_____ the Quartermaster himself.

"That [here the good Quartermaster used a word I'll not repeat] dared threaten me with flogging when I told him truly we have no good steel bayonets for his company. He'll have the same as the rest of us, and I'll be damned if I let some New Yorker threaten me like that. You'd think he was George the Third himself the way he was making demands."

"Careful with that one," I told him. "I've heard tell he has his own men flogged on the regular, or worse. The ones he suspects of insubordination aren't seen again."

"[Our Quartermaster uttered another unrepeatable phrase], he'll get his good steel bayonets tomorrow, only they'll be on the end of a Hessian musket and pointed his way."

I bade old P_____ good evening then, for I had an appointment with a bottle of rum a good friend of mine had squirreled away for the eve of battle. I'd not told the Quartermaster all I'd heard, for it was not pleasant. I had another friend in Redmarch's company, and he swore to me that when a sergeant reported for duty one morning reeking drunk, Redmarch had had his Lieutenant, a bull of a man named Morris, drown him in a horse trough, all while Redmarch himself sat and watched like he was passing an evening at the theater.

That next morning, we marched out to meet the Loyalists at the Brandywine, and I forgot the whole affair. I never did hear what happened to old P_____ though, even years after the war.

—Excerpt from *His Soldiering Days: Recollections of a Continental Soldier,* by Elias West
From the library of Tom Morris

VIII.

The next day, I woke up feeling like the living dead, but I still managed to be up and ready in time for my first full day at the café. I walked to town so I wouldn't leave my father stranded without a car. A chill fog still clung to the trees, and the forest was as dark and imposing as ever. The sun was rising, filling the eastern sky with a bright band of gold, but under those trees, it was still night. I made sure to walk on the side of the street where all the houses were.

The town center was empty in the gray light before dawn. It was empty most of the time, but this was another level, a new degree of stillness. The lake was completely invisible from the town square, a bank of gray fog obscured both land and water. Something made me afraid to walk down into that fog. I imagined it would be like walking out into the lake until the water covered me. I looked away and headed straight to the café.

Lady Daphne left me a list of things to do before opening. Most of them were easy enough to take care of. I cleaned all the coffee machines a second time, ground the beans and brewed the drip coffee, and scrubbed down the tables. As the rich, earthy smell of coffee brewing hit me, I felt better. A near-sleepless night full of bad dreams wouldn't slow me down. I helped myself to the first cup of dark roast—I had to test it out, right?

As I took a sip, I thought I saw a face at the front window, out of the corner of my eye. I quickly looked up, but there was nothing there. I even checked outside, but the street was empty on either side of the café. I told myself it had just been my reflection.

I arranged the sandwiches Lady Daphne had made last night into the display cases, and got Clyde the cat his food, just as she had specified. Clyde, looking the most energetic I'd ever seen, came trotting to his dish, furry belly swaying. He gave me a single, indignant meow when I didn't put his food down fast enough.

"There you go, your highness. I hope you like chicken parts platter," I said.

He certainly seemed to like it—I think it was gone before I turned around.

With everything on the list complete, I flipped the sign on the window from closed to open. I knew the customers wouldn't suddenly come stampeding in, but even so, I was surprised how quiet my first hour was. The two ladies who'd come in yesterday as part of their power walk were my first customers—just getting drip coffee this time. Once they had their to-go cups in hand, they hit the sidewalk again.

No one else came in after that, and I was feeling pretty useless. I wondered if I'd scared Hector off for good. I reminded myself that it was his own fault if he felt bad about not helping me. I wished I didn't want his help so badly in the first place. I kept picturing his stupid cocky smile when he said, *you have fun with that.* Who did he think he was?

When the door chime rang, I caught myself hoping he'd changed his mind. It wasn't him though; Lady Daphne had come to check on me.

"The place looks wonderful, dear. Keep up the good work."

I made her a latte, pouring the foam in another fancy leaf design just because I felt like showing off.

"Delicious," she said. "I'm lucky to have found you. Ashley always does her best, but she doesn't drink coffee so I don't think she knows how it's supposed to taste."

"Is she all right? Did she complain about me or anything?"

"No, dear, why would she?"

"No reason," I said, trying quickly to change the subject. "It's been pretty quiet in here. Maybe you should have a poetry night or something. Not that you should do anything like that during my shift. I'm sure Ash could cover it."

"My patrons like their quiet," said Lady. "I have an advantage when it comes to customer research."

She tapped her temple, pointing at all the psychic secrets trapped in her brain. Her powers didn't work that well, though, because she took my silence as a request to tell me more about the wonderful world of clairvoyance.

"I've seen the whole world without leaving my room," she said. "The Taj Mahal, the Great Wall of China, Niagara Falls . . ."

"That's just a few hours from here," I said.

"Still, easier with clairvoyance, dear. Saves me quite a bit on gas."

"So you can see anything anywhere, any time you want?"

"Oh no, sadly it doesn't work like that. It comes only when it wants to, just like Mr. Clyde here." She extended her hand, beckoning to the cat, who raised his head from his cushion, only to yawn and return to napping.

Ask her if she's ever seen anyone on the toilet, I imagined Zoe saying. Before I had a chance to think better of it, I'd already asked the question.

She was quiet for a moment, and I was afraid I'd crossed a line, but then she smiled.

"So far I've been lucky," she said. "I'm a little afraid I'll see something I can't unsee every time I feel it coming on, but such is the burden of the gifted."

With a dramatic sigh, she left me to my work. I was sorry to see her go. Beneath all the theatrics, I liked her—she was nicer than anyone else in this town who wasn't dead or related to me, and she seemed to think I was doing a good job.

The old man came in at noon, still smoking his cigarette. He ordered his coffee, paid, and left with barely a word, only a brief nod by way of goodbye. My only other customer was the pregnant woman from the New Again shop, the same one who tried to throw me out of her store. She seemed not to recognize me, or to pretended she didn't, at least. I made her decaf coffee with low-fat vanilla syrup without complaint, though I thought about secretly using the full fat. I imagined Zoe whispering for me to put something even worse in it.

I kept looking up at her, expecting her to glare at me, or look at the floor, but she genuinely seemed to not remember me, or she just didn't care that she'd been rude. Thankfully she decided to take her coffee to go.

Ash came in a little later for her shift. She walked in gazing at the floor the whole time, not looking me in the eye once.

"Hey," I said. I don't know why I forced the issue, I probably shouldn't have, but after the smoking man and the New Again lady, I was desperate for someone to at least acknowledge my existence, and both of us could definitely use a friend right now.

"Hey."

She looked up for half a second, then went back to get her apron on and pin her hair up. All this was hard for her, I knew. At least she didn't seem to hate me anymore, or blame me for throwing the town out of balance. She didn't have anything more to say, but we actually got into a pretty good rhythm working together, cleaning everything up and making new batches of the drip coffees. When my shift ended, I hung up my apron, let my hair down, and headed out. I made sure to wave to her, and she gave me a tiny ambiguous hand motion that might have been a wave in return.

Deputy Harry was parked near the café again. I could feel his eyes on me as I left. I had to seriously restrain myself from flipping him off.

I was done with work, but not ready to go home yet. Reading those passages my father had left next to the computer gave me an idea. I might not be able to read his book, but nothing was stopping me from doing my own research. There was a little public library not far from the sheriff's station—I noticed it when they brought me in for questioning. It was a good place to start. I was tired of all the secrets, and books at least couldn't change the subject or ignore my questions.

The library was a plain little brick building. Inside it had the same musty smell every other library had. The librarian was an old man with a bushy gray thatch of a mustache and eyebrows to match. He glared at me, squinting his eyes behind a pair of reading glasses, but he didn't say anything.

Someone else sat in the library's little reading area, hard at work behind an impressive stack of books. I tried to sit down without disturbing them.

I stopped short when I saw the face behind the wall of books belonged to Hector. He looked up at the same moment, surprise and what I hoped was guilt flashing across his face, before he recovered and gave me his usual aloof, cocky look.

"What the hell?" I said. "You won't help me, but you'll spend your time studying over summer vacation?"

"Shhh," said Hector, "this is the library."

I almost punched him, I swear. He dropped the smirk when he saw the look in my eyes, which was lucky for him.

"Okay, it's not for school. I'm trying to launch my baseball stat app."

"Right, you mentioned you were a big baseball fan before you had to take a phone call in the middle of a party."

He bit his lip, looking genuinely ashamed.

"Yeah, sorry. I'm used to everyone just ignoring me anyway. I was expecting some stuff I ordered to be delivered. To make up for it, I'll tell you an embarrassing secret: I'm not actually that big of a baseball fan. I'm more of a math fan. Baseball has all these stats and percentages that interact in interesting ways—but it's a lot easier to just tell people you're a baseball fan."

"I never would have guessed," I said. "Now everyone will know you're a huge nerd."

His smirk was back.

"What will become of my popular reputation? Wait, before you keep making fun of me, what are *you* doing here?"

The old man from the library desk was glaring at both of us, clearing his throat every so often. We lowered our voices.

"I'm going to learn what's really going on here any way I can," I said.

Hector was suddenly very interested in the reams of baseball statistics he was poring over. So much for second chances. It looked like I really was on my own.

I went over to one of the computer terminals and typed "Redmarch Lake" into the search field. Not a lot came up: a few regional guides and books on local ecology. Scrolling down a little further, I found hits for the name Redmarch in a few local histories. One of the titles stuck out: *Black Widows: A History of Women Who Poison*—that sounded like something I'd read just for the fun of it. It had a hit for the name Redmarch; I didn't know if they were the same family, but it was worth a shot.

It had a lurid cover with a glass of wine and a bottle sporting a skull and crossbones, and it seemed like something in between serious history and trashy true crime. I skimmed the index until I found the right passage.

Cordelia Redmarch, of the upstate New York town that bears her family's name, was similar in that no poisoning was ever proved conclusively. She was an only child, her mother having died giving birth to her, and the family name was expected to die with her. She had two children with her first husband, a prominent industrialist, before he passed away of a mysterious wasting illness. There were wild rumors of slow poisoning, torture, and a number of wilder things involving hexes and evil spirits, this all having occurred during the nineteenth-century revival of Spiritualism. No charges were brought, however, until Cordelia's second husband succumbed to an identical wasting illness shortly after she gave birth to her third child.

According to the crude medicine of the day, both men died of profound and sustained stress to the heart and nervous system, with no telltale signs of poisoning. It was put forward by the defense that both men had suffered from weak hearts, despite the fact that Cordelia's second husband had been a decorated cavalry officer in the Civil War. In a trial that caused considerable scandal, Cordelia was found innocent. Newspaper accounts portray her as the very picture of a beautiful, heartbroken widow, evoking pity from all, though apparently there was much whispering behind her back. Later she quietly petitioned to have all her children's names changed back to Redmarch, which the judge granted without complaint—an almost unprecedented occurrence given the era.

When I looked up, Hector was staring at me. He seemed surprised and a little nervous. He quickly lowered his eyes and went back to his book, pretending it was the most fascinating thing in the world.

"You'll never believe the stuff I'm learning," I said.

He pretended not to hear me. *What a jerk*, Zoe whispered in my head.

"Is it really this bad?" I asked him.

"What?"

"This town—it's got to be bad if you're spending your summer in the library."

He was silent for a moment, his mouth a hard line. I'd found a crack in his sarcastic exterior.

"Don't you dare feel sorry for me," he said. "I don't need this town. I won't be here forever, and when I leave, I'm going to do great things."

"What things?"

"I don't know. . . . Save the world. Whatever I do, I won't get there by poking this hornet's nest. You should learn from me. I'm serious. I've seen things . . ."

"What things?"

He got quiet again, realizing he said too much. I could tell he wanted to talk—if for no other reason than no one else would talk to him here. Things must have been bad if he was still maintaining the code of silence. It wasn't just that, though. I could tell he was mad at how much he wanted companionship—and stubbornly determined to stay quiet just for that reason.

You two have a lot in common, I imagined Zoe whispering to me.

"Shut up."

Hector looked at me with a raised eyebrow, and I realized with horror I just said that out loud. The embarrassment on my face finally made him crack a smile.

"See, you've only been here a few days, and you're already talking to yourself."

The librarian glared at us again. I went back to get another book from the list, still cursing my lack of inner monologue. The next book was a much more conventional history of the local Native American reservations. Paging through the index, I found a reference to a petition signed by leaders of the Oneida, Onondaga, Seneca, Cayuga, Mohawk, and Tuscarora nations to rename the town of Redmarch Lake, due to ". . . the perpetration of atrocities on nations of the Haudenosaunee in the aftermath of the American Revolution by one Captain Broderick Redmarch, founder of the town of Redmarch Lake, which greatly exceeded in both frequency and viciousness even the other historical crimes committed against the Six Nations by both unauthorized settlers and agents of the United States Government at the time and in the region."

The book didn't go into detail on any of these atrocities, which was a relief. The petition itself had been summarily dismissed by the state assembly, which made me ashamed but not exactly surprised. The book did include a portrait of Captain Redmarch, though, and the statue in the town square wasn't far off. There was a wild look in his pale blue eyes, and something cruel in his smile. He had the same dark blonde hair as Keith.

"You're really doing this, aren't you?" Hector said suddenly.

"What made you think I wasn't serious?"

He scrunched up his eyebrows, giving me a look of profound unease and frustration.

"Damn it, I can't do this anymore. What happened to Neil bothers me—it makes me sick and it freaks me the hell out, and of course I want to do something about it, but the only reason people even tolerate my family in this town is that we don't ask questions."

The old man at the front desk raised a bushy eyebrow at this.

"Keep it down, you two. Miss, I've never seen you before, so I doubt you have a library card. If you don't stay quiet, I might have to ask you to leave."

We had been whispering. How he even heard us I had no idea.

"See what I mean?" whispered Hector. "I'll help you, but we've got to be quiet about it, okay?"

I tried not to smile. I was glad he was helping me, but it shouldn't have taken this long.

"Sure, I'll help you with your school project," Hector said louder. The librarian shook his head and went back to surfing the internet behind his desk. "Once I snuck a look at what he reads all day," Hector whispered. "It's a message board for people who think world leaders and CEO's are secretly lizard men from another planet."

"If you ever meet my dad, don't tell him about that one," I whispered back. "He reads enough of that paranormal stuff."

"Around here we just call it normal stuff," said Hector with a lopsided grin. He was really cute when he wasn't driving me up the wall. I told myself this wasn't the time to think of stuff like that, but I couldn't help sneaking quick glances at him as we pulled books from the shelves, and once I thought I caught him doing the same to me.

I showed Hector the two passages I'd found already, and he went to work on the search database. He had the layout of the whole place memorized. I wished he'd been on board sooner.

"If it weren't for the library and the café, I don't know what I'd do in this town," he said.

We took out a few more local history books, but Hector also wanted to check the town's birth and death records, business registry, and regional crime data, which hadn't even crossed my mind.

"I remember looking into this myself once," said Hector. "I . . . I don't know why I stopped, I just remember getting really nervous about it. I felt like I was doing something wrong."

"Do they make you sign a pledge or something? 'I promise not to ask too many questions?' Because I sure as hell haven't signed anything."

Hector paused for a moment, thinking. His expression was worried.

"I-I don't know. It's not like me to not want to learn something, I just . . . it's hard to explain. I remember being interested in it when I first moved to this town, but the longer I lived here, the more I felt, I don't know, worried . . . afraid? It's like there's this voice in my head that says, 'You don't want to know.'"

He shivered.

"My dad's a mechanic at the quarry," he said. "He specializes in the kind of heavy machines they have out there. They approached my parents with an offer, back when we lived in the city. They already had a house picked out for us and everything. If we'd just tried to move here randomly, I don't think anyone would have sold to us. If we piss everyone off, who knows, maybe they'll kick us out. I wouldn't be surprised if there wasn't some shady clause in the mortgage we signed. It's that kind of town."

We split up the books we'd pulled from the shelves and started poring over the indexes. As we read, one disturbing fact after another emerged.

The Redmarch family really did own most of the lakefront property, along with the quarry, known for its rosy-hued marble, and the Redmarch Savings Bank. But they'd been rich for a long time, before starting either business. Before the Revolutionary War, Broderick Redmarch had been a fur trapper, starting a company with a merchant named Wallace Clyburn. The two had made a fortune, even when the fur trade was drying up in the region. Through all the ups and downs of history, the Redmarches always seemed to come out on top, always one step ahead of a downturn, or primed to take advantage of a boom.

Redmarch Lake also had dramatically higher rates of violent death and disappearance than the surrounding area. Most of this was attributed to things pretty common to small towns throughout America: alcohol, the collapse of local industry, and the rise of drugs like methamphetamine and heroin. But that didn't explain why it was so much worse here than anywhere else.

"This is crazy," said Hector. "There's more unexplained deaths in this town than anywhere for miles, and it's constant across time. It doesn't seem to be related to national trends at all."

"You mentioned human sacrifice back at the party," I said.

"That's an old story. I was just trying to freak you out, I'm sorry."

He didn't sound convinced, though. In fact, it sounded like he was the one freaked out right now.

There was more. We found cause to tie at least some of that violence to the Redmarch family; besides founder Broderick Redmarch and the infamous Cordelia, there was a Lyman Redmarch hanged for a series of grisly murders in the region. This was in the late 1800s, before people really knew anything about serial killers. Still, one of the local papers had given him the wildly original title of Finger Lakes Ripper.

It took me a moment to realize Lyman was Cordelia's youngest child. Given what she got away with, his crimes must have been spectacularly bad if he was actually executed for them. The anecdote I found about him only mentioned a "chamber of horrors" beneath the Redmarch manor that "dismayed many a stouthearted lawman normally unfazed by man's inhumanity to man."

What's more, Lyman Redmarch was widely suspected to have two accomplices from the two other most prominent families in the town. I caught my breath when I saw their names: Wendell Clyburn and Theodore Morris. Both men were cleared due to lack of evidence, but a cloud of suspicion hung over them their whole lives—rumors of "black magic and blasphemous native rites." I winced at the vintage racism, but I couldn't help but wonder what that gruesome threesome had been up to, even if I didn't want to know the gory details.

That made me think of something else. There were obviously ruins here, but no matter how hard I looked, I couldn't find anything on the tribe that built them and when they lived here. The tribal history I'd read just made a vague remark about the Six Nations of the Iroquois staying well away from Redmarch Lake and its surrounding woods. They'd called the lake *Otkon Okàra*, which means the Spirit's Eye.

There was one passage, the statement of a Seneca war chieftain after he'd surrendered, claiming the Americans fought with "a viciousness not seen since the fearsome Two-Shadows," but I could find no other reference to this name anywhere. Just as I was about to mention this to Hector, the old librarian heaved himself up from his desk.

"Library's closing," he said, "if you're actually going to check any of that out, do it now."

"Your mother was a lizard person," Hector said under his breath.

"What was that?"

"Nothing, sir, we're on our way." He turned to me, whispering again, "I feel like he closes up earlier every day."

Our houses were in the same direction, so we walked back for a ways together as the sun set and the shadows deepened in the trees around us.

"Thanks for helping me," I said. "It can't be easy living here."

"Now I'm mad at myself for not doing it sooner," said Hector. "I don't like the idea that this town is messing with my head that much. What if I can't readjust to normal life?"

"That might not be the town's fault," I said, giving him a playful punch on the arm.

I was nervous for a second—he didn't know me well enough to know I said stuff like that even to my good friends—or pretty much only to my good friends. Luckily, he laughed.

"I've got an idea for what we do next," he said. "No promises, it might not work, but if it does, I think it'll really help."

"Don't keep me in suspense," I said. "What is it?"

"Uh-uh, it's a surprise. I don't want to look lame if I can't pull it off. If it works, I'll let you know at the café."

I nodded. We had come to his house. Another old wooden place like my dad's, but this one looked freshly painted and better cared for, with a lush garden in front.

"Have a good night," I said. "And thanks for the help. I'm glad you're here."

"Me too," he said. "Glad you're here, I mean. I'm not glad *I'm* here. . . . You know what I mean—I'll see you later."

He blushed a little as he said this. All the way home, I tried not to think of how cute it was, and I totally failed.

You like him, just admit it, Zoe whispered in my head.

"Shut up," I muttered, glad no one was around to hear me this time. I felt a sudden twinge of sadness as I walked. Zoe had left me too early to talk about boys together. I had to try to imagine what kind of guys she'd like, if she'd even like guys at all. My memories of her could only take me so far.

My father was just getting dinner ready when I came in— spaghetti with jarred sauce, which Mom would never have even allowed in the house. Instead, whenever we had pasta, she tried and failed to replicate my grandmother's sauce— which was one of the best things I'd ever tasted. Mom made a good sauce, but it never matched up to Grandma's, and that put her in such a bad mood I kind of dreaded having pasta with her. Dad's spaghetti was the opposite of *al dente*, and the sauce was practically sloppy joe, but at least we could eat it in peace.

The next day, I rose at dawn again and walked the misty street into town. I cleaned everything, fed the cat, and made the coffee, just like I had the day before. As the coffee was brewing, I thought I saw someone at the window again, but when I went to look, there was nobody there. Was this town making me lose my mind? Had Neil seen the same thing every morning?

I kept hoping to see Hector that day, and the day after, but he didn't turn up. Instead, I served the power walk ladies, the old man from the bus, and a few other locals who barely acknowledged my existence, then worked in silent détente with Ash in the hour or so our shifts overlapped.

I noticed Deputy Harry outside the café again on the second day and tried to tell myself he wasn't keeping tabs on me.

I was starting to think Hector's fear of the town had gotten the better of him, or the whole thing had just been a ruse to get me to stop asking. Then, four days after our visit to the library, Hector came rushing through the door, breathless, like he'd run the whole way here. His expression was hard to read—one part triumph, one part pure panic.

"What can I get you?" I said.

"Never mind that," he said. "Do you want to know how Neil really died?"

IX.

"What did you find out?" I said.

"I got a copy of the county coroner's report. I haven't read it yet, I figured we should do it together."

My jaw dropped. I didn't expect Hector to pull off anything like this.

"How'd you do that?" I said. "Did you hack into the county system or something?"

"That's a lot harder than on TV, plus it's like mad illegal—this town already feels enough like prison. No, I spoofed an email address from the *Finger Lakes Monitor*, which is much easier. I said I was a reporter writing a story on the incident, and they sent me the redacted coroner's report—they said I was the only one who'd even requested it."

"Isn't that also illegal?"

"Yeah, but the *Finger Lakes Monitor* has barely heard of the internet. I think their average reader's like eighty years old. Not much chance they'll find out. Plus, this town likes to keep to itself, and the surrounding area is only too happy to oblige."

"That's—" I could see him waiting for me to say *brilliant*, which it was, but I couldn't resist messing with him a little. "—that's not bad."

He looked offended for a moment, before he saw me smirking, and smiled back. Then we remembered what we were about to look at, and any amusement drained from our faces.

The document Hector opened had been scanned badly—all the text was slightly skewed on a diagonal, and parts of it had been blacked out with permanent marker. Even so, the parts that were still legible sent a chill down my spine.

"He didn't drown," Hector said, "he *was* drowned. It says they think someone held him down. He was fighting back. It's hard to tell from the stuff they redacted, but it looks like someone cut him up first. The cuts must have come from a serrated knife, or . . . or some sort of animal claw."

We were both quiet as the awfulness of this sunk in. I thought of the note, and what I thought had chased me in the woods, and I shivered. Just what the hell was going on here? I almost told Hector about the note, about Zoe, but I had no idea where to begin, and I was afraid he'd think I was as bad as the librarian with his lizard-people conspiracies. Who wouldn't, given the circumstances?

I barely knew Neil, but I was already thinking of him as my friend on the night he died. I thought of him right here in the café, laughing or talking about going away to college. I couldn't think of my friend dying in such an awful way.

Hector emailed me a copy of the report. We exchanged phone numbers as well, and I couldn't help but imagine a more normal situation, where he was asking for my number to take me out sometime. Thoughts like that were so far away from what we were dealing with that they might as well have been happening in a movie—a movie I wished I was in right now, instead of here where someone could die so horribly.

Neither of us could handle talking about what happened to Neil, so we tried to think of what we could do to find out more. It wasn't much.

"We need a contact on the inside," I said. "There's only so much we can find out without someone who knows how this place works."

"Good luck with that. It's like they've all taken a vow of silence. Most of the time, they don't even acknowledge my presence. You might have better luck, though, since you're family's in the founders' club or whatever. Why don't you just ask your father?"

"Whenever the town comes up, he acts just like the rest of them. He'll tell me little things now and then, but any time I ask a question, he avoids it, or makes some kind of answer that doesn't really answer anything."

Hector looked sincerely disappointed.

"That leaves the junior detectives with a dead end. I was . . . I was starting to think things would change here for a minute."

His sarcastic smile was back, but now I could see the hurt and anger he masked with it. Hector had been stuck in this place he hated for so long, he didn't want to start hoping—but I couldn't let him quit now.

"Things are already different here—now there are two of us, and we can learn more than either of us could alone. I'm not giving up."

"Why do you care so much about this? You barely knew Neil."

"It's more than that. My family is tied up in this town somehow. I have to know what that means." I hoped I could tell him about Zoe and the notes at some point. I wanted someone else to know—and if I was honest with myself, I wanted that someone to be Hector, but he'd probably think I was nuts.

The bell on the door rang, startling us both. Ash was here for her shift. She walked to the back, looking at the floor the whole time—pretending we didn't exist. I could see how much she was hurting. If anyone in this town would want justice, it would be her.

"I think it's my turn to do some investigating," I said to Hector. "I'll let you know when I find what we need."

In the few hours we worked together, I tried to be helpful to Ash while still giving her space. She just went on pretending I wasn't there. It was better than outright hostility, but it was a long way from breaking through this town's wall of silence, and I still thought she was our best hope.

I felt a twinge of guilt, like I was plotting to manipulate her, but I genuinely did want to help her. It seemed to me she'd want to know the truth more than anyone. I only started to come to terms with losing Zoe when I learned more about my feelings and the enormity of what I'd lost.

Maybe Ash was content to bury her head in the sand like most of the people here, but I doubted it.

"I just wanted to say again how sorry I am about Neil," I said.

She only nodded her head at this.

"I hope we can move past how we got started."

She stopped scrubbing the counter and looked at me. Not hateful, at least, but not exactly friendly, either.

"How long are you going to be here, the summer?"

"Yeah, but my dad lives here. I'll be back to visit. I like it here."

She looked at me like I'd just said I enjoyed gargling battery acid.

"I'm out of here as soon as I turn eighteen," she said. "If it weren't for my mom, I'd be gone now."

"Is she all right?"

"She's got a condition. She mostly just needs help around the house. She can find someone, though, or she can deal. There's nothing for me here, not anymore."

She let that last thought hang in the air between us. Neil's restless spirit might as well have been haunting the place, whipping up a spume of ghostly latte foam. Before now, I thought I was done with death, at least until I was older. How many people make it through their youth without losing more than a grandparent? I had lost the person that felt like half of myself, and now someone I knew had died in a way more horrible than I could imagine. It was like losing Zoe had opened a black hole in my life that just drew more death into its orbit.

And somehow, all of it was connected. I had to know how Zoe fit in to all of this.

"You never stop feeling it when you lose someone," I said, "but it does get easier. If it didn't, I wouldn't be here."

She looked up. Her mouth moved like she was going to say something, but nothing came out. She was silent for a moment, as if fighting back more tears. Then she gave me a brief nod.

"Thanks," she said. "I forgot about your sister. Sorry . . ."

"It's okay. You just have to find what helps you keep going, whatever it is."

She nodded. It might have been my imagination, but she seemed a bit more at ease around me now.

Our last hour together passed in silence, but it was a more comfortable silence. When my time was finally up, I hung my apron and waved goodbye to her. Once again she gave me a little wave back—progress.

Deputy Harry was nowhere to be seen today. Instead, a Jeep was parked on the street in front of the café. I did a double take when I saw the driver—Keith Redmarch. What's more, he was apparently waiting for me, because when he saw me, he leaned his head out.

"Clara, hey, I'm glad I caught you. I heard you were working at the café now."

"You heard right," I said, trying not to be too sarcastic. Keith was nice, but why was he waiting for me, and what more did he know about what had happened that night in the woods?

"So, I hope this isn't too weird or anything, but when

my father heard I'd met Tom's daughter, he insisted I invite you up to the house. He'd like to meet you."

He wasn't wrong about the weird part—why would his father want to meet me? Was he like, the king of the town? Would I insult him by saying no? My father's warning to stay away from the Redmarch clan seemed a little less strange now, especially given everything I'd read about their ancestors. Then again, my ancestors had been a part of that, too.

"Um, I know I'm a riveting conversationalist, but why exactly does he want to meet me?"

Keith looked troubled for a moment, caught between an awkward situation and a duty to his family.

"I didn't ask him why, but I think he was good friends with your dad when they were kids. They don't really talk anymore, though. Maybe he wants you to give him a message. Look . . . my dad is a nice guy, but he's used to people just doing what he says. I'm sorry to put you up to this; it's clearly awkward. I'll head out."

He turned to go, shaking his head.

"No, wait. It's okay," I said. "I'll come."

He mentioned two or three times that I didn't have to, but I had made up my mind. If someone in this town actually wanted to talk to me, I wasn't about to pass up the opportunity. I hopped into the passenger side, and we were off. The wind whipped around us as Keith drove along the road that wound around the lake. We were headed for the big house on the opposite bank, by the island.

"Did the deputies talk to you about Neil?" Keith asked.

"Yeah, you?"

"They came up to the house to talk to me. Not fair, I know. I should have had to go to the station like everyone else. I'm not sure what good it would have done—I lost track of Neil that night—but all the 'family perks' really make me want to punch someone. I don't want special treatment."

Easy to say when you're used to getting it, I thought. Still, points for even acknowledging it.

"Listen, thanks for being all right with this. I hate letting my father down." The way he said this made me wonder just what his father was really like. "Plus, it's nice to meet someone new here. It doesn't happen very often."

The road wound up as we went around the lake, hugging the edge of the cliff. Past Keith, I could see out to the calm water below. Before long, the house was in view, bordered by terraced slopes of grape vines strung on poles. The Redmarch mansion definitely did not disappoint— somewhere along the way, the road had become a long driveway flanked by hedges, which ended in a dry marble fountain. The house itself was brick, with white stucco columns in front—built in what I think was a Colonial style. Keith parked his Jeep in front and we went inside.

The house was dark in the way only old houses were; like it was built when people worried about warmth and safety, and light was just a trifle. The walls were dark wood and old, patterned wallpaper. A massive staircase stood in the front room. Portraits lined the walls—Redmarch ancestors. Most of them had Keith's ethereal good looks: graceful, symmetrical features, piercing eyes, hair like a saintly halo or a dark cloud, depending on how the light caught it. Others in the Redmarch clan were pale and sickly. Even with the artist's idealizing touch, they looked tired and old beyond their years. I saw a portrait of a stunning blonde woman in an old-fashioned ball gown that might have been Cordelia Redmarch. I looked for her son Lyman, the Finger Lakes Ripper, but couldn't guess which one he was. I wondered if his chamber of horrors was still under our feet. I tried not to dwell on it.

"Dad's in the winery, I think. I'd give you a tour of the house, but honestly, most of it's closed off under sheets and like a desert's worth of dust. It's just dad and me here."

Keith led me through the kitchen toward the back door. I caught a brief glimpse of a massive dark wood table in the dining room, and past it what looked like a study or library before we were outside again. We walked through the rows of grape vines. As we passed a perfect green cluster of grapes, Keith picked a few and handed them to me. They were delightfully sweet. Not wanting to seem rude, I spat the bitter seeds quietly into my hand and dropped them beside the path.

The winery was an old building like a barn behind the main house, made with heavy wooden beams. Inside it was even darker than the mansion, lined with racks and racks of wooden wine casks. There were a few beams of pale light shining down from the high windows, each filled with dancing dust motes.

"Dad?" Keith called out. We caught sight of Mr. Redmarch with a glass in hand, sampling wine from one of the casks. He was swirling the wine in his glass around with a spiral motion, gazing into the golden liquid. He looked up and smiled when he saw us.

Jonathan Redmarch was supposedly the same age as my father, but he looked at least ten years younger. His age was only visible in the crinkle at the corners of his eyes. His hair was the same dark blond as Keith's, without even a trace of gray.

"Clara Morris, wonderful to meet you."

"Hello," I said, suddenly at a loss for words. I had come here with grand plans of finding out more about this town and what happened to Neil, but something about Keith's father made me want to hold my tongue. In old stories, I'd heard people describe the regal bearing of kings, the way something in their nature made you want to listen and obey. I thought it was all propaganda, but that's what Mr. Redmarch seemed like: a king. It was hard to describe, but it felt like there was more of him there than you could see.

"Your father probably hasn't mentioned me. He used to be my best friend, you know, but we lost touch when he moved to the city. I'd hoped, when he came back last year, that it would be like old times again."

Mr. Redmarch took a deep whiff of the aroma from his glass of wine. He took a small sip, savoring it.

"I'm worried about him, you know. He won't talk to me. Then I heard you were here, and as luck would have it, my son's already met you, and I thought, well that's certainly a sign if there ever was one."

He smiled. Beside me, I noticed Keith had relaxed a little.

"Come, try some of this, it's coming along nicely. I know you're underage, but it's just a taste."

He poured us each a little bit right from the barrel. Before we could taste, he insisted we smell the wine's aroma, which I learned is called the bouquet. The smell was stronger than I expected, fresh strawberries with just a hint of something rough and raw underneath, almost like gasoline. Mr. Redmarch held his glass up for a toast.

"To friends old and new."

I felt a little quiver of panic—I'd been so firm about not drinking before that even a sip seemed wrong, somehow. I was afraid of losing even the tiniest amount of control, but I didn't want to be rude. It was lusciously sweet, like strawberries with honey.

"It's a late harvest Riesling," said Mr. Redmarch. "The trick is to leave it on the vine just long enough. A little rot preserves the sweetness."

"Do you sell this?" I asked.

"Oh no, it's just a vanity project. We don't have room to grow that much. Tell me, how's your father doing?"

I was worried about him, he was spending too much time at home, and not talking to the people who cared about him, but I didn't want to tell Mr. Redmarch any of that. Somehow it seemed like the wrong thing to do. Instead, I told him about my father's work, and the time we spent together on his visits to the city. Mr. Redmarch asked me a little about my life and my mother, too, and our time in New Jersey where we'd lived before losing Zoe. He nodded as I spoke, though he barely seemed interested in anything outside of the town that bore his family's name. After a while, he suggested Keith show me the view. As we turned to go, he pulled his son aside for a few more quiet words. I tried not to eavesdrop, as much as I wanted to. "Visit your mother, she misses you," was all I could make out.

"Everything all right?" I said as we walked out toward the front of the house.

"Yeah, hey, thanks for coming. I know it was a weird request."

"No offense, but everything seems a bit weird in this town."

On the front lawn, we could see out over the lake toward the town on the other side. The sun was setting over the mirror-smooth water, leaving a golden trail in the lake as it drew closer to the horizon. There was a path leading down the slope of the front yard to a little dock. Not far from shore, I could see the island with its ruins. Closer now, I could make out what looked like a mound of earth crowned by the single broken column I'd seen before. Something about it made me uneasy. Hector's human sacrifice stories were a little more believable now that I knew something of the town's history.

"I can see how this place might seem strange, but it's all I know," Keith said. He glanced once over his shoulder, making sure his father wasn't there. "I'd love to see New York City. I mean, I don't know if it's anything like on

TV, but it seems like the kind of place where you can, you know, be yourself."

I suddenly had the horrible, sinking feeling that all this time I'd been on some sort of arranged date. Keith hadn't made it sound that way, but his father had been awfully glad we'd met. I wondered if the deputy I saw outside the café had been watching me for the sheriff's office, or for Mr. Redmarch. And now Keith couldn't look me in the eye, just like a boy at a seventh-grade dance—shocking, considering he was the town's angel-faced heir apparent.

What's his problem? I imagined Zoe whispering. *He should be grateful you put up with his weirdo family in his weirdo town.*

"Look, you don't have to talk to me just because your father wants you to."

Keith looked like I'd just given him a swift kick in the family jewels.

"Oh my god, no, I like you, I mean . . . I mean, it's not like that . . ."

I didn't expect him to be this nervous. I laid a hand on his shoulder and he seemed to relax a bit.

"I'm sorry about all this," he said. "I knew I'd find a way to make it awkward. Being who I am, I have certain things expected of me, things I have to live up to. My family is very old-fashioned; they expect you to carry on the bloodline. But I don't think I'll ever be able to. It's just not who I am . . ."

I wasn't absolutely sure what he meant, but I had a pretty good idea. It made me feel better about him not

132

seeming very interested in me, and much more sympathetic toward this boy who seemed to have everything. The sun was lower in the sky now. It was starting to slip behind the clouds, lighting them up in pink and orange like paper lanterns, which were mirrored in the lake below.

"Nice view," I said.

X.

By the time Keith dropped me off at my father's house, the sun had slipped behind the trees, and I could see the first flicker of fireflies in the darkness of the forest.

"Be careful at dusk around here," Keith said.

I didn't bother asking him why; I knew he wouldn't answer. I waved goodbye to him and walked toward the house. I could see the edge of the curtain in the front window was pulled back—I'd been spotted. There would be no getting out of this. I opened the door braced for an argument, but as usual, my father looked more disappointed, even afraid, than angry. I wished in that moment that he'd just yell like Mom.

"No wonder you drive your mother crazy: everything we ask of you, you do the exact opposite. I don't think I was demanding too much, just to stay out of the forest and stay away from the Redmarches. You haven't been in the forest, too, have you?"

"No, Dad."

Guilt twisted up my stomach like a wrung-out cloth. I wanted to take back everything I'd done, but some stubborn part of me still felt justified in doing it. My father was right: he really wasn't asking a lot, but he'd offered me no explanation, just "don't do this" like I was a child. What was I supposed to do when Keith and his father showed up acting like perfectly nice people? Not exactly normal but no weirder than anyone else in this town.

"Dad, I'm sorry, he came by the café saying his father wanted to meet me, that you used to be best friends. What was I supposed to do? I didn't want to be rude."

"Sometimes being rude is the right thing to do."

I felt anger welling up in me, washing away the guilt. One thing I never let go was being talked down to, and both my parents were experts at it.

"Maybe if you told me why, instead of just forbidding me like a kid with a hot stove, I'd know what to do in situations like this."

My father sighed. He took a moment to collect his thoughts before speaking again.

"All right, as you wish. I'm sure you noticed the Redmarch clan is rich, and they seem to stay that way no matter what happens They own half the valley and they pretty much do as they please. They've got connections in the county, and all the way in Albany—their money goes a long way to keep this town isolated.

"It's true that Jonathan Redmarch used to be my best friend, but the rest of his family was different. When I was a boy, everyone knew not to leave children alone with his uncle. The parents in town would all warn each other when they saw him hanging around the school, but no one ever called the sheriff. As for Jonathan's father, he seemed nice enough, but every time I saw his mother, she had a fresh bruise from a different household accident. And where's Jonathan's wife now? Some fancy facility in the Hudson Valley, but no one knows what she's there for—"

I thought of all the portraits in the foyer of that house. All those beautiful faces now seemed hard and cruel, their spouses next to them were pale and haunted. History in the library had been one thing, but I had no idea it was so recent.

"Keith's not like the rest of them."

"They never are at first. Jonathan Redmarch was the nicest person I ever met, once. Now—"

The phone rang with a loud buzz that made both of us jump. My father looked at me, as if I somehow knew who was calling. He picked up the receiver.

"Hello? Jonathan, hi."

My father's voice stayed friendly, but his face went white.

"Yes, she mentioned. Yes, it's been much too long. I'm glad you're well. Things . . . things are all right with me." I could see my father trying to keep his voice steady. His free hand was shaking slightly.

"Well, I've got a lot of work lately, so I don't—what's that? Well, I'm sure I could find the time. I'll see you next week, then. Looking forward to it."

My father hung up the phone. He looked like he'd just been fired and diagnosed with cancer in the same phone call.

"We're having dinner with the Redmarches next week, at the old Clyburn hotel."

My father said this as if it were my fault. I guess I gave Jonathan Redmarch an excuse to call. I was about to ask dad what had happened between them, but I could see the silence settling over him like a heavy blanket, and I knew I'd be lucky to hear two more words from him tonight. Without saying a thing, he left the room to start dinner.

The next morning was quiet at the coffee shop, as usual. I saw the same silhouette in the window while I was getting ready to open, but this time I knew not to go looking for anyone in the street. It was probably just a trick of the light—still, I doubted I'd ever get used to it, or anything else about this eerie little town.

I was hoping to see Hector again, but he never came in. My only customer all morning was the old man from the bus, who arrived exactly at twelve with his cigarette blazing, ordered his coffee, filled it with enough cream and sugar to give a horse type-2 diabetes, and left with a friendly nod.

I thought that would be it for customers today, but just as I was getting to the last hour before Ash joined me, Deputy Chief Elaine Cross River walked in. I froze.

"Hi, Clara. You remember me, right?"

"Of course, um, what can I help you with? Did you have more questions?"

A voice in the back of my mind was screaming, *She knows you and Hector are looking into things. She knows about the coroner's report*, but Elaine Cross River just shook her head. She actually looked a little annoyed.

"Can't I just order some coffee?"

"Oh, of course, what would you like? I can make you an espresso . . ."

"Just the regular kind. Black."

I poured her coffee. I'd have liked the chance to make her something special, but at least she didn't load it down with cream or sugar. I expected her to take it to go, but she pulled up one of the stools at the café counter and sat down.

"Can I ask you something, Clara? Off the record, I mean."

"Of course."

"What the hell is wrong with this town?"

She smiled when she said this, but I could tell it was really getting to her. I couldn't blame her.

"I wish I knew. My father moved back two years ago and this is my first time visiting. Even he won't talk to me about the town. Sometimes it feels like he's closer with the people here than with me, except nobody here seems to like each other that much."

"I know what you mean," said Elaine. "This place has a bad reputation in the home office. Nobody likes to come here. If something's happened, they know the locals won't talk. And between you and me, more than the usual share of bad things seem to happen here. You work with that Ash girl, right? I'm positive she knows more than she told us, but I couldn't get it out of her. And of course the two deputies stationed here are local boys. The town likes it that way."

"Bill and Harry?"

"Yeah. The poker faces. Bill's nice enough." She left her opinion of Harry unsaid, but it was easy to guess. "I shouldn't be talking to you about stuff like this, but it's nice to see someone else from outside the cone of silence. I'll tell you what—keep your eyes open while you're here. If you see anything strange, call me. I don't think anyone else here will."

She gave me a card with her phone number before heading back to work. I wished I could help her more.

I waved hello to Ash when she showed up for her shift, and she gave me a shy little wave in return. I couldn't help but wonder what she knew that she wouldn't tell the sheriff's office.

"Slow day today," I said.

"No complaints here, as long as her Ladyship can still pay us."

We worked in silence until my time was up, but by now it felt normal, like we were working together instead of awkwardly avoiding each other. Then, as I was mopping down the floor, I looked up to see Ash staring at me, working up the nerve to talk.

"I-I thought he was such a loser," she finally said, "at first, I mean."

". . . Neil?"

She nodded.

"This is a rough place to grow up. It's . . . there's a feeling here. Everyone's always on edge. You learn to keep your defenses up all the time. No one trusts each other. Then there's this guy—this guy who smiles all the time like it's all nothing. I thought, what an idiot. Then we worked together every day, and it was like I couldn't help it. . . . He just made everything a little brighter."

"I'm sorry," I said. I rested a hand on her shoulder. She didn't flinch, which was progress.

"I should have known," she said. "I should have known something like this would happen. It's how things work here."

We were quiet for a moment then. I had dealt with more grief than most people my age, but now that I had the opportunity, I couldn't think of anything to say that would actually make it better. Things here were bad in a way I barely understood, and I didn't see how I could comfort someone who'd lived with it all her life. Especially when I barely had things together myself.

"I saw you get in the car with Keith Redmarch yesterday," she said. "You need to be careful."

"Why?" I said. "My father said the same thing."

"Not him, I mean, his family. They—" She looked around her in a panic. Everyone in this town seemed to do that when they were about to say something true. "They're in charge. This is their town, in more than just the name. I'm just getting used to you here, I'd hate to . . . just don't try to change things here."

"Is that what Neil tried to do?"

She nodded. She didn't say much more after that.

"When he broke up with me, he said he'd done something wrong. He wouldn't tell me what. He seemed afraid.

I heard his friend Danny teasing him about some new girl-friend, so I just figured he dumped me for her. When I saw you at the party, I—well, I thought it was you. Now I don't know what to think."

Things were quiet for a week. I served the same regulars at the café, only now I looked forward to Ash showing up in the afternoon. We actually talked now, not about anything that shed light on the town or its secrets, but it was still good to have someone to chat with. She asked me to tell her about living in New York, and she seemed to know more about the city than I did. I guess she read a lot about it online.

"I thought about moving there," she said. "Maybe trying to sing in a band or something."

I asked her to sing something, and she refused for days, finally crooning along with a pop song on the radio and rolling her eyes the whole time. Her voice was great, though, a sultry alto. I never would have guessed.

If anything, my father withdrew even further into himself. We barely talked. I knew he was dreading dinner with the Redmarches. I wished he would tell me why. I met up with Hector a few more times at the library, but we didn't manage to find anything new.

Then, on the day we were supposed to have dinner with Keith and his father, Ash stopped me as I was about to leave work.

"I've been thinking a lot, and I want to apologize for the way I acted when we met. It was out of line."

"It's okay. You lost someone. I know what that's like."

"No, I shouldn't have blamed you. This town makes you afraid of anything new or out of place, and I hate it. I don't want that to be my life anymore. Friends?"

She stretched her arms out toward me. The whole thing was so unexpected, it took me a minute to realize she was trying to give me a hug. It was an awkward embrace on both our parts, but it felt really good to clear the air with Ash. I liked to think I didn't care what other people thought of me, but of course I did.

"Listen," I said. "I don't know if you want to be involved in this, but—"

"You're trying to find out what happened to Neil," she said. "What really happened. I know you found something. I know it seems like no one talks in this town, but there are rumors. I heard you were working with Hector. I-I guess you won't stop trying to change things, just like Neil."

"I can show you what we found, if you like," I said.

I expected her to say no, to push me away. I'd done exactly what she told me not to do. Instead, she nodded. She looked spooked, like she couldn't believe she was doing this, but when I looked her in the eye, I was surprised at the resolve I found there.

I took out my phone and found the police report in my email. Ash turned even paler than normal as she read, one hand clamped over her mouth to stifle a gasp.

"I knew it. He'd never just get drunk and drown, and he'd never pick a fight with anyone. He was the nicest guy . . ." She was quiet for a moment, trembling slightly. "I want to help you. I-I know I'm going to regret this, but I can't just let it go."

I nodded.

"We'll talk tomorrow," Ash said. "I think I can find someone who might know what happened that night."

My father was pacing nervously around the house when I got home. He'd probably been that way all day. I took a quick shower to wash off a day at the café while he puttered around the living room. I hadn't really packed any dressy clothes, but I had a skirt and a nice top that were probably good enough. When I walked out, my father was wearing slacks and a rumpled dress shirt. I had to help him fix the collar.

"Thanks," he said, "stupid thing . . ."

"I'm sorry I got us into this, Dad."

"Don't worry about it. I owe Jonathan a visit. It's been too long."

He smiled, but his eyes were still panicked. It was unnerving to see my father so afraid, especially when I didn't understand why. I liked to tell myself I didn't need other people to be strong for me, but right then, I wished my father was confident like fathers are supposed to be. Or that he'd at least tell me why he was so afraid.

We don't know what he's been through, I imagined Zoe whispering, *we have to be patient.*

She was right, but if he didn't tell me what was going on, I wasn't sure how much longer I could stand it.

The Redmarches hadn't arrived yet when we came to the Clyburn. There were a few other people eating dinner, but the big dining room was mostly empty. The host almost pounced on us when we walked in, even before my father mentioned we were meeting the Redmarches. I was amazed someone in this town actually looked glad to see us. In fact, the whole restaurant had an out-of-place feel. The staff was all young and eager to do their jobs, and the décor was surprisingly modern in a town that felt so stuck in the past. Yet under it all was a faint odor, like old wood when damp and mildew have set in. No amount of candles and new white tablecloths could erase what lay beneath. And just like that book of ghost stories had said, I couldn't see a mirror anywhere.

The menu was the same as what you'd see in half the fancier places in Brooklyn these days—heritage pork belly, roasted brussels sprouts, heirloom tomatoes—which always made me picture a smiling grandmother passing on a mummified old tomato to her disappointed granddaughter. Everything was locally sourced and farm-to-table.

"A restaurant group from the city bought this place a while ago," my father said. "They want to open up the old hotel above it, too."

I felt sorry for whoever's bright idea that was. They clearly didn't know what they were getting into. My father seemed to be thinking exactly the same thing without saying it.

A moment later, everyone in the restaurant fell silent as Keith and his father walked in. It was good to be the local royalty, though I could tell the attention made Keith uncomfortable, and his father barely seemed to notice. When Jonathan Redmarch caught sight of my father, he smiled in a sincere, almost goofy way that was totally at odds with the cool, reserved man I'd met yesterday.

"There's Tom. God damn, it's been too long!"

In a flash, he was by my father's side, shaking his hand. The difference between them was even more stark up close—my father looked tired, his hair thinning and his midsection getting thicker, while Jonathan Redmarch looked like he'd stepped off a movie set. They sat down, and Mr. Redmarch pulled out a bottle of wine, which the waiter swiftly uncorked and poured two generous glasses for him and my father.

The effect was almost charming, except that everyone else in the restaurant, my father included, was watching Mr. Redmarch as if he might snap at any moment.

"I bet you haven't told your daughter what a troublemaker you used to be," Mr. Redmarch said with a laugh. "This guy was always getting me in over my head. Remember when you talked me into stealing apples from the McReady's farm? Then old Mrs. McReady came after us with her shotgun?"

Sure enough, I didn't remember that story, or any stories from my father's childhood, but he was nodding along with Mr. Redmarch and even smiling a little.

"Is that true, Dad?"

"I guess it is, except it wasn't apples we stole, it was a jug of her extra-hard cider."

"Right, right," said Mr. Redmarch. "You'll have to forgive me. Those years are a bit of a blur. Sometimes they almost feel like they happened to someone else."

Mr. Redmarch looked troubled for a moment, as if trying to capture a memory that was just out of reach.

"Yes, well it's a good thing I got you in trouble with me. She had me dead in her sights. They'd have been pulling buckshot out of me for weeks if she hadn't seen you with me."

Mr. Redmarch frowned like he'd just smelled something bad. I guess he didn't like anyone calling attention to his special status. Then he grinned.

"Those were the days. Shame we got old."

My father looked old, Mr. Redmarch did not. With a cheerful flourish, he handed the menus back to the waiter, asking instead for whatever the chef thought was best. Jonathan Redmarch and my father spent the rest of the night talking and laughing about old times. It was a side to my father I never imagined; stealing hard cider, racing cars on country roads at midnight, trying to make moonshine in the woods. I had trouble squaring it with the quiet man I knew, and I wished he'd told me even one of these stories. Mr. Redmarch seemed to love every moment of it, savoring it like he couldn't remember any of it without someone else there to remind him.

Even my father seemed to be enjoying himself, though he remained uneasy, and as the night progressed, I noticed a wistful sadness creeping into his voice, as if there was a painful side to all these happy memories. I knew how he felt—my childhood with Zoe had been happy, but now even my best memories were a source of pain.

"Do you remember the time you had dates with Marcy Barrows and Sue Stevens on the same night?" Mr.

Redmarch pointed a mock accusing finger at my father, who protested his innocence.

"An honest mistake. Dating was a nightmare. You were lucky you and Anne were so steady. How is she, by the way?"

Everything was suddenly silent. There was so much I didn't know about this history, but it was plain to see my father had forgotten himself. The color had vanished from his face, and Mr. Redmarch was looking at him with a hard, penetrating stare.

"She's well. We should all get together sometime. Perhaps we should take a boat out on the lake."

Mr. Redmarch's words sounded normal, but they were full of cold menace. My father couldn't look him in the eye. I glanced over at Keith, but he had shut his eyes tight as soon as his mother's name was mentioned.

"But that's something for another time," Mr. Redmarch's easy smile was back. "Tonight, I want to catch up with my good friend who I once thought had left us behind for the big city. You know, the rest of us felt a bit betrayed when you ran off. This town's not the same without the Morrises."

My father nodded.

"Who do I have to thank for bringing you back?"

"Well, I got divorced," my father said quietly.

"I'm sorry to hear that," Mr. Redmarch said, "but glad to see you never forgot your ties to this place. Those ties go double for families like ours. Our ancestors bled and died for this land, and who are we to spurn their gifts?"

Judging by what I'd read, they'd done a lot more killing than dying for it.

My father nodded, but he couldn't meet Mr. Redmarch's gaze. I waited for him to say something about Zoe, about how losing her had driven my parents apart, but he never brought her up. It hurt how little my parents talked about her. Sometimes I felt like I was the only one keeping her memory alive, even though I knew that wasn't true. I didn't want that to happen again tonight.

"My twin sister died eight years ago," I said. "Things weren't really the same after. We moved from Jersey to the city after that."

Mr. Redmarch raised his eyebrows in alarm.

"I'm so sorry to hear that. You never told me you had twins," he said to my father.

My father seemed taken aback when I mentioned Zoe. He looked like he had no idea what to say to Mr. Redmarch. Finally he nodded.

"It's hard to talk about," he said.

"In any case, you have my deepest condolences. I can't imagine what it's like to lose a sister or a daughter."

He didn't look sorry. His expression was somber, but there was something else in his eyes. Something I didn't like. My father had noticed it, too, and it made him even more nervous.

"I-I'd rather talk about something else, if you don't mind," my father said. I glared at him, but the creepy feeling I was getting from Mr. Redmarch kept me from getting too angry.

"Sorry," I said quietly. "I wasn't trying to depress everyone."

"You have nothing to apologize for," Mr. Redmarch said.

Quickly, I cast around for something, anything to change the subject, but all I could think of was the hotel we were in. "This hotel is named for the family that owned it, right? Are there still Clyburns in town?"

Mr. Redmarch's expression was back to what passed for normal again—friendly, in a stiff sort of way, with something odd and inscrutable beneath. Apparently he was always happy to talk about the town that bore his name.

"They were one of the town's original families, along with the Redmarches and the Morrises. They were quite rich in the hotel's glory days, but they were too focused on the outside world. Our families' strength has always been here, in Redmarch lake. They lost everything in the Great Depression. My mother, Pearl Clyburn, was her parents' only child." Mr. Redmarch made a gesture interlacing the fingers of both hands. "But now our bloodlines are joined, and both are stronger for it. My father always said the old families are strongest when we stick together."

That got him reminiscing about what the town was like when he was younger, and a moment later, my father and Mr. Redmarch were both talking about old times again while Keith and I ate forkfuls of heritage pork. Our brief discussion of my sister had brought up a riot of emotions, and I couldn't sit here and listen to them much longer. After a while, I excused myself to use the bathroom.

The ladies' room was all porcelain tile and dark wood stalls. The mildewy old smell was stronger here, and I thought I could almost smell the lake. When I washed my hands, I saw the water was cloudy, and when I looked up, there was no mirror above the sink. Whoever had bought the hotel probably thought superstition was good for business.

Outside I could hear Mr. Redmarch, still going on about old times. I noticed there was an unmarked door open just a crack between the bathrooms. I couldn't resist a quick look. It opened on a short hallway, which led to the old hotel lobby. The smell of mold and mildew was thicker here, and I felt a sneeze building in my nose. The old carpet had once been lush and intricately patterned, but it was now water damaged and half eaten away. The front desk was fine old wood, just like the bathroom. It was such a shame this had all gone to rot.

Something next to the front desk caught my eye—an old glass display case, like you'd see in a museum. Inside were three intricately carved stone figures. They were old, but they didn't look like anything I'd seen before—nothing like European art, or the Native American artifacts I'd seen in museums. They looked like miniature statues or idols, but I couldn't tell what sort of figures they were supposed to represent—the forms looped and bent back on each other in what seemed like painful contortions, and I couldn't tell which parts were arms, legs, heads or both.

Then I realized I *had* seen something like them before, briefly—the weird statue I saw in the consignment store on my first day in town. The stone looked like it almost flowed in a sinuous, organic way, and it glistened with an oily sheen. Some of the statues were carved with what looked like letters or symbols, though I couldn't recognize the alphabet. I'd seen them somewhere before, too, though—the plaque on the statue of Broderick Redmarch in the town square.

As I stared at the sculptures, I started to get a queasy feeling in the pit of my stomach, just like in the consignment store, and I quickly turned my eyes away. There was a tiny placard below the display case. All it said was *Double Shadow, c. 1200 a.d.? Purpose and material unknown.* Double shadow? Was that anything like the Two-Shadows from the book I'd found in the library?

Feeling my stomach start to settle, I turned my attention to the big windows that stretched along the back wall. They had a sweeping view of the lake—there was even a row of moldy old couches arranged so that guests could enjoy the sight. The Clyburn hotel must have been something in its day. I walked over to look out the window. The lake was as eerily placid as ever, calm and silvery in the dusk. It was hard to tell as the light was fading, but I thought I could see a figure down by the lakeshore, standing at the edge of the town's little esplanade—the same place I'd stood on my first morning here.

I couldn't be sure in the half light, but I think it was a woman, or a girl. Her hair was dark brown, almost black, and hung down to the small of her back—just like mine. My heart started to beat faster.

"Wow, I had no idea this was back here."

I whirled around to see Keith standing behind me.

"Sorry, I didn't mean to startle you. I just couldn't take the 'glory days' talk anymore—I was getting jealous you managed to escape."

"I guess I did," I said. "Sorry to leave you there. I don't know what it is between our dads, my father won't talk about it. They sound friendly enough, but I couldn't deal with whatever was going on underneath."

"That's like every day of my life," said Keith, glancing out at the lake. "Here, there's always something going on underneath."

I looked back out at that calm surface. It might have been my imagination, but I thought I saw something stir beneath it, the faintest ripple, gone just as quickly as it came. The figure was still there by the shore, her back to me. I wondered if I should run out there—if she'd still be there if I did.

"My dad warned me to stay away from your family," I said. It just slipped out, before I could think better of it, and I cursed myself for saying it, afraid I'd offend him somehow or make things worse. Instead he nodded like he understood.

"Sometimes I wish I could do that, too."

"I guess we should go back before they get suspicious," I said.

Keith sighed, but he agreed. As we walked back, I took another look over my shoulder at the lake. The figure by the shore was gone.

1934

. . . It was all a grift. Strictly small time, you understand—you won't lock me up for something so little, right? Not after you hear what I got to say.

Dennis was the medium, I was the skeptic—Dr. Ephraim Wright of the Reason Institute—I don't have to tell you there's no such place. We'd go from town to town, performing "investigations into psychic and paranormal phenomena." We'd argue and debate, Denny would do his spirit talk act. We had it just right—enough mystery the believers went home happy, and enough science that the doubters did the same. Even when a man's only got two nickels to his name, he'll give you one if you show him what he wants to see.

We hear about this town called Redmarch Lake—just rumors, I'd never heard of the place before, and I thought I'd hit everywhere in New York. Denny told me it used to be rich folks would vacation out there, before everything went to hell in twenty-nine, pardon my French. It's got everything—a haunted lake, a creepy hotel with no mirrors—perfect spot for a show. But as soon as we get there, Denny starts acting all cuckoo-bird, saying this place ain't right. He won't even go down by the lake.

I never suspected he actually bought this stuff, but he tells me once when he was just a boy he heard his aunt speaking to him, telling him she felt cold, and when he ran to tell his mother, he found her crying, reading a letter saying his dear Aunt Gladys had died the week before. He told me he hadn't heard a thing like it since, until now. "The lake," he says, "they're lost in the lake. So many people. And that's not all. There's things here, things I never felt before."

"What the hell does that mean?"

"Ghosts . . . ghosts used to be alive," he says. "There's things here with no bodies, only they ain't never been alive."

I tell him to pull himself together. We don't eat if we don't perform. I put on my Dr. Wright getup and go to drum up some interest in the town square, but nobody will give me the time of day. Unfriendliest town I've ever seen. I thought, well, we're not eating tonight even if Denny gets his head on straight, but when I get back to the hotel, he's not even there. Someone else was, though, and I swear to you this is true. A tall man with dark blond hair, said his name was Frederick Redmarch—just like the town, I swear to you.

"Your friend had a nervous fit in the lobby," he says. "Don't worry yourself, we'll see he's well taken care of. I must insist you not perform your little show tonight, though. Our residents don't go in for that sort of thing. I've taken the liberty of buying you a train ticket. Your friend will join you as soon as he's well."

I know when I'm being run out of town, even when they use nice words. I took the message. The thing is, I believed him about Denny, but it's been weeks, and I ain't even got a telegram.

—Testimony of Albert Wiley, a.k.a. Ephraim Wright, arrested on an outstanding charges of fraud in New York City, 1934. From the library of Tom Morris.

XI.

"Every time I see him, there's less of my friend left," my father said as we left the restaurant. I waited for him to explain, or at least say more, but he was silent for the rest of the drive home, a distant and morose expression on his face. I thought again of him smiling and laughing as he went on about old memories with Mr. Redmarch, a hint of wild terror never leaving his eyes. Keith's father had to have seen it, too. Was all that we witnessed just some sort of game? My father didn't say another word until we'd made it inside the house and he'd locked the door behind us.

"I-I wish you hadn't mentioned Zoe."

These were fighting words, and my father knew it. He wasn't angry, more like scared and depressed, but he felt compelled to say them anyway. I clenched my hands into fists. I tried to tell myself to stay calm, or at least not to yell. I wanted to, but I knew it would get me nowhere.

"Why would you say that to me, Dad? You and Mom both never bring her up, and you know how that makes me feel. It's like you're erasing part of who I am."

"I'm sorry, sweetheart. I just—I remember how hard it was, after . . . and I never, ever want you to go through that again. You're doing so well now, friends and good grades and everything . . ."

This was a lie, or at the very least it wasn't the whole truth. I remembered the look on Mr. Redmarch's face, and I shivered. I was still angry, but I just couldn't bring myself to have another fight. I wanted my father to tell me what was going on, why he'd left New York and moved back here. I wanted my family back again. More than anything, I wanted Zoe. Without her beside me, even after all these years, I felt so unbearably alone.

"Good night, Dad."

Hector was my first customer the next morning, and he listened in awe as I told him about my awkward dinner at the old Clyburn Hotel. His eyes narrowed a bit when I told him about sneaking off to look at the lake with Keith. I was surprised by how good I felt when I spotted what I thought was a little flash of jealousy on Hector's part.

See, he likes you, too, he totally does, I imagined Zoe whispering.

"I've got good news, though," I said. "Ash is joining our investigation. She has an idea of who might know more about Neil. Can you come by after we close up?"

"No way I'd miss it," Hector said.

Our speculation about what the rest of the day would hold came to a sudden halt when we smelled smoke. I checked the coffee machines, but they were all in good shape, and I was too early for the cigarette-smoking man. Then we saw the strangest thing outside: a procession of townsfolk were slowly making their way down the street. I saw the power walk ladies, the pregnant woman from New Again, the old man from the bus, even the librarian. They carried lashed bundles of leaves, all burning at the tips, and as they walked, they waved them around to spread the bitter smoke, acrid and pungent. No one sang or even spoke as they marched—they all continued in glum silence, as if they were taking out the trash.

"Any idea what's going on?"

To my surprise, Hector nodded.

"They're burning sage and tobacco—kind of an old world meets new world idea. No one told me this, of course, but based on stuff I've read, I think it's supposed to protect the town."

"From what?"

"Everything they refuse to talk about. It's almost Midsummer's Eve—that's one of the nights you have to be extra careful."

With all my anticipation, the day ticked by at a snail's pace. I served the few regulars that came in, which included the power walk ladies after their herb-burning duties were finished, and later the old man at noon as usual. I ate a tofu sandwich for lunch and eagerly greeted Ash when she arrived. She was happy to see me, too. I was glad things had changed between us.

"I called around a little to see what I could find out," Ash said. "Neil and I broke up a month ago, which made working here hell. Neil was friends with almost everyone, but Danny Harris was his best friend since kindergarten, and the only one I heard mention his new girlfriend. No one else had even seen her."

"Maybe it was just a rumor," I said. "The old Canadian girlfriend, just to make you jealous. It'd be hard to not know who in a town this size. No wonder you assumed it was me."

Ash nodded.

"Yeah, sorry about that again."

For some reason, I thought of the ghostly figure I'd seen every morning at the café window. It was hard to tell, but if I had to guess, I'd say it was a girl.

"Don't worry about that now," I said. "We're well past it."

The power-walk ladies strode back in for their afternoon coffees, and Ash and I served them quickly. Once they left, we resumed our planning.

"If anyone knows what was up with Neil, it's Danny. I haven't seen him for a while. I went by his house the other day, and apparently his folks haven't either, which is nothing unusual in the summer. No one from school's seen him either, though, and that worries me. He doesn't usually go to the parties, but he sometimes hangs out at the Excelsior."

Ash clearly saw the question in my raised eyebrow.

"Don't let the name fool you," she seemed a little embarrassed. "It's just an old house where some young guys live. They usually have beer and throw parties for the high school kids."

Of course, this was a time-honored tradition. Rayna always said it should be an elected position—the Wooderson, another of her movie references, I guess—so you could vote for the guy who was least creepy (which usually wasn't saying much).

I stayed with Ash through her shift, helping her run the café, even though she didn't have many more customers than I did. While we worked, she asked me more about growing up in New York. I told her it was a mixed bag, exciting but stressful, and way too crowded.

"It's crazy," I said. "This town feels so small, but all the interior spaces feel huge. You have no idea how small bathrooms get in the city."

"I think I could get used to it," said Ash. "This place is stressful too, in a way nowhere else is."

"Stressful how?" I said.

Ash frowned. I'd seen the same look on my father, on Keith, even on Hector. It was like everyone here had a sixth sense for the things they couldn't talk about. A sixth sense much more accurate than Lady Daphne's.

"You have to be careful about where you go at what time, and what you talk about. There are lots of rules to follow, and no one will tell you why, except that bad things will happen if you don't. And if bad things do happen, no one wants to know why or how . . ."

All this time, I'd assumed everyone knew more than me. Now I wasn't so sure. It seemed like most people in Redmarch Lake wanted to know as little as possible.

"My mom always says I need to remember where I come from and know my place," Ash said. "She doesn't want me to leave, or to break any of the stupid rules. Some days this whole town feels like a jail without any jailers. We could walk away at any time, or live how we want, but no one does because this is all they know."

"Only one way to find out if that's true," I said.

"If we keep this up, that's just what we'll do," said Ash. She was smiling, but I can't say that made me feel much better. Neither of us mentioned that's probably what Neil tried to do, too, though I could tell we were both thinking it.

When closing time finally arrived, Hector was waiting for us outside.

"I told my folks I was going to a summer study group. I don't know if the fact that they bought it means they're too gullible or I'm too nerdy."

"They're not mutually exclusive," I said, giving him another little punch in the arm.

"I don't think I've bothered giving my mother an excuse for anything for years," said Ash. "I almost envy you."

We hopped in Ash's old Honda while I filled Hector in on the plan.

"I hear about that place all the time. I've never been invited."

"You're not missing much," said Ash.

"Thanks for doing this, by the way," said Hector. "I mean that sincerely. I know my default tone is sarcastic jerk. I feel like I can't turn it off even when I want to."

Ash nodded.

"I'm sorry for how people are here. Most of them suck, even when they will talk to you. For the rest of us . . . all I can say is that we're cowards. We're too afraid of anything that sticks out or goes against the grain that we just pretend it's not there. It's nothing personal, but that doesn't make it okay."

Hector's mouth hung open. It was the first time I'd seen him speechless.

"I never thought I'd hear anyone say that out loud," he said. "Thanks."

A second later, he had his phone out, loading up a voice recorder app.

"Hey, could you say that again?"

Ash laughed. Hector put the phone away.

"But seriously, while you're here and talking to us out-of-townies, there's one thing I'm seriously dying to know. Is there like an organized conspiracy, or is it just a *de facto* thing?"

Ash frowned.

"The second one," she said. "Unless there's a conspiracy I'm not a part of."

She was quiet for a moment, just like my dad when he was trying to think of how to answer something he didn't want to.

"This town . . . I'm sorry, I know it must be hard to come from outside here, but trust me, it's hard to be born here, too. No one answers our questions either; they just tell us what to do. You hear it enough, and it sort of gets inside you."

In a few minutes, we arrived at a crumbling old clapboard house with a weed-knotted lawn that could only be the Excelsior.

"This is it, huh? Pure class," Hector said.

I peeled back the rusty screen door and walked in, Ash and Hector following me. It slammed shut like a bear trap behind us. Inside, the windows had been hung with old bedsheets, blanketing the interior in gloom. Dust motes danced in the rays of light that peeked in through the gaps. Everything smelled like pot, both stale and fresh. From the next room, I could hear hushed voices and the sound of a bong bubbling. A song was playing on an old record player—points for being music snob creeps, at least—something slow and eerie I'd never heard before. It gave me chills.

Hector and I froze in the hallway, suddenly conscious of the fact we knew no one here. Ash walked toward the living room, motioning for us to follow. I recognized some of the people splayed across the various couches and chairs from the party in the woods. A few of them looked older, especially a guy with long, curly hair and a goatee who probably lived here. When we walked into the room, he raised an eyebrow at us. Everyone else seemed to defer to him.

"Hey, Kyle, have you seen Danny around?" Ash said.

"Ash, hey, why don't you stay and party with us?"

He indicated a big glass bong on the floor among them.

"No thanks, it's really important I find Danny now. Has he been here?"

Kyle frowned.

"Moving on to Neil's little best friend, eh? I don't think he plays for the right team."

Ash looked like she desperately wanted to shout something back at Kyle, but she couldn't find the words. Her mouth hung open. Kyle turned toward me.

"What about your friend here? Maybe she wants to party."

He flashed me a wolf grin. Beside me, I was surprised to see Hector's hands curl into fists. I hoped he wasn't about to do something stupid—Kyle was almost twice his size, but he hadn't even looked at Hector since we came in. I guess he saved all his attention for the girls. I gave Kyle my best *drop dead* glare, the one I saved for street creepers in the city.

"Why don't you just answer her question before I report you to the sex offender registry," I said.

"Damn, okay. The one rule of this house is be mellow. If you can't abide by that, I'll have to send you on your way. Danny was here a few days ago. He said he had a fishing trip planned. Neil was supposed to go, too, but after what happened, I guess he went alone."

"You're right, I wasn't missing anything," Hector said when we got outside. "It was pretty cool to see that guy almost crap his pants when you told him off, though."

"Yeah, thanks for that," Ash said.

"Don't mention it," I said. "So where to now? Do we check the lake?"

"No one fishes in Redmarch Lake," Hector said. "My father has to go two towns over when he goes fishing."

"Yeah," said Ash. "That was code for getting drunk at their spot by the lake." She looked at her feet as everything she'd lost caught up with her again. "Neil used to take me there a lot. I doubt he or Danny have been fishing for real since they were little kids."

Ash drove down a little winding road I'd never been on before, wending around the lake in the opposite direction I'd gone with Keith. As we drove, the shadows lengthened around us. The last rays of sun behind us glinted in the rear-view mirror. Every so often, I'd catch a glimpse of the lake through the trees. I had a queasy feeling in my stomach. Somehow I knew we were headed for something bad. It was like the drowning dream—right now I was floating above the surface, but I knew any minute I would plunge into the depths. I almost asked Ash to turn the car around, but I couldn't. My fear held me just as still as the ocean in my dream.

Ash turned down a little dirt track I never would have noticed from the road, driving through a gloomy tunnel of close-grown trees to park at a little clearing.

"We're here," she said.

The queasy feeling hadn't left my stomach, but I opened the door and stepped out. Hector seemed to be thinking the same thing—I saw an echo of my own fears in his face. Ash had been calm and confident driving us here, but now she looked just as nervous as the rest of us. Slowly, we made our way down a worn dirt track to a little sheltered cove on the lake shore. A few logs and stumps had been stacked along the edge to make places to sit, and an empty case of light beer sat next to the black and gray ashes of a campfire. The ashes were still warm, but there was no sign of Danny.

Then, behind me, I heard Ash scream. I looked out where she pointed and found Danny, floating face up in the shallows of the lake, a horrified gasp frozen on his pale face while the water around him was calm as glass.

Memories flooded over me—being pulled from the ocean by the lifeguard, the relief of air and light, but through it all wanting to dive back in to get my sister. I saw Danny out there in the lake, and though it was the last place I wanted to go, I couldn't leave anyone there alone.

I waded out to him.

"Wait, don't—" I heard Hector curse behind me, then he was wading out beside me when he saw I wouldn't wait. I wasn't ready for what I saw when we reached the body. The coroner's report we'd read said Neil had been attacked with a knife or claw, but if it had been anything like this, they didn't do it justice. Danny's stomach was mostly gone, a red ruin. There were slashes all along his chest in some kind of cruel, whorled pattern. The knife had traced red spirals down his shoulders, and on his cheeks. Some sort of letters or runes had been cut into his arms. They looked eerily like the glyphs on the statues at the hotel, and on the statue of Broderick Redmarch.

On the bank, Ash was screaming into her phone, calling the sheriff, or whoever answered emergency calls out here. Hector was tugging on my arm, trying to pull me in to shore. I couldn't hear either of them. All I could hear was my own breath rushing in and out like the tide. I had never met poor Danny, but it had to be hell to die this way. Who would do this to another person?

When I couldn't bear seeing Danny's body one more minute, I turned to the lake itself, still so clear and still. I saw my reflection staring back at me, beside Danny's corpse. Then I felt a chill run down my spine. I recognized someone I hadn't seen in a very long time. The reflection staring back at me had my dark brown hair, my almost-black eyes, but she wasn't me. She was my sister, Zoe.

Identical twins are never perfectly identical. There are always differences, quirks that change and intensify as the twins grow. But Zoe and I were almost perfect mirrors. Even our own parents often couldn't tell us apart. The differences were hard to spot—the line of the lips, the way she narrowed her eyes—but I would know her anywhere.

I could see blue and red lights flashing from the shore. The sheriff had arrived. I could barely hear the sound of someone shouting my name over my pounding heartbeat. I couldn't move. After all this time, my sister had appeared to me here. Looking down at the lake, at that face that was so like mine in every way, I could see her lips were moving. It was hard to follow, I was no lip reader. I could only make out the last two words.

Efra mir.

Help me.

I felt hands take hold of me, pulling me back to shore. My father's friend Deputy Bill was guiding me, gently but firmly.

I didn't want to take my eyes off my sister, but Bill's grip was too strong. Slowly he pulled me back toward shore. On the bank, Deputy Chief Cross River was on her phone.

"No, I don't care what they say, I need the state forensic team back. We don't have the resources. Yes, it's the same MO, markings and all."

She hung up with a single, ferocious curse, then spent a minute staring out at the body in the lake, shaking her head.

"Bill, take the other two back to the station. I'll take this one with me."

Bill nodded and left with Ash and Hector in tow. Hector looked back at me, concern on his face. I tried to give him a reassuring wink, but it probably looked like some sort of nervous twitch, given the state I was in. He made the *call me* gesture with his fingers before Bill pushed him into the back of his patrol car.

As I waited for Deputy Chief Cross River to finish, I caught sight of something I'd missed before, a little notebook fallen beside one of the log benches. I flipped through the pages—it was some sort of diary, written in a messy, haphazard hand. I slipped it into my pocket.

As soon as she was done looking around, Deputy Chief Cross River motioned for me to get in the car with her. She let me sit in the front, next to her, which surprised me.

"We'll get going as soon as the crime scene team shows up," she said. There was a tense moment of silence as she seemed to be gathering her thoughts. Then the cool, competent shell she projected every time I saw her suddenly cracked, and she punched the steering wheel.

"I can't stand this damn town. Everyone tried to warn me about it, it's my own damn fault. The county tried to stick me on the Tribal Liaison unit when I joined up after the army. If I wanted that job, I would have stayed on the Rez. This was the first promotion that opened up, and no one else wanted it. You know why? Because of this god damned town. No one talks about it, no one says why, because no one wants to come out and admit this place is wrong. It shouldn't exist. The goddamn Addams Family on the other side of the lake is tight with every politician in the region. And everyone that lives here is convinced that if they just pretend it's normal, that'll make it true. Tell that to these poor kids."

I could see she was venting, and not really talking to me, so I kept my mouth shut. I knew exactly how she felt. After a moment, she regained her composure and turned to look at me.

"I know you're just trying to help your friend, and you did the right thing to call us here. You're not in trouble, but do me a favor. Promise me, no more junior detective crap. I don't want to lose any more kids. Stay out of trouble, and if you hear anything, or if trouble finds you, you call me. Can you promise me that?"

I nodded, though I knew I couldn't. I liked Elaine Cross River, and I didn't want to lie to her, but something in me knew I couldn't keep out of trouble. Not if I could see my sister again.

XII.

By the time we got back to the station, my father was already there. The only other time I'd seen him this pale and tight-lipped was when they pulled me from the ocean that awful day eight years ago. He didn't say a word as Elaine explained I would have to give a statement after what I saw.

They led me back to one of the little rooms in the Sheriff's station, and my father and I sat with Elaine and Deputy Bill as I went over the events that had led us to finding Danny at the lake. I left out Hector getting his hands on the coroner's report for fear that would land us in more trouble.

"Thank you," said Elaine, "you've done a good thing, I want you to know that, but remember, no more good things. Being a normal teenager is hard enough, trust me, you don't need to go looking for more trouble."

I nodded, the picture of responsibility. I felt bad—I actually liked Elaine a lot, and I wanted to make her proud, but I knew I couldn't. Not after what I saw in the lake.

Hector and Ash had both given their statements, and their parents had arrived to pick them up, as well. Hector's mother ran to him and hugged him, which he clearly found horribly embarrassing. After the love, though, came the anger—I could tell from her face that he was going to get an earful on the way home, and I felt sorry for him. His dad looked like he'd rather stay far away from the whole mess. Ash's mother was a big, tired-looking woman who just shook her head when she saw her.

"What'd you do this time?"

Ash gave her a dark look, then waved to us as they walked away.

"I'll talk to you later," Hector said as he walked off with his folks. That left just Dad and me. He still wasn't talking, which definitely was not a good sign. As soon as we were in the car, he felt ready to speak to me again.

"Clara, what's wrong? You're starting to scare me with this behavior. This is serious, people are dead, and I don't want my daughter mixed up in it."

He was coldly furious. I had never seen him like this, and it freaked me out.

"I know, Dad, I know but—"

"But what?"

"Everybody was just going to turn their back on this and pretend it was just some drunk accident. And who knows when anyone would have even found Danny? I couldn't let that happen."

I could feel the thickness of a sob in my throat. This conversation was dredging up things I had learned to keep well-buried—things that could land me back in the hole I'd lived in after losing Zoe. The hole that had almost swallowed me up.

"Why not? Neil was a nice kid, and so was Danny. I'm sorry they're dead, but you barely knew them, Clara. I'm sorry, but this is not your fight."

"I couldn't let it happen because that's what happened to Zoe." There were tears in my eyes now. "Or am I still not allowed to talk about her?"

At the mention of Zoe's name, my father went pale. He put a hand on my shoulder as he drove home. If anything, he looked even more worried after I brought her up.

"I'm sorry, honey. Really, I am. We-we can talk about Zoe anytime you want. But please don't put yourself in danger any more."

"Except with the Redmarches. You just told me not to talk about Zoe there."

"You should be very careful of anything you tell that man. You shouldn't talk to him at all, or his son."

"You know more about this than you're telling me. How do you even know I'm in danger?"

We pulled into the driveway.

"I only mean that people are dead and we don't know who did it, and I don't want you anywhere near a crime scene. It's probably drugs. Meth or heroin or something. The country is worse than the city with that these days."

"Neil drank, and maybe smoked a little pot, but that was it," I said. "No way he was a dealer or anything, either."

We walked into the house. My father locked and bolted the door behind us.

"Those are the kinds of questions it's not our job to answer," he said.

"And what if no one answers them?"

"It's sad, I know, but questions like that go unanswered all the time. There are thousands of unsolved crimes in this world, millions," he said. "And some things are better off staying that way."

I was surprised at the vehemence in his voice. Something about this was touching a nerve for him, too, but I had no idea what, and at this point I was too angry to care.

"What the hell does that mean?" I said.

"Don't speak to me that way. You didn't grow up in this town. You don't know what it's like! People go missing all the time. Strange things happen, but no one talks about it. No one dares to say a word, because if you do, you'll be next. That's how it works."

My father was shouting. I'd never seen him like this. He saw the shock in my eyes, and suddenly realized what he was doing. He clapped a hand over his mouth, as if wishing he could cram everything he'd just said back inside.

"I'm sorry, I'm sorry . . . forget I said that. It's not true. This place, it just makes people paranoid."

I took a deep breath. My father's apologies had been more for the air around us than for me. For just one second, he had broken the town's code of silence, and that scared me, but it also filled me with hope. If anyone could help me find Zoe's connection to all of this, he could.

"There's something I have to show you," I said.

Back in my room, I pulled out the letter from Zoe from the dresser drawer where I'd hidden it. I was afraid this was a mistake, but I had to take the chance. I took the letter back out and showed it to my father.

He gave me a blank, hopeless look after reading the words on the page. He'd heard Zoe and me use our language before, when we were small, but he'd never seen it written down. It had never been written down until now. Who knew if he even remembered?

"I found that note in the stump in your back yard, after I heard a noise near it. It's written in the language Zoe and I made up."

My father looked back at me, utter disbelief on his face.

"No, look here, let me translate it." I wrote out the English words below the original *Deep in the wood, far from the town, they spilled his blood, they made him drown.*

"Sweetheart, I'm sorry. That can't be true . . ." my father said.

In an instant, my hope burned off into rage and despair. I knew this would happen. That's why I hid the letter away in the first place. Why was I crazy enough to think I could trust anyone with it? Would I have believed it if anyone had shown it to me? Still, I was trembling with fury. My own father couldn't just believe his daughter, or even make an attempt? Right now, he was probably thinking of putting me back on all the meds I'd been on after Zoe's death.

"I'm not calling you a liar, sweetheart. Sometimes our minds play tricks on us. Sometimes we do things without knowing . . ."

"So I'm crazy?"

"Dear god, no, that's not what I mean. I just . . . I don't know, Clara. I'm just trying to keep you safe."

I snatched the letter out of his hand and stormed back to my room. I couldn't listen to him for another minute. He seemed so pathetic, just throwing up his hands and refusing to do anything. I knew I'd regret it later, but I hated him just then. If he'd been stronger after everything that happened, maybe things would be different. Maybe my parents would still be together. While I was at it, why not just wish for Zoe back again? That's what I really wanted. I had almost come to terms with my parents' divorce, but I would never come to terms with being half of twins, like spending the rest of my life as a one-arm scissor.

I stared at the letter again. Could I have been fooling myself about it? I didn't see how. I'd seen more strange things in my short time here than I had in my entire life before, and it couldn't all be in my head.

I thought about calling my mother, but my parents always backed each other up, even after the divorce. It was probably written into the settlement. She'd just tell me I'd be happier back in the city. Maybe I would be, Woodchuck or no, but I couldn't leave yet. I had to know what was behind the note.

Instead I texted Rayna, *My dad is the worst.*

A little while later she wrote back, *You can't win with either parent, am I right? Tell me what's up.* She was the best. I was tempted to spill everything to her, just launch into the crazy stuff that had happened here, but I limited myself to *The country is messed up, I'll tell you everything soon, I swear. Long story short, my dad is paranoid and won't treat his depression.*

That stuff's no joke, Rayna wrote. *Speaking of the crazy country, if you see the townsfolk building a big wicker man, just run, all right?*

Girl, you don't even know, I wrote back.

Tell me later I hope. I gotta go. Korusawa Festival tonight at Film Forum.

I sighed. I really did miss Rayna, and the city. At any other time in my life, I'd have said I love New York because it was big and crazy and there was always something happening, but now I missed it because it felt sane and understandable.

I tried the rest of the gang, but I guess they weren't around. If I was honest with myself, they were really more Rayna's friends than mine. She was the one who'd taken a chance and talked to the weird new kid years ago, the girl from the suburbs who'd lost half of herself just a year before. The other girls just let me tag along.

With no one to talk to, I threw on the loudest music I had on my phone and lay there, unable to sleep. My father knocked on my door a while later, saying dinner was ready, but I ignored him, and after trying again, he went away. I wasn't hungry and wouldn't have come out even if I was.

When I was little, I used to put myself in timeout when I knew I'd done something bad. I figured my parents couldn't get mad if I was already punishing myself. Zoe never did this, even though she had a hand in almost everything I got in trouble for. She'd come to me while I sat in the corner, solemn in my self-imposed exile.

"Come on, Clara, I thought of a new game."

"I can't, I'm in timeout."

"So put yourself out of it. You feel really bad. You've learned your lesson. Now let's go play."

She would have been a good lawyer, always ready with a sly smile and a loophole, but I knew it was really because she hated seeing me sad. I wished she were here right now more than anything. I tried to think of what she would say to me now, like I always did when I missed her, but I couldn't think of anything. All I could do was picture her staring back at me from the lake, silently begging for help.

It was then that I remembered Danny's diary, still in my pocket. I'd forgotten to mention it to Elaine, or even look at it myself, and I felt a flush of shame—I'd been withholding evidence the whole time. I wondered if it was too late to suddenly "remember" the diary and turn it in.

Of course I opened it. I felt bad about that, too, but I couldn't resist. And I'm sure Danny would have approved if it helped find his killer.

His handwriting was a mess, but after a little while, I got the hang of it. Most of the diary was records of his workout routine—how much weight and how many reps, and that sort of thing. There were a lot of song lyrics copied out, and scribbled ink doodles. Then I noticed a cryptic little note:

Saw K in the hall today. I had to look away. He never even noticed.

There were more notes like that scattered through the diary, but I wasn't seeing anything that could relate to the murder. I was just about to stop looking when I saw something that made me catch my breath.

I can't believe Neil talked me into this, it goes against everything they say. We're supposed to keep them at bay, not go looking for one, but Neil says this is the only way to change things. He says we're not looking for the bad ones, only the ones they hold captive. I don't even know what that means. Who the hell knows where he found the stupid 'instructions,' either? Probably some musty old book or crackpot website. I should stay home, tell him to forget the whole thing. We'll deal, just like our parents did.

I flipped through frantically, looking for more on whatever Danny was talking about. There was nothing but workout logs for the next few days, then this:

Nothing happened. Of course nothing happened. Half this town runs on hearsay and superstition. I actually feel better that we tried it now. It makes this whole place a little less scary. Neil is still convinced it worked, somehow. I'm worried about him. He says he keeps catching glimpses of someone, a girl, sometimes when he's alone, at sunrise and at dusk. Now whenever I see him, I ask about his girlfriend, and he tells me to go to hell.

After that it was all workout logs again, punctuated by another sighting of the mysterious K. Then, a few pages before the last entry, there was this:

Neil is gone. I can't believe it. He was like a brother to me, and the only one who helped me get by after . . . [Danny had started to write something here, then scratched it out]

How could we have been so stupid? The power in this place is real, and I wish I could take back every second I doubted it. I've started seeing shadows out of the corner of my eye, following me. There are things that move in the woods—all I can see are their eyes. What have we done? I need to get away. I need to clear my head.

Just then I heard something, a faint tapping or knocking sound. I stuffed the diary back in my pocket and popped the earbuds out of my ears. Dead silence greeted me. I stayed frozen still for a moment, scanning every corner, not sure if I'd been hearing things.

Then it came again, three loud taps on the glass of my window: *tap, tap tap.*

I jumped, unable to move for a moment. The yard outside was just a square of darkness with the light on in my room. I reached up and flicked the switch off. Without the light to contrast, I could make out the blue-black mass of the forest. The green lawn looked gray in the darkness, but the yard was empty. There was nothing else I could see.

I slowly edged the window open, my heart hammering in my chest. Wedged between the window and the sill was a folded piece of paper. Trembling, I reached out and grabbed it before it blew away.

It was the same paper as the other letter, freshly torn from a notebook. The handwriting was identical, forming the words of our private language.

"If you're not Zoe, who the hell are you, and what do you want with me?" I said. There was no answer from the darkness outside. I read the note, afraid to see what I'd find:

Iyr spat flenn
Dreg bar a hir snek
Noo sen harn vlanna
Flek faash a lenn rash

I caught my breath. This was bad, and there wasn't much time. In English, the note read:

The eye has fallen on your friends
The hounds will bay and feel the lash
Tonight they ride to bloody ends
To spark the fire and clear the ash

Clear the ash. I had to leave now. I had to get Hector. I hoped he knew where Ash lived. I hoped we could get there in time. I scrambled out the window and into the night.

XIII.

The houses I passed were all dark. Here and there, a crack of light peered out from under curtains. There were no street lamps on my father's street, and the night was darker than I thought possible in a place where people lived—dark like the bottom of the sea. I used my phone as a flashlight as I walked. The crickets sang out from every side, and I prayed they'd keep singing.

In the distance, I heard what sounded like a howl—someone's dog, I hoped. It was answered by another, further away. I quickened my pace, searching out Hector's address in my email, trying to map it out. I shook my head at how crazy this was. People were dead, and if I didn't hurry, another of my friends would join them.

I froze as I suddenly found myself bathed in the beam of a headlight. From behind, I heard a car slowing down.

"Clara?"

It was Keith, leaning out of his Jeep.

"Oh my god," I said. "You scared the hell out of me."

"Jesus, so did you. I was just coming to try to talk to you."

I slipped into the passenger side.

"We have to hurry," I said. "Please, I'll explain later, we have to get Hector, and then go find Ash."

Keith swallowed whatever questions he was going to ask when he saw my face. I probably looked as terrified as I felt. I told him how to get to Hector's.

"I came as soon as I heard. You-you guys really saw Danny?"

"Yeah," I said.

Keith shuddered. I realized then that I didn't know anything about Danny until I read the diary—just that he was Neil's friend. I clearly didn't know his history with Keith.

"He and I, well, we were good friends a while ago. We didn't really hang out anymore, but—"

He shuddered again.

We pulled up to Hector's house. I texted him, *Get out here now, we have trouble.*

What, where are you? he texted back.

Outside, come here. Explain later.

We sat for a tense, silent moment in the car, hoping his parents wouldn't see us waiting and blow the whole thing. Then I heard the creak of a screen door from the back yard, followed by a muttered curse, then Hector emerged from the back of his house. His eyes widened when he saw Keith at the wheel.

"What's the crown prince doing here?"

Hector flashed Keith a resentful glare, and to my surprise Keith looked down, ashamed.

"I heard about Danny—"

Keith's voice was thick with emotion, and that seemed

to be enough for Hector to let his guard down at least a little. He hopped in the back.

"Ash is in danger," I said. "I think she's going to be next, unless we can stop it."

"Next, as in what happened to—" Hector looked grim as he realized what I meant. "How do you know that?"

I was a second away from full on panic, and I had no idea how to explain.

"I need you to trust me, please. I hope I'm wrong. Do you know her address?"

"No, but I can find it. Take us down the street in case my parents look out."

Keith took us slowly down the road as Hector whipped out his phone, working the touchscreen with frenzied fingers.

"Let's see, PTA records. They always put too much online. . . . Here, got it: 1820 Cedar Street."

Keith nodded, and we were on our way, speeding through the darkened streets. The address was on the other side of town. I gripped the arm rest until my knuckles turned pale, thinking *please let us not be too late*. None of us spoke on the way over, terrified of what we might find. Keith's Jeep raced through the black streets of the town, headlights bathing the trees ahead in a ghostly glow.

When we finally pulled up in front, I was afraid we'd found the wrong house. The yard was overgrown, and even on the pitch-dark street, the house's peeling paint and cardboard-patched window were obvious. There were no lights on.

"Are you sure this is right?' I said.

"Of course it's right," Hector said, though he didn't look as sure as he sounded.

Then I saw Ash's car in the driveway, the cigarette butts in the front yard. I knew she had a hard life, but it was something else to see it like this, without being invited. I just prayed she was all right. I couldn't handle losing her just as we'd become friends. I was about to walk up to the front door when Keith stopped me.

"I don't know if anyone's home," he said. "Let's check the back. Maybe her room's on that side."

We crept through the narrow side yard to the rear of the house. The back yard was strung with a clothesline, and part of it was set up as a garden, but the rest was mostly mud. Ash's backyard bordered directly on the forest that surrounded the town, just like my father's. The back door was ajar, creaking faintly in the breeze. Then I saw the footprints.

"Look!" I said.

They made a trail through the mud from the front door out to the tree line. They were made by sneakers, about the same size as Ash's feet, from what I could remember. Immediately I thought of my promise to Elaine to stop the junior detective stuff. I'd broken promise after promise to the adults in my life, but I had to break one more. Until now, I'd been hoping we'd just find Ash at home with nothing amiss, but now there was no choice but to believe the note. I followed the footprints to the edge of the forest, Hector and Keith behind me.

We stopped for a moment at the tree line. We all knew what we might find at the end of this trail, but none of us wanted to say it, or even think it. The darkness of the forest ahead made the street look bright. The trees were hulking gray shapes in the purple gloom. The wind whipped my hair into my face and made an eerie rustling sound as it blew through the branches.

"We have to go," I said.

Hector and Keith nodded, and we set off down Ash's trail. Her footprints were soon lost in the darkness and the uneven ground. Not even moonlight penetrated the canopy above us. We had to take out our phones to see the way forward.

I thought of my first trip into the forest and shivered.

"Stay together," I said. "No matter what you hear, don't run off after it."

"This isn't a path," Keith said. "This is no good . . ."

"No choice now, man," said Hector.

The crickets were still chirping around us, and I gave silent thanks for that. The undergrowth here wasn't dense, but the tree roots were hard and gnarled and seemed to rise up out of the ground on purpose to trip us unawares. There was a heaviness to the air that grew as we got deeper in. The trees ahead were shrouded in a pale mist.

"We're getting close to the lake," Keith said.

Just then, an ear-splitting howl rang out from somewhere in the forest. It froze us all to the spot. It was answered by others further off, savage growls that rose to a frenzy of high-pitched baying yips. We took off running deeper into the forest. Wherever we were going, I hoped it was toward Ash.

We were almost at the lake—I could see a silvery ribbon of reflected moonlight ahead. Then I caught sight of a lone figure walking between the trees, making for the water. She moved slowly, swaying as if she were still half-asleep. The cascade of matte-black hair was unmistakable.

"Ash!" I shouted.

She didn't even turn around. She was clear of the trees now, walking down the rocky shore toward the lake's edge. We ran toward her. The lake was a pool of utter blackness, like a second sky, with its own near-full silvery moon to match the one above. I thought of all those times I'd seen the lake during the day and thought there was more to it I wasn't seeing. . . . At night, it's true face was visible, a dark, yawning void, like deep space. I couldn't look directly at it—I was afraid it would swallow me whole.

Ash was almost to the edge when I caught up with her. "Stop!"

I grabbed hold of her shoulder, wrenching her back. She stopped, shaking her head, then stared at me, bewildered. The question she was about to ask me died on her lips, as her eyes suddenly went wide with terror. My eyes followed hers, a shape even blacker than the darkness of the lake had risen up from the water, towering above us. It was like a cloud of dense shadow, standing twice the height of a full-grown man. We stumbled backward as it advanced toward us. From around us in the forest, the howling rose up again, closer this time. We tripped over rocks and roots,

186

scraping our arms and legs, running back toward the trees. Hector and Keith both saw what followed us, their faces pale with fright.

"Run!" I shouted.

Hector took off with us back into the trees, but Keith stood rooted to the spot, unable to move. The rest of us drew back in terror. My mind raced, trying to think of some way to help him, but what could we do against something so unreal? I threw a loose rock at Keith, hoping to stir him from his trance, but it only bounced off his shoulder.

"Keith, run! You've got to fight it!"

The shadow drew closer, drawing itself up even taller. The howling around us in the forest had risen to a gibbering chorus, and I knew then we wouldn't be safe, no matter how fast we ran. The shadow stood there in front of Keith, a negative stain like an afterimage burned into the eye. I felt certain it concealed something, something even worse than what we could see.

The air around us was electric. I could feel my hair stand on end. Keith still hadn't moved. He was staring right into that mass of darkness. It moved toward him slowly, as if it had all the time in the world. All of us could feel the same rank, animal fear that rooted Keith to the spot. We were all holding our breath.

Here it comes, I thought, *do something.*

I fumbled on the ground, looking for a rock, for anything that could help. Then I remembered the old iron clasp in my pocket. I pulled it out and hurled it at the cloud of shadow, hoping that for once in my life I could manage to throw something straight.

The clasp arced over Keith, striking the darkness as it rose above him. There was a terrible hiss, like a nest of snakes, and the darkness drew back.

It hovered there for a tense moment. I was afraid it would come back toward us, and I was about to scream for everyone to run. Then, slowly, it withdrew, sinking lower to the ground like an animal on all fours, backing slowly down to the lake. In a moment, it was gone, and it was as if the whole forest breathed out at once. The crickets burst out in a frenzied chorus. In the trees, a flock of night birds took panicked flight. In the distance, I could hear one last mournful howl fade to silence. We caught our breath. Ash almost fell to the ground, catching herself on a nearby tree branch.

"Thanks," she said, "thank god you were there. I-I don't know what happened."

"Yeah," said Keith. "Thanks. I don't—I couldn't—"

I looked back into the depths of the forest. The iron clasp my father had given me was out there somewhere, but I couldn't bring myself to take one more step in that direction.

"Let's get out of here," I said.

We walked back toward Keith's Jeep in hushed silence. My head was brimming with questions, but I didn't feel ready to speak yet. It took us until Ash's back yard was in sight for the fear to even start to lift.

"What do you remember?" I asked.

"I was here, at home. My mother had gone to bed, her medication makes her sleep like the dead. I was just sitting up, watching something stupid on TV. Then-then everything after was like a dream. I heard a voice whispering to me, telling me to come outside. I knew I shouldn't, but it was like I wanted to so badly. I had to.

"When I opened the door, it wasn't my back yard. I was walking down a garden path. The flowers were glowing just like the moon. I heard singing in the distance. A voice I wanted to follow. It was beautiful." She shuddered.

"What—" Hector began, his voice hoarse. "What the hell was that back there?"

Keith had been vacant-eyed the whole way back, walking in a daze just like Ash had, but at Hector's question, he seemed to come around.

"I've seen it before, when I was a child," he said. "It's called the King of the Wood."

1725

. . .After the requisite niceties had been observed, we were brought before the Sachem at the Onondaga council fire. Members of the Bear Clan spoke against us, and asked that we answer for the indiscretions of our countryman. Louis and his troops bristled at the words, being unfamiliar with the ways of the Haudenosaunee. They had likely heard wild tales at the settlement, and expected to be flayed alive or some such nonsense.

The Turtle Clan counseled patience and spoke in our favor, and I was permitted to present an entreaty from the Commander of Fort Frontenac, inquiring as to the health and whereabouts of his foolish young nephew, who had ridden this way some months before with a company of *coureurs du bois* after furs and gold. When I had said my piece, the Sachem frowned. He motioned to two of his warriors, and they brought forth a body wrapped in a shroud. He had been given all the respect of their funerary rites and our own, such as they knew them. Louis hissed that this was surely treachery, but I told him to be silent.

"I have ill news," the Sachem said. "Your Commander's kinsman did not return."

"Then who is this?" I said.

"The Spirit's Eye is forbidden for good reason. Your man would not heed our many warnings. He ventured there, and he did not return. What did was not a man as you or I know them. He slew two of my best warriors, and he died cursing all men and all their gods."

I thanked the Sachem, and told our men to ready the body for transport to Frontenac. Louis whispered to me that I was abetting murder, and that he could not countenance how a man of the cloth could be so taken in by pagan superstition. He promised the Commander would know all when we returned, and I would be hanged.

Perhaps I would have been if Louis had shared his tale, but one look at the dead man's face and he fell silent. The features were that of our commander's nephew, but twisted into a look of such unearthly malevolence that none could say he was the youth they remembered. I heard nothing from Louis all the ride back to Frontenac.

—*Confessions of Fra. Benoit Giraud, Societas Iesu*, 1725
From the library of Tom Morris

XIV.

Keith and Ash exchanged fearful looks. The name King of the Wood meant something to them it didn't mean to Hector and me.

"We're all in this together now," I said. "We need to know what you know."

"It-it's just supposed to be a story," said Ash. "He steals children that don't obey their parents, or go walking in the woods at night. He and his hounds hunt the souls of sinners on All Hallows Eve."

"I saw him before," Keith said as we walked toward the Jeep. There was something hollow in his voice, like he was trying to hide from his own memory. "I was just a kid, I don't remember how old. I was wandering in the grape vines, pretending they were a maze I had to find my way out of. I lost track of time. Before I knew it, the sun had set, and it was dusk. Everything was caught between light and dark, and I saw this shadow, big and darker than the rest of the shadows, rise up out of the lake and creep along the ground t-toward my house. I couldn't move. I've never been that afraid in my life. As it passed, it turned toward me, and I knew it could see me crouched there between the grape vines, holding my breath. It just looked at me like-like it did now by the lake, and I could see it, too, beneath the darkness, it . . . I can't remember. I don't want to."

I laid a hand on Keith's shoulder, and all of us stayed there for a moment, silent, while he buried his head in his hands. Ash also put an arm around him, and even Hector laid a hand on his shoulder. Finally, he seemed to come back to himself.

"What now?"

"I don't want to go home," said Ash. "I need to be somewhere with light. I . . . can you all come with me?"

"Light," said Keith. "I think that's a good idea."

Keith took us down the road I'd first come into town on, past the bus stop. He was driving us out of Redmarch Lake. All the time I'd been here, I'd never thought of just hopping in the car and leaving town. It seemed wrong, just like throwing a pebble into the lake had. Part of me was afraid we'd hit an invisible wall, or realize we'd somehow turned around and were right back where we started, but Keith kept driving until we were outside the town limits, on a dark road lit by the silvery circles of streetlights.

"The only thing open now is a gas station out by the state road," said Keith. "I hope no one minds."

"Nothing numbs the unspeakable horror like beef jerky," said Hector.

We all managed to laugh a little, which was good. It was funny—leaving the town and the lake felt like letting out a breath I didn't even know I was holding. It was nice, and almost made me want to head back home, but I couldn't go now. Despite the horrible things I'd seen, I didn't want to leave the lake. Not until I knew what it had to do with my sister. It was more than that, though. This lake had a hold on me, somehow, and even now I felt a disturbing urge to be near it again.

As we drove, Hector and Ash talked about the town in the back seats. It was like something had come loose in Hector—now that a few of the locals acknowledged his existence, he couldn't stop talking.

"For real, no one sits you down one day and says 'don't talk to any outsiders,' or anything?"

"My mom didn't tell me much besides shut up and sit still," Ash said. "Maybe other people's parents did. Sometimes this place feels like one of those old Hollywood sets of a Wild West town—like it only looks real on the surface. I don't know what's underneath, and I'm not sure most of the adults do either."

"Wow," he said. "All this time, I thought I was the only one on the outside of this big secret."

"If there's a secret, I think we're all outside it," Ash gave Keith a sideways look, which he couldn't see with his eyes on the road. "Well, most of us, anyway."

I felt a sudden flush of jealousy at Hector and Ash's new little mutual-respect society. Was he only talking to me because the locals ignored him? I told myself I was being crazy, and it was good they were becoming friends.

The gas station was a little oasis of red-white-and-blue neon. There were a few trucks refueling at the diesel pumps, but otherwise it was empty. We parked well within the station's halo of light and walked into the mini-mart,

which was lit up like high noon. I think all of us appreciated that. We bought big armfuls of junk food—sodas and
chips and candy bars, not caring how bad any of it was. The
sleep-deprived young man behind the counter rang us up
without saying a word, or even opening his eyes beyond
a painful squint. None of us minded. The bright artificial
light made this the best place in the world right now.

We sat in the parked car, opened our feast of junk, and
shared everything. I mixed salty and sweet without second
thoughts until my stomach ached and my teeth hurt, but I
was finally starting to feel normal.

"So I just want to get one thing out there," said Hector.
"Out of all the small towns in America, why did I have to
move to the haunted one?"

"I'm sorry," said Ash. "For everything, for the way we
all don't talk to outsiders and all that. I hate it. Neil was the
only one who refused to do it . . ."

And look what happened to him, we all added silently.

"We didn't ask to be born here, either," said Keith. "I
know, the town's named for my family, cue the world's
smallest violin, but—I hate it, too. It feels good to say that.
I don't think I ever have before."

Both Hector and Ash seemed a little nervous around
Keith. I guess for them he still represented everything they
feared about the town, but I hoped they were starting to
see him like I did.

"Let it out," said Hector. "Don't be shy. I used to count
any word someone said to me in this town as a victory,
even if it was 'shut up, nerd.'"

195

"Ouch, see I feel bad for complaining already," said Keith. "They made me captain of the football team. I didn't even have to try out. I was terrible, but no one would tell me that. It was hard to resist, but I could see what kind of person I would be if I let that continue, and I didn't like it. I quit the team. I couldn't take it anymore."

"I never thought of it that way," said Ash. "Half the kids in school are afraid of you, I mean, of your family. No one wants to get on your bad side, even the teachers."

"Don't remind me," said Keith. "I do all my homework, even though I'd get the same grades if I never turned anything in. My whole life is like a really comfortable cage, but the cage is so nice I feel awful for complaining about it."

"Why don't we just keep driving?" said Hector. "We could stay with Clara's mother in the city."

Keith and Ash agreed enthusiastically to this decision. They were already planning out new lives in New York. They were only half joking, I think. I wished right then that I could bring them all back with me, Ash and Keith and especially Hector.

"You don't know what you're getting into," I said. "You haven't met my mother, not to mention her loser boyfriend."

"That's a good point," said Hector. "If your mom's as tough as you, we're all in trouble."

I felt my cheeks get hot. I hoped Hector couldn't see my face in the rearview mirror. I wasn't even sure that was a compliment, but my body already seemed to think it was—clearly I wasn't as tough as I liked to think. Maybe it was just that Hector was the one complimenting me.

I looked away, catching sight of my reflection in the passenger side window, against the darkness of the road and the forest. It made me think again of Zoe at the lake. Every friendship, every night spent with people I cared about made me feel guilty, because I should have been spending that time with her. It's not what she would have wanted, I know—but nothing can replace a twin. If only she were here beside me.

It had been her, not me, in the lake. I was certain. All this time I'd been half-pretending she was still with me, trying to think of what she'd say about everything in my life. Then I started receiving these clues in our secret language, and when I actually saw her, it was in the water beside a dead boy—begging for my help.

What did it mean? I'd thought a lot about ghosts since coming here, but even after all I'd seen tonight, I couldn't bring myself to believe in something like that. Just thinking about it made me feel like the ground was about to open up and swallow me whole.

The others had fallen silent around me—their conversations gradually petering out in the face of returning memories. We could only distract our minds for so long before we started seeing the darkness between the trees again.

"Oh, right," said Hector, "we have to go back, don't we?"

"My father is probably going to ship me back to the city in a crate," I said, "but after what I saw tonight, I can't go. Not if you all are still here."

And, I added silently, *not if in whatever impossible way my sister is here, as well.*

Ash squeezed my shoulder.

"You're the craziest person I've ever met," she said. "Thank you."

I clasped her hand in mine.

"Anytime," I said.

"No, I mean it," she said, whispering now, "you saved my life. How did you know I was in trouble?"

I wanted to tell her everything then and there—the notes from my sister, the thoughts and questions that were driving me completely crazy—but I couldn't find the words to even begin.

"I just had a feeling," was all I said instead.

Reluctantly, Keith drove us back into town.

"It's not too late to make for Cali," said Hector. "Come on, coast to coast?"

We all sighed. I was hoping my father slept through the whole thing, even though I knew there was no way my escape had gone unnoticed.

We came to Ash's house first.

"Is your mother still asleep?" Keith asked.

"Yeah," said Ash. "Like I said, the medicine knocks her out. She missed the whole thing. Thanks, everyone, I don't even want to think about what would have happened if you hadn't come for me. I'm not good at this sort of thing, but . . . it's good to have friends like you."

"You, too," I said. "Are you going to be okay?"

"Not sure what okay means anymore, but I'll be safe for now. The sun's coming up."

"And when it goes down again?"

None of us wanted to think about that, I could tell, but that wouldn't stop it from coming.

"I don't know, I'll barricade myself inside, or just stay up all night with a baseball bat."

I gave her a hug before she went inside.

"You could always stay with me, I mean it."

"Thanks, I might take you up on that," she said, though I doubted she would.

We came to Hector's house next. As Keith pulled to a stop, the sound of furious barking erupted from inside the house..

"Oh crap," he said. "If you don't see me tomorrow, it's because I haven't thought of a creative way to get out of being grounded."

"I hope—" I said.

"Oh, I will, don't worry." He tapped his temple, flashing me a cocky smile. "Get her home safe," he said to Keith—a surprising edge to his voice.

"Who's gonna get *me* home safe?" Keith said as we drove away. He started to drive back to my father's house. I pictured Dad waiting up for me, furious and yet unable to properly express his anger, or even tell me what was going on in his head. It made the whole thing so much worse.

"Hey, I don't think I'm ready to go home yet." I said. "I'm sorry, I don't want to keep you up, but could you just drop me in town?"

"I know how you feel," he said. "I'm in no hurry to get home either."

Keith parked near the town square. There was a gray strip of light in the eastern sky. Soon the sun would rise behind the veil of morning mist. Without thinking, Keith started walking down to the little lakefront promenade.

"Wait, you're going back down by the water?"

"You can't avoid the lake," Keith said, "but it's almost sunrise."

He spoke as if all of that should mean something to me.

"Does that mean it's safe?"

"Nowhere is safe, but it's safer here in town than in the forest."

"How do you know?"

The lake was swathed in gray mist, blurring water and sky into one eerie in-between. The only thing that stood out in the gloom was a faint line of pre-dawn light on the other side of the water, where Keith's house was.

"It's not good to talk about . . . no one ever sits you down and says 'hey, these are the rules of the town.' No one even talks about it if they can help it. You pick things up, that's all. Your mom won't let you leave the house without something made of iron, you know not to drink the lake water, you don't go into the woods at night, unless you stay on a path . . ."

"I was never good with rules," I said.

"I can see that."

For a moment, we just sat in silence, watching the pale disc of the sun creep up above the horizon through the shroud of mist.

"I loved Danny," Keith said suddenly.

I looked at him, his mouth twisted into an anguished grimace. I put a hand on his arm, trying in vain to reassure him.

"We used to be on the football team together," he said. "He was actually good, good for our little town, anyway. I-I thought he would hate me because of who I was, but he always tried to encourage me, help me play better. Then, well, we spent more time together, and one day, out at my family's vineyard, I kissed him. I just reached out and did it, because it felt right, and he kissed me back. It was the best few moments of my life."

He wiped away a tear from one eye.

"We didn't have long, a few weeks maybe. Then my dad found out. He sat me down, and he said, 'Son, I want you to know I'm not doing this because of any small-minded bigotry, or anything so pointless, but you're a Redmarch, and that comes with certain obligations. You are, we all are, bound to our blood. Do you understand? You aren't to see that boy again.'"

He spat those words out, a guttural parody of his father's baritone.

"Danny had to quit the team, even though he was good. Even though I was the one who wanted to quit.... He fell in with the stoners. I'd catch him looking at me sometimes, not angry. He was never angry, and it killed me. If what happened to him is somehow my fault ..."

"It's not," I said. "I don't know why they died, but ... I think they broke one of those unspoken rules you mentioned—a

201

big one. Neil had a new girlfriend, or there was a rumor about it, anyway, and Danny was the only one who knew anything about her . . . and then Ash was connected to Neil, as well. I don't understand it, but it's not your fault."

Saying it out loud like that made it clear just how little I knew. Keith wasn't convinced.

"No, the thing we saw last night—"

"The king—" I started to say, but he put a finger to his lips, a terrified look in his eye.

"Don't say it. Not here. You don't understand, it's tied to my family somehow. My father won't tell me any more than this. 'Not until you're ready,' he says. Whatever is going on here, my family is somehow responsible for it. We're . . . I don't know how to say this, it sounds ridiculous, but I think we're cursed. We go bad. It goes way back."

I shivered as I thought about what Keith said, and I remembered everything I knew about his family.

"You're not bad," I said, giving him a pat on the shoulder.

"Thanks."

"Hey, I think you should have this," I said. "I found it at . . . where we found Danny. I read some stuff in it I'm not sure I understand, but I don't think Danny ever stopped caring about you."

I handed Danny's diary to Keith.

"Thanks," he whispered. "I can't look at it. Not yet . . ."

We sat still for a moment, while Keith shook with silent sobs. I put my arm around him and tried my best to comfort him—I wished I was better at that sort of thing.

Everything I thought of saying sounded so flat, a platitude. I had no idea what would make this or anything else okay. Nothing had worked for me when I lost Zoe, not at first, at least. Loss was loss, and sometimes the best thing was just to acknowledge it.

"It's hard, I know," I said. "It's hard for a long time, but it gets easier."

A little while later, the sun rose above the mist, and the first rays of light hit us with a wave of warmth. Keith gave me a sad little smile.

"I guess it's a new day now," he said.

"I'd better get home before my father organizes a search party," I said.

"Mine can take his bloodline straight to hell," Keith said, but he didn't look like he believed it.

As he drove me home, a placid mask came over his features. I didn't realize it until now, but the Keith I met that first night at the party, or even most of the afternoon we spent at his house, was not the real Keith. He was getting ready to see his father again, putting the facade back in place. It was hard to watch.

"I'm so sorry," I said.

"Don't be. Just-just let's get to the bottom of this."

He dropped me off in front of my father's house. The blinds were up in the front window. Dad had to have seen me by now.

I walked in, knowing trouble was waiting for me.

XV.

My father was on the phone when I walked in, his voice on the verge of hysteria.

"No, wait, call it off, Bill. She just walked in. She's okay."

His voice on the phone was equal parts relief and pure fury. After he hung up, he ran over to me, both emotions fighting for dominance in his face. He hugged me tight.

"You're okay. Please tell me you're okay."

"Dad, I'm sorry, I'm really sorry. Yes, I'm okay—"

"Good, because now I'm going to kill you. Seriously, what the hell, Clara! What the hell! This can't go on anymore. Go to your room and pack your bags. I'm going to march you to the bus stop and make sure as hell you are on the first bus back to New York, and your mother will be there to pick you up at the station. Believe me, I have loved having you here, but I can't—I just can't—you're going to give me a heart attack . . ."

"So you're pawning me off on Mom? Just like you moved back here to get away from us after the divorce?"

Since I arrived, I'd been trying to find the words to ask him this, but I hadn't wanted it to come out now—not this way. I wished I could take it back, but then I remembered how he'd refused to believe me about Zoe's notes, and I was furious all over again. My father gave me a pained look, but it wasn't enough to make him forget his anger.

"You know it's not like that. It's not just me; the sheriff's office gave you a warning, for chrissakes. You are going back to the city, and that's all there is to it."

"I'm not going anywhere."

My father's face turned pink, then red. He just sputtered for a second, unable to even speak. I'd never seen him like this.

"Y-you're going. I mean it. Get packing now."

I stared right back at him, my own anger wiping away my guilt. I couldn't leave, not now.

"What is the King of the Wood?"

My father's face went from red to white so fast I was afraid he'd pass out.

"Don't! Don't you say that out loud. Where the hell did you even hear it?"

"What is the King of the Wood?"

"It's nothing, all right? Just a stupid story to scare kids."

His eyes darted nervously to the left and right.

"What is the King—"

"All right, all right, stop!" he shouted, nearly frantic. "We are not going to do this here. Get in the car."

He hurried me out the door, looking around nervously the whole time.

"You're not driving me back to the city."

"I'm not, not right now anyway. But if you want me to tell you anything, it can't be here."

He opened the car door for me. As I sank into the seat, I was conscious for the first time of how tired I was, but I fought to stay awake. The last thing I wanted was to wake up on the road back to the city. My father got in the drivers' seat, still on the verge of panic. He backed out of the driveway and sped off, and for the second time in twenty-four hours, I found myself on the way out of Redmarch Lake. As we left the town behind, I called Lady Daphne, leaving a message letting her know I was really sick and couldn't make it in to open the café. I hoped she would understand.

As we drove out of town, the rhythm of the car and the same unconscious feeling of release I'd felt last night combined to put me to sleep. I fought to keep my head up, but I could only manage to delay the inevitable a little longer.

I started awake when the car came to a stop in a gravel parking lot. In front of us was a big red barn, with racks of fresh produce on display in front. My father shut off the engine and we walked through the rows of strawberries and raspberries. It was still too early for apples, the other thing they grew most out here besides wine grapes and corn. My father didn't speak, and I decided to let him work up to whatever he was going to say. I was still half asleep anyway.

The farm was like a child's drawing come to life: blue sky, green fields, and a bright yellow sun. I almost expected a friendly tractor to come rolling by with a big happy smile, then we could all sing a song about ducks. Inside the barn was a little country store with cheese, butter, and baked goods, along with a bunch of hokey handcrafts that were probably made in China. At least the food looked good.

We bought some bread and cheese to go with a big carton of fresh raspberries, and a bottle of sparkling cider to wash it down. For a second, it felt like a weekend trip when I was much younger, all of us packed in my parents' old hatchback for a day of hiking or apple picking. Only my mother was still back in the city, and Zoe was gone. I pictured her in the lake again, mouthing words to me, a silent cry for help. It felt so far away right now, but it was etched into my mind. I would never forget or stop looking until I knew why she came to me there.

The sky was a pale blue, almost too bright to look at, and the sun was starting to singe my pale arms, but I still shivered.

"I'm sorry," my father said. "Maybe a lot of things could have been avoided if I did this sooner."

"It's okay, Dad. I'm involved in this, no matter what, and I'm glad I am." I couldn't tell him why, of course, not really, after the way he'd dismissed Zoe's note. I hoped he'd just assume it was because of my friends—that was just as true. I couldn't leave Hector, Ash, or Keith behind any more than I could leave Zoe.

"Damn, this is still hard to talk about," my father said. "It's like reaching out to pick up a red hot coal. Your body keeps telling you not to. I don't even know where to start."

"Start at the beginning," I said. "Wherever you start in your book."

He frowned for a moment longer, then he spoke.

"I would wager that before the lake even had a name, it was a haunted place. Even the animals seem to know it. We don't really have words to describe what it is, but the best I can say is it's sort of a hole or a membrane between this world and . . . somewhere else."

"Where?"

"I don't know, and I don't want to. Sometimes things come through the hole, though. Their notions of life, and of right and wrong, are very different from ours. To us, most of them seem horribly cruel. They live by different rules. Some you only see at night, or dawn or dusk—even midday. Most you never see at all, but you know they're there. Some can never break a promise, but others can never speak the truth. They hate the touch of iron, just like in fairy tales—in most old stories, it's tied to the earth and to blood, or maybe they just don't have it where they're from. No one tells us any of this, but as children in Redmarch Lake, we all learn it or we disappear."

"What are they?" I said. "Fairies? Demons?"

"Those are just words. The French and British had names for them—so do the Mohawk, Cayuga, Oneida, Onondaga, Seneca, and Tuscarora. Spirits, Fey, Otkon, Manitou. Names don't really get at what they are, but even so, they don't like to be talked about."

I couldn't be sure, but I thought I saw something move at the edge of the field, where the forest began. I told myself it was probably just a bird.

"At some point, long ago, a tribe of indigenous people came and settled by the lake. Whatever name they called themselves is long lost, but the name the Iroquois gave them loosely translates to 'Two Shadows' or 'Double Shadow.' You can still see their artifacts some places in town, and on the island in the lake. I'm sure they were a normal tribe once—in fact, the fragments of song and poetry that remain before they came to this area paint them as gentle farmers— but that soon changed, thanks to the place they'd chosen to settle. The stories after that point aren't pretty. People making up nasty stories about their neighbors is nothing new: the Iroquois call themselves Haudenosaunee, or the Long House People. Their old enemies, the Huron, called them Iroquo, which means rattlesnakes.

"The stories about the Double Shadow are different, though. They're too strange and too specific to be rumor or libel. It's gruesome stuff, I . . . I couldn't bring myself to put much of it in the book. One story says they liked to drive their captives mad before they killed them. They may have believed madness was imprinted on the soul, and it would mean that person would never have final rest. When their minds were finally broken, they would drown them in the lake, where their soul would be trapped, and their ongoing torment would nourish the spirits. The other stories are worse. It was said that at some point in their lives, every member of the tribe, as soon as they came of age, was possessed by a malevolent spirit. The strongest one, the one you insisted on naming this morning, always possessed their chief."

I shivered despite myself. All of this would seem like just another story, if not for what I'd seen last night.

"The stories say, in the right light, the spirit's shadow is visible with the man's—that's where the name comes from. It was a grand bargain: the spirits gave the Double Shadow extraordinary gifts—long life, strength, speed and beauty—and the Double Shadow paid them back with 'tributes,' like their poor mad captives. The spirits don't eat normal food. Some of them feed on passion or joy, but most feed on fear and pain. Every suffering soul cast into their lake let them enter this world more fully, which also made the Two Shadows stronger.

"By the time the Iroquois came to the region, the Two Shadows had become decadent, better at torture than war. They still fought fiercely, but eventually the Iroquois Confederacy overwhelmed them. They never occupied the land, even though it was within their borders. They called the lake *otkon okàra*, the Spirit's Eyes, and they had the good sense to stay well away from it."

"What happened then?" I said. "The spirits had no hosts, and no . . . no food?"

"I don't know any of this for certain," my father said, "but according to the stories, the Two Shadows believed their victims would never find final rest. Maybe their lost souls, trapped in the lake, helped the spirits stay connected to this world. Still, they waited hungrily for hundreds of years. Then, around 1756, along comes a young Englishman named Broderick Redmarch, a deserter from the colonial regiments during the French and Indian War. He spent the war hiding from both armies by the lake. While he lived there, the—" It was hard for my father to say the words. Even here, he barely spoke above a whisper, "the King came to him."

At the tree line, a flock of birds suddenly took to the air. My father turned to look. He didn't relax when he saw it was just birds.

"It offered him whatever he desired, if he would let it enter the world more fully through him. It taught him rites that had gone unperformed for centuries, and it grew strong again. They were both colonists, in different ways, and both greedy for this land. It was perhaps the worst thing that could have happened.

"When the war ended in 1763, Redmarch made a fortune in the fur trade, even as beaver pelts grew scarce. None of the men he served with remained alive to report his cowardice—he probably took care of whoever the war didn't. By the time the American Revolution broke out thirteen years later, he'd built enough wealth and connections to get commissioned a Captain in the Continental Army."

I remembered the statue in the town square, and the cruel look in its eyes.

"The Revolution split the Six Nations of the Iroquois Confederacy apart. Some tribes sided with the British, and some with the Americans. When we won, the colonists used this as an excuse to take their land by force, whether they supported the British or not. Broderick Redmarch led a number of 'local militias' that were infamous for their brutality. In return, all he asked for was title to land on a little lake with no river access and no edible fish, which the colonists were all too happy to give him. He married the unfortunate daughter of one of the settlers, and brought along two other families he was close with: his business partner, Wallace Clyburn, and his trusted lieutenant, Nathaniel Morris."

I felt a queasy twist in my stomach, being reminded of our family's connection to all this.

"We're not like them, though. . . . Are we?" I asked. I knew the Morrises had done bad things, but it was suddenly very important for me to know we weren't as bad as the Redmarches.

"We were one of the town's founding families, which means we had a big role in stealing the surrounding lands from their rightful owners, and in other things that are harder to explain. It's important to remember the sins of the past. We're all complicit in things from long ago that echo into the present day. But we're not exactly like them. Redmarch's unholy bargain is passed down through his bloodline. Anyone with Redmarch blood is strong, beautiful, long-lived. Anyone who marries into that family withers away. Not by accident, either. The King still needs to eat. It's become much more careful since it consumed and discarded the Two Shadows—only the King has a human host, and it will not share."

"And Jonathan Redmarch is what, possessed?"

"I don't know," said my father. "Whatever it is, it's not so simple as that. All I've managed to read on the subject is hints and conjecture. The Redmarch heirs change some time in adolescence. The-the king will take men or women, though it seems to favor the men, if only because powerful women draw more scrutiny from society. It acts through them, but they're not puppets. It changes them somehow, brings out their worst qualities, and even when it moves on to their heirs, they're still left twisted and wrong."

I remembered Cordelia Redmarch and her serial killer son. I thought of everything Dad had told me about Jonathan's family. This all sounded so crazy, sitting here on a picnic bench while my father talked about things that might have come from his conspiracy books. If not for what I saw with my own eyes last night, I would have laughed.

"I know how this sounds," my father said. I guess it was pretty obvious what I was thinking. "I know it's true, though. Jonathan was my best friend once. He was the kindest person I ever met, even though his father was a terror who beat him within an inch of his life more than once. When we were young, he promised me he'd never be like his father. He told me that I should kill him if he ever became like that.

"The woman he married, Anne, was my good friend, too. The two of them were high school sweethearts. Then Jonathan started to change. There was a darkness in him. He was different with Anne, cruel. I told him what was happening, what he was becoming, and he didn't like it. He . . . he took me boating on the lake the day after I brought it up, acting like everything was normal, and he was back to being the Jonathan I'd grown up with. He took me out on the water, and he changed. There was this awful, cruel light in his eye. He threw me overboard. He was so strong, I couldn't fight it, and I'd always been stronger than him. He still had his hands on me, and he was holding me underwater, trying to drown me. I fought with everything I had, but I couldn't get free. He stopped just short of killing me. He heaved me back up into the boat to watch me cough and sputter like it was grade-A entertainment. And while I was catching my breath, coughing up lungfuls of that foul lake water, he leaned in close to me and said, 'Don't you ever question me or my affairs again.'"

"What happened then?" I said.

"I stopped seeing him, cut myself off. Not long after that, I moved to the city. Anne wasn't so lucky. The two of them were already engaged. I begged her to leave him, but she didn't. I think she was too afraid. He kept one promise, at least—I don't think he ever raised a hand to her physically. The thing is, there are all kinds of ways to be cruel to a person without ever touching them. . . . I don't know everything that happened between them, but Anne voluntarily committed herself at a treatment center years ago."

I could see the regret etched in the lines of my father's face. Mr. Redmarch seemed so calm, jovial even. I had trouble squaring my picture of him with what my father had just told me, even with everything I knew about the family. Then again, I'd always had the feeling that there was something *more* to him, like an iceberg whose mass was mostly below the surface.

We were quiet for a moment. I hoped the sun and the warm breeze would make me feel normal again, after everything I just heard, but it wasn't working. How could any of this be real, and if it was, why would my father come back to it? Even after he and mom split, why return to a nightmare place like this? If I didn't get an answer now, I probably never would.

"Dad, why did you leave the city and come back to this place?"

He was silent for a long time.

"I-I'm sorry, sweetheart. I know how it must have felt. I've asked myself the same question, and I don't have a good answer."

"Try," I said.

"This place is in my blood. Ever since I moved away, I've felt it calling me back. I would dream I was back here, or find myself thinking about it every day. After the divorce, it got worse. Once I even started to drive here in the morning without thinking."

I remembered the odd pull I'd felt about this place, too, the sense I always had that I'd come here. I was a Morris, too, even if I was born in Jersey.

"So you had to come here?"

"I thought if I could just figure this place out, get my head straight, then I'd be able to come back to be near you. Believe me, it's what I want."

I thought of my father's book—his attempt to make sense of this place that refused to make sense. I had been so mad at him, and part of me still was, but now I thought I understood. After all, I still felt that same need to understand this place, and not let it overwhelm me. I got up and gave him a hug. I felt the sun and the breeze and his arms around me and for one moment, it felt just like I was a kid again, before all the hurt.

"There's more," he said, a nervous edge in his voice. "I didn't have a good childhood here. My father wasn't as bad as Jonathan's, more of a garden-variety abusive drunk, but we have a history of that in the family, and worse, especially when connected with the Redmarches. They have a way of bringing out the worst in everyone around them. I was . . . I was really afraid I'd turn out like my dad."

I'd never met my grandfather on Dad's side. He died when Zoe and I were still little. I couldn't remember, but I don't think my dad even came back for the funeral. My father was always so gentle, I couldn't imagine him hurting me or Mom, but I hadn't known what he grew up with until now.

We took a walk through the fields while I tried to sort out everything my father had said. We passed through rows of apple trees, their apples just hard little green lumps this early in the year. My phone buzzed and I saw it was a voicemail from Lady Daphne, telling me not to worry about staying home, and to be sure to let her know if I was still feeling bad tomorrow. Good thing she hadn't used her clairvoyance on me.

As we walked, I found myself gazing nervously at the forest every so often. I didn't see anything weird, but it wouldn't be long before I was always checking behind my back like a paranoid local. I tried to think of how Zoe fit in to all of this. Why had I seen her in the lake? The figure I'd glimpsed sometimes in the distance, or at the café window

216

in the early morning, had looked like her, too. Had her soul somehow migrated here, lost and trapped in that horrible lake? Or were the spirits lying to me, using my sister's face and our language, trying to tempt or trick me? Either possibility felt too frightening to bear, but I knew I'd have to keep looking until I found the truth.

I couldn't put any of this into words yet, but one other thing was bothering me.

"Dad, if talking about this is so dangerous, why are you writing that book?"

I understood now why he kept it hidden away, afraid to show anyone, and why he refused to talk about it even with me. I understood his need to make sense of this place, and to free himself from it, but why do it if it was such a big risk?

"They don't like to be exposed, or talked about—that's why they're so sensitive about names. The book is . . . well, I hoped it would free me of this place once and for all, and if I couldn't free myself, maybe exposing this place, telling the truth, would free us all somehow."

He didn't sound convinced. In fact, he sounded terrified of the very idea of going public, but I could see how badly he wanted to be free of this town.

My sleepless night was starting to catch up with me again, though I was amazed I could even think of sleeping after learning what I'd just learned. We shared some homemade fudge, then headed back to the car.

I had been so angry at my father since the divorce—angrier than I'd admitted even to myself. It had felt like being abandoned all over again after losing Zoe. It was like a muscle I'd been clenching all this time, and now, slowly, it was beginning to release. I don't think I could have grasped what my father was going through until I came here myself, and I was glad I did, ghosts and spirits be damned.

"Thanks for breakfast, Dad," I said as I sank into the passenger seat.

I thought I would pass out the moment I lay back in the seat, but my mind was racing with thoughts of family curses and evil spirits and all the brutal history of this place. I kept coming back to Zoe, staring back at me from that horrible lake. Zoe who needed my help. I had learned so much in the past few hours. Maybe now my father would finally help me make sense of it all.

"Dad, I saw Zoe."

My father gave me a shocked look as he drove.

"I know you don't believe me about the notes, but I saw her. I've seen her in the distance, and at the café window early in the morning. She looks like she wants to come to me, but she can't. Something's holding her back. Then, when we found Danny in the lake, I-I saw her there. My reflection wasn't me, you understand, it was her looking back at me. I can't explain it, and it's tearing me up inside."

My father turned to look at me, and I was stunned to see the anguish in his face. He wiped away a tear as he swung his gaze back to the road in time to keep from drifting into the shoulder. When he finally spoke, his voice was thick with sadness and with fear.

"Clara, there's something else I have to tell you."

XVI.

As he drove, my father bit his lip, searching for the right words. He was biting so hard, I was afraid he'd start bleeding.

"Tell me," I said.

He looked at me, and there was such worry in his face that I started to feel afraid myself. But it was different than his panic when I named the King of the Wood out loud. This was a slow, creeping dread, as if something he'd feared for a long time were finally coming true. I was silently freaking out as I waited for him to speak.

"There's something we should have told you a long time ago. We wanted to tell you, but we were afraid it'd do more harm than good. Your mother . . . your mother wanted to. She was always stronger than me. Oh, Clara, honey, I hope you can forgive us. You see, you never had a twin sister."

He whispered the words at first. I couldn't believe I heard them right.

"What?"

"You never had a twin sister," he said louder. "Zoe . . . Zoe wasn't real."

I looked into his eyes, expecting some sort of sick joke, or at least an explanation, but he was deeply, sadly serious.

219

What the hell was he trying to tell me, that I was delusional? That I'd hallucinated a twin sister, only to hallucinate that she died?

"Why would you say something like that? It makes no sense."

"I'm so sorry, sweetheart. We should have done things differently. . . . There's so much I should have done differently."

As we drove, I looked out into the blue-green shadows between the trees, dark even in daylight. I wished I was there, alone with whatever lurked in the woods around Redmarch Lake, rather than right here listening to this. Slowly, painfully, my father tried to explain.

"You told us about Zoe almost as soon as you could form sentences. We thought she was your imaginary friend. You would tell us all these stories about the two of you and all the adventures you had. It's not uncommon to want a twin."

This sounded like so much nonsense to me. All of the memories I had, good or bad, Zoe was there. Every night when we went to sleep, every day out with our parents, or at school. We had been inseparable.

"We went along with it at first, but as time went on, we started to worry. You wouldn't talk to other children, you spent all your time with Zoe. We-we took you to therapy, we even tried medication. It wasn't working. They wanted to take you out of school—they said you scared the other children. The therapists said it would only get worse as you got older. We were afraid if it went on too long, you'd completely disassociate from real life, and we'd have to put you in-in an institution somewhere. We had no idea what to do. . . . We just wanted our daughter to have a normal life. We took that vacation because we prayed a change of scenery might help. We were ready to try anything."

I sat there, numb. I remembered spending long hours with a rotating cast of doctors and therapists. I thought it was all after losing Zoe, but I couldn't be sure. So much of my life from those years was a blur. I remembered mornings as a little girl, my parents getting me my vitamins—were they giving me drugs? I remembered my mother reading hospital pamphlets with tears in her eyes.

"Then the accident happened," my father went on. "I'll never forgive myself for that day. I don't know how I let you out of my sight. When I heard the lifeguard's whistle, I came running, but they held me back at shore, saying I'd only make things worse.

"They pulled you out of the ocean, beat the water out of your lungs, but you kept insisting that they go back for Zoe. You kept telling us that Zoe drowned. The lifeguard was panicked, saying he only saw you out there, no one else. We had to tell him Zoe wasn't real."

This was too much to bear. All of the pain and stress and confusion I'd felt since I'd come here was crashing down on me in one giant wave, and I felt like I was drowning all over again, sitting in that passenger seat. Only the speed of the car stopped me from opening the door and running away.

"Zoe saved my life," I said. "I-I was the one who started drowning, she saved me, pulled me up so I could breathe, until a wave knocked us apart. Of course she's real."

"You were in so much pain after. We wanted to tell you that you didn't have to be, but we were too afraid of how you'd take it," my father said. "You weren't speaking, or listening. You barely ate. We took you to therapist after therapist. We pulled you out of school. We were afraid we would have to go through with committing you to a mental health facility."

"I had just lost my twin," I said. "I didn't want to feel anything anymore. All of that time is a blur for me."

My father looked at me, tears in his eyes.

"Finally, a new therapist we took you to mentioned something called Vanishing Twin Syndrome. She said we should speak to the doctor who delivered you. Sure enough, the doctor told us that in the early stages of your mother's pregnancy, there had been twins in her womb, but one of them didn't make it. He said when this happens, they don't tell the family because they don't want them to be traumatized—and they especially don't want the surviving twin to know. We didn't think it could have anything to do with Zoe, but the therapist thought the imaginary sister, and her imaginary death, were all your way of coping with this first subconscious loss, compounded by the trauma of almost drowning.

"You never had a chance to mourn the first time, so we thought it would help to let you make up for that now. She had you draw pictures of Zoe, write about her, and soon you were eating and sleeping again, even talking a little. She told us to make pictures of you and Zoe, to help you grieve, and so we made some.

"Once you had improved enough, we moved to the city. We didn't want you spending another day in that school, dealing with the same kids who—they never understood that Zoe was real to you. They could be so cruel. We found a place in Forest Hills, near where your mom grew up.

"You were always strong, and in time, you mentioned Zoe less. You made friends with Rayna, and we thought things were better, that you had healed—but all that time you were grieving, and you still are. We felt so guilty for lying to you. Please believe me, we only did it because we thought we were losing our little girl. It wasn't supposed to be forever, but as time went on, it only got harder to tell you. I'm so sorry, Clara."

"The divorce . . . I thought it was because you guys couldn't keep it together after losing Zoe."

"Things between us hadn't been working for a while," he said. "Please never think it was your fault. We argued about . . . about Zoe, and about how best to help you, but your mother and I just didn't work together, and on my part, I was afraid I'd hurt you or your mother. I was angry at the world for what had happened to you, and I saw too much of what anger can do growing up here."

A cold weight was settling inside me. If what my father said was true, how could I trust anything I saw or felt again? How would I know what else was real if Zoe had felt so real to me? No, it had to be wrong. There was no other way.

A half hour later, we pulled into the driveway. As soon as the car came to a stop, I was out the door. I ran into the house, my father calling after me. I didn't listen. I tore through the bookshelves, looking for where he kept the photo albums. All of the drawings and collages I'd made were back in Queens, but my father had to have pictures.

I finally found a stack of old leather albums, not on the shelves but in a cardboard box tucked underneath. I supposed it was hard for my father to look at them after all that had happened, but I didn't care about that now. I skipped past all the recent pictures of me, and the awkward middle school years with my braces and my glassy eyes and flimsy fake smile—all those years I'd been more dead than alive. I paged through until I found younger photos. The vacation where Zoe drowned was a gap in the timeline. There were no pictures from that trip, but before it . . . before it should have been nothing but me and Zoe.

I turned the pages, and there we were, two little girls in matching dresses, alike in every way. I looked closer. The flaws weren't hard to spot, the altered photos—the duplication of my image. It was easy to see in the face, maybe not for anyone else, but for me. The little differences that set us apart, the things only we knew, just weren't there. How had I not noticed before? Had I just seen what I wanted to see?

I tore the fake photos out, throwing them on the floor. I couldn't stand to look at them. I knew my father was hovering somewhere behind me. Without looking, I could picture the sad, nervous expression he had on his face. I didn't care.

I flipped faster through the pages, hoping for something real. I had to—if I didn't find it, I would explode—or

I'd vanish, undone by the changing past like someone in a time travel movie.

Then one photo made me gasp. I was maybe six years old, my hair in braids with the barrettes I was so proud of back then. I was looking at the mirror, smiling, and my mother had taken the picture so that both me and my reflection were captured by the camera—two girls smiling back at each other. Only the girl in the mirror wasn't me. She was almost exactly the same in every way—most people could never tell the difference between us, but it was always clear to Zoe and me.

Beneath the picture, a caption written in my mother's sloppy handwriting said only *Clara and "Zoe."*

I felt the room spin around me. This was too much. I felt sick, my stomach cinched into a terrible knot. I took deep breaths, closing the photo album. When I opened it again, the picture was still there, still the same. The only true record of my twin's existence was a reflection in a mirror. Every time I'd seen her, was I seeing someone who wasn't there?

My father laid a hand on my shoulder, but I shook it off. Just a short time ago, I'd felt closer to him than ever in my life, but with those words in the car, he'd opened an impassable rift between us.

"I'm so sorry," he said. "I can't imagine how this must feel. I-I hope you can forgive us. We thought we were doing what was best."

"I don't care what you say," I said. "She's real."

My father stared at me, speechless. I could see the panic behind his eyes, searching in vain for the right thing to say to his daughter, like there was a magic word to fix this. All he could manage was to sadly shake his head. I couldn't look at him. Just when I thought I finally understood him, he tore my whole world apart.

"Maybe there's more to it than you know," I said.

I pushed past him, headed for the exit. I waited for him to stop me, to tell me I was grounded or that he was sending me back first thing tomorrow, but he only watched as I walked out the door.

The sun was setting, turning the clouds in the western sky a deep red-gold that lightened to pink at the edges. It would be dark soon. Under the forest's canopy, it was already practically night. I walked faster, texting Hector on the way. *Can you meet me at the diner? Had to get away from home.*

I walked quickly, keeping one eye on the forested side of the street, wary for anything moving in the shadows. This town's paranoia had officially infected me. My phone buzzed with an incoming text, but it was my father, *Please, Clara, please be safe. Don't put yourself in danger. Stay in town, stay out of the forest.* As if I would just wander off into the woods for no reason after what I'd seen here.

My head was full of memories of Zoe, our late nights telling stories when we were supposed to be in bed, or summer afternoons playing in the park, buying ice cream from the Mister Softee truck. I wondered how sad I'd looked, a little girl all by herself, convinced she was with her best friend in the world. Had I just been hearing her voice in my head, like now when I tried to imagine what she'd say? No, it had been different. She had been there—somehow. All I felt now was her absence. Doubting your own memory is a terrible thing. I felt like my sense of self was breaking apart, like there was an earthquake ripping through the landscape of my life. No memory was safe.

And as I walked, I thought of everything else my father had told me about the lake and the beings that lived here, and the lost souls they trapped. I thought of Zoe, glimpsed in the mirror, or in those still waters. Maybe I had been talking to a reflection every time I spoke to her—but what if your reflection talks back?

Things were racing through my head I couldn't yet bring myself to put into words.

By the time I reached the diner, Hector texted to say he was on the way. I sat at a booth and ordered a chocolate milkshake. I didn't care about calories at a time like this. Outside, the sun finally slipped behind the clouds and the sky darkened. I wished Hector would hurry. Then I pictured him running afoul of the thing we'd seen that night on the way here. I told my mind not to go there, but of course that was the first place it went, and each second passed with an agonizing tension as I waited for him to walk in the door.

Finally, the chimes on the door rang as he pulled it open. He must have sprinted here, because he was winded and twitchy. I wasn't the only nervous one after what we'd seen in the forest.

"Hey," I said.

"This better be good; I had to make up a big summer essay project you're supposedly helping me with before I could leave the house, which means I'll actually have to do the project or my folks will get suspicious. That, and after last night, I was seriously considering never leaving the house again. So what is it?"

He saw the fear and the hurt in my eyes, and his expression immediately softened.

"I'm sorry. We've all been through hell, and I don't even know what's real anymore. How can I help?"

All of a sudden, without thinking, I threw my arms around him. I was as surprised as he was by my own actions—I was never much of a hugger, but I couldn't believe how good it was to see him. Just hearing his voice was a warm wave of relief, even when he was being a jerk.

We sat down and he ordered a soda. I wasn't sure where to start, so I started at the beginning, telling him all about Zoe, and our life together until the day I lost her at the beach. Then I softly told him what my dad had told me earlier today, about the town and about Zoe. I felt eyes on us from other parts of the diner, but I didn't care. I spoke in an urgent whisper. I had to share.

"Jesus," was all Hector could manage. "I don't even know what to say but I'm sorry."

"You don't think I'm crazy?"

"No, Clara. Of course not. Even if I hadn't seen all the crazy things last night, I'd still believe you, because I trust you."

I felt such shocking relief when he said this that a chill went through me. I never guessed how badly I needed someone to believe me, especially if that someone was Hector. I reached across the table and put my hand in his.

"This might sound weird," he went on. "Math nerds are supposed to be rational types, but I've always sort of believed in ghosts. There used to be this dog—a real monster—back in Inwood, all the kids on the block were scared of it, even when it was old and half blind. There were rumors it had mauled one kid so badly his mother didn't let him outside, or that it ate the old man who had owned it and now it just did what it wanted. When it finally died, we were all relieved—except, I never was. Every time I walked by the lot it used to hang around, I still felt it there, watching me, like it never left." He shivered. "Now this place makes that ghost dog look like a shih tzu in a tutu."

"There's more," I said, "and it's even stranger. Zoe is here. I don't know how, or in what way, but I saw her in the lake. I've seen her before, too—indistinct, in the distance or as a blurred shape looking in the café window in the morning. I think . . . I think she's one of them, or one of the souls they trapped. I don't know, but somehow I can feel it."

I showed him the notes, explaining the language we had made up together. I could see doubt and worry cross Hector's face like a bout of nausea, and I was briefly afraid it was too much for him to accept, but then he nodded his head.

"Sorry, keep going. It's just—it's hard to talk about this stuff out in the open. I guess I'm more a part of this town than I thought."

"When I first came here, Neil seemed to recognize me," I said. "He did a double take, like I was somehow familiar but not. There was a rumor that he had a new girlfriend, but no one had ever seen her. I think Zoe was trying to contact him. There was something in Danny's diary about him and Neil trying some sort of ritual, trying to contact a soul from the lake."

"Why in the hell would they do that?" said Hector.

"I think-I think they wanted her help, or she wanted theirs, to change the way things are here, and I think that's why they died."

Hector was silent from a moment, and I thought *oh god, he thinks I've lost my mind.* Then he squeezed my hand and smiled—not the cocky, sarcastic smile he usually wore. This was shy, almost sad.

"I think you're right."

Just then I could have jumped across the table and kissed him.

"You know," he went on, "since you came along, I've gotten way over my head in stuff that I don't understand and that could seriously kill me. I may be nuts, but I'm still glad you're here."

"Glad you're here too," I said.

I was happier than I'd been in what felt like forever, but I couldn't ignore the gathering darkness outside the diner. Sooner or later, we'd have to leave. "So what do we do now?"

"Do you think it'll come back for us?"

That was exactly what I'd been trying *not* to think about.

"I've been wondering why it stopped when it saw Keith."

Hector frowned when I mentioned Keith.

"It stopped when you hit it with cold iron."

"I don't think that did more than slow it down," I said. "It could have come back for us."

"Keith's family is bad news," Hector said. "Who knows how they're tied in to this. Keith seems like a decent guy, though. All this time, I assumed he had to be the biggest jerk in this town. Are you and Keith . . . ?"

The question caught me by surprise. How could he have thought that? *Maybe when you showed up in Keith's car, and then you were the last one he dropped off, dummy,* I thought.

"Oh, no. I don't feel that way about Keith."

I caught the ghost of a relieved smile on his face before he quickly tried to look serious.

"I was one of those kids who never stopped asking questions," he said. "My mother would always tell me to look something up when I didn't know it, so I kept doing that. You can't look any of this up, though, not really. There's no Ghostopedia out there, not a real one anyway."

He paused for a second—I could tell he was making a mental note of the idea.

"I don't recommend making one. They don't like being talked about," I said. "And I don't think they're all ghosts, at least not the bad ones. Spirits, maybe, but not of anyone that used to be alive as we know it."

He shook his head. I doubted any of this would ever feel normal, or even comprehensible. We both glanced out the window. The night was deep black outside the diner's circle of light.

"We should probably get back," he said.

I had been trying not to think about the walk home. Whatever Zoe was, I wished she were here with me again, ready to face what was coming. She was always the braver one. All those years, my parents must have thought she was my impulsive side, or the excuse I made up to cover bad behavior. Even the idea of that made me furious. Whatever the truth was, she was so much more than any of it.

The town was dark and silent outside the neon halo of the diner's sign. It felt like we were stepping out of a magic circle. As we walked through the empty streets, Hector's hand reached out and found mine. It felt good to have him beside me.

As we walked out of the town center and along the road that bordered the woods, I started to worry. There should have been armies of crickets chirping on a night like this, but everything was dead silent. The air had that eerie stillness it sometimes gets before a thunderstorm, though there were no clouds in the sky. The moon shone out big and near-full, but it brought no light to the forest below.

"I think they're watching us," Hector said.

I held a finger up to my lips. Whatever these things were, I knew talking about them wouldn't help.

"Stay on the road," I said. "Not even one foot in the woods."

"Trust me, I wasn't planning on it."

We walked like that for another few blocks. Once in a while, I thought I could see shapes moving in the forest, shadows that seemed darker and denser than the surrounding night. We quickened our pace, and soon Hector's house was up ahead.

We stopped outside his front door. It looked like his parents were already asleep.

"Let me walk you home," he said.

"I'll be okay as long as I move fast and stay on the road."

He didn't look so sure, but he was prepared to trust me in this new reality.

"Be careful, Clara. I mean it. I couldn't stand it if anything happened to you."

I looked into his intense brown eyes. All the aloofness and sarcasm he usually guarded himself with were long gone, and suddenly I felt like I was melting, like I didn't care about what was waiting out in those woods, if only for a second. His hand stroked my cheek with just the slightest touch, bringing our faces closer together. Our lips parted.

Then, from the depths of the forest came a bone-chilling howl, answered by several more in the distance. The sound sent waves of panic through me. Hector looked toward the forest, then back at me.

"Get inside!" I said.

"What about you?"

"I'll run home. Go!"

He hesitated one second, then ran toward his front door, checking over his shoulder to make sure I was all right.

I ran like I never had in gym class, or for any other reason, and I kept running even as my ankles started to ache and a stitch burned in my side. I could hear things moving within the woods, keeping pace with me in the darkness. I wished I still had the iron clasp I threw at the King of the Wood.

My father's house was close now. I prayed whatever rules governed these things' behavior still kept them from leaving the woods. My breath was ragged, but I only ran faster, racing to the front door.

I stopped for a second before running in and looked back over my shoulder. I wished I hadn't. Behind me, the shadows were full of eyes that glowed like burning coals.

c. 1400

Let these words tell of our little sister, who gave her life for ours when we took shelter here.

When the Two Shadows came to our village, we fled.

They took our food and our possessions. They burned our homes. They fouled our hearths, but still they came.

We fled to the hills, but still they came, hunting us among the trees. We heard the screams of those they found. The most fortunate ones were killed quickly.

We fled to the mountains, and sought shelter in this cave, but still they came.

We heard them outside, calling for us.

"Send us our tribute, or we will take you all."

Father bade us all be silent.

"We gave you our food, our homes, and all that we possess."

"Send us our tribute, or we will take you all."

The Two Shadows would not kill us quickly. They would break our bodies and our spirits, and then drown us in their foul lake. We huddled in fear.

"Send us our tribute, or we will take you all."

Then little sister spoke out among us.
"I will be your tribute, if you spare my family."
We tried to stop her, but she would not listen.

She was wild and free as a fox in moonlight.
She was as kind as rain to growing things, as gentle as
the dawn.
She was our sister, who gave her life for us.
Her will was strong, her heart was pure.
We prayed they would not break her spirit.
We prayed her soul would find true rest.
She was our sister, who gave her life for us.

—Approximate translation of an inscription found in a
cave near Deer Hollow, NY. Believed to be created circa
1400 A.D. From the library of Tom Morris

XVII.

My father was asleep when I came in. I felt briefly guilty for the pain he must have been feeling—I knew how hard it was for him to finally come clean—but that didn't last long. When I thought of all the years he and my mother had lied by omission, letting me think they were mourning my sister with me, hoping my memories would just fade away . . . I was furious, and I probably would be for a long time. The worst part was, I couldn't prove I wasn't imagining everything like they thought. All I had was a feeling, deep in my bones, that what I saw and felt was somehow real.

I texted Hector so he knew I made it home all right, then headed to bed.

After everything I had lived through in the past two days, I was overwhelmed with exhaustion, but my heart was still racing and my mind too troubled by thoughts of Zoe and whatever was watching me in the woods for sleep to come easily. When it finally came, I tossed and turned, dreaming of fleeing through the forest, branches snapping in my path, until I was almost at the lake. I didn't want to see it again, that darkness that was more than just night, and so much worse. I dug my heels in, tried to run the other direction, but I couldn't move. Something invisible grabbed hold of me, pulling me foot by trembling foot toward that vast emptiness, until everything around me was lost in its darkness.

The next day, I woke to the alarm I forgot was still set. I was due at the café in an hour. I almost laughed, worrying about something so small and normal as being on time for my summer job. I showered and dressed, still half-awake, and was out the door before my father was up. The less I saw of him, the better.

The walk back to town was tense in the half-light of dawn. I kept checking the shadowy edge of the forest for the things I had seen last night. The more I was aware of what went on in this town, the more I was shocked people still lived here.

Cleaning up, feeding Clyde, and making the coffee brought the calm feeling of routine. I could see much more of the appeal of boring summer jobs now than when I started here. I was glad Lady Daphne had been so understanding about the day before.

Then, when the store was almost ready to open, I saw the familiar shape outside, blurred against the glass. She was my height, my build—it could have been me standing there on the other side of the café window. I dropped what I was doing right away, a chill running down my spine. I ran outside, Zoe's name on my lips. A wild hope was rising inside me, along with a terrible fear that this was somehow wrong, or not what I thought. I didn't care. I raced out the door, heart hammering in my chest, but when I looked outside, once again, the street was empty.

"Zoe, if you're here, know that I love you," I said. "I miss you, and I'm trying to help you. Just . . . just tell me what I need to do."

There was no response from the silent street.

When I got back inside, I slumped down at the cash register. She'd been so close, I knew it. More than ever, I had to see her, to know she was real in whatever strange way she was. If only I could talk to her and understand what kind of trouble she was in.

Then I noticed a folded piece of notebook paper wedged under the cash register. It was just like the others.

Trembling slightly, I unfolded the paper and looked down to see three short words in the language Zoe and I shared:

Naa ong issah.
Don't go to the island.

That chilly edge of panic laced with faint hope stayed with me all day. I still didn't know how these notes were coming to me—if somehow Zoe could write but she couldn't speak, or if she was somehow making the words come through me—but I treasured them all the same, even as they filled me with dread.

The only people I served in the morning were the two ladies on their power walk. All these days I'd seen them and I didn't even know their names. Then again, that was hardly surprising in this unfriendly town.

Then at noon the old man from the bus stop wandered in, cigarette still smoldering in his hand. He wore a beat-up old baseball cap and a T-shirt, both with words that had long since faded to illegibility. He ordered his usual coffee, then proceeded to load it up with cream and sugar. Just as he was about to head out, he stopped, as if remembering something that had almost slipped his mind, and walked back to me.

"They say things might change around here. That sort of thing don't come easy. The wrong folks have been in power for a long time, and they don't wanna give up. Best watch out. Full moon tonight."

My jaw hung open. He was looking at me like he knew me, or knew all about me from somewhere. All I could think to do was say, "I'll be careful," but he was gone before I could even finish talking.

Hector came in a little while later, and I rushed over to tell him about the note.

"Oh my god," he said. "Well, I hope you weren't planning on going to the island."

"Yeah, no way."

Hector asked how I'd slept, and I told him about the dreams. Disturbingly, his dreams had been almost exactly the same—being dragged against his will toward the darkness of the lake. I made us both lattes, and we sipped them together until we felt calmer.

"You really don't put sugar in this?"

"The milk should be enough, it's a beautiful combination."

"If you say so. It's not bad."

Before long, Ash reported for her shift. It had only been a day, but even so, I had missed her. She looked like she hadn't been sleeping well since what happened that night, and I couldn't blame her. She gave me another awkward hug as soon as she saw me.

"I've learned a lot," I said to her when she asked me how I was doing. ". . . a lot I guess I'm not supposed to talk about out loud. That's how it works, right?"

"Before everything that happened I thought it was so stupid," said Ash. "Now I'm ready to obey every rule, at least until I can get the hell out of here."

No one else wandered into the café that afternoon, and even when my shift was over, I stayed to sip coffee and share a cookie with Hector and Ash. For a little while, at least, I could pretend to be normal and just spending an afternoon with my good friends, even if we were all trying not to think about the horrors we'd seen in the woods. If only Keith were here, our little group would be complete.

Thinking of Keith shattered the illusion of normalcy. I thought of him, up in his big weird house with his father, and worried about what he might be going through right now. I knew it couldn't be anything good.

A middle-aged couple came in to the café, and Ash went back to the counter to help them. As soon as she left, Hector turned to me, a nervous look on his face.

"Hey, I wanted to talk to you about last night—"

"I know," I said, "I've been trying to forget it, but—"

"No," he looked even more nervous, "I don't mean the-the things in the forest, or the dreams. I mean, I wanted to tell you that I-I mean—"

This was new; I'd never seen him so hesitant about anything. I felt a sudden hope fluttering in me, catching me by surprise. Even the things in the forest and the terrible dreams hadn't been enough to make me forget almost kissing Hector.

Then the café's telephone started ringing.

In all my time here, no one had ever called the café's land line, not even Lady Daphne. We let it ring three times, struck still by the sound and the sudden unease it created in all of us. Then Ash picked up the receiver. Hector turned back to me.

"What I wanted to say was—"

"Clara?" Ash's voice was panicked. She held the phone like at any moment it could turn into a giant spider. "It's for you."

I took the receiver from Ash's trembling hand, terrified of what I'd hear on the other end.

"Hello?"

"Yes, is this Clara Morris?"

The voice was deep and sonorous. I recognized it immediately, though I wished I didn't.

"Yes."

"Hello, Clara, this is Jonathan Redmarch. I hope you're doing well?"

There was a strange sound on the other end of the line, suddenly muffled. I thought I could hear someone speaking in the background.

"I'm . . . fine? How can I help you?"

"Wonderful to hear. You know, your father dropped by this afternoon, and I was thinking, since he's here, and so is Keith, and you're nearby, why not just have the two of you over for dinner?"

I felt like he had dropped a lead weight into my stomach. I didn't know what to say or do. My father was there at the Redmarch mansion—and I doubt he had just decided to drop by—and here was Mr. Redmarch making small talk.

"Um, can I talk to my father please?" I said.

There was silence on the other end of the line for a moment, then what sounded like shouting, muffled by what might have been a hand held to the receiver.

"I'm afraid he can't come to the phone right now, but he would love to see you for dinner here tonight. Are you coming?"

There was another muffled sound on the other side of the line.

"I think you should come very soon."

"O-okay."

I hung up the phone, shaken. Hector and Ash were both beside me in a second, and I told them what had happened.

"We have to call the cops," said Hector.

"They won't look into anything at the Redmarch house," said Ash. "They never have before."

"I have to go," I said. "I know it's a bad idea, but I have to."

They both nodded. I was glad I didn't have to argue or explain myself.

"I'm coming with you," said Hector. "Whatever it is, you shouldn't have to face it alone."

I nodded. Even now I felt a little thrill that he was willing to follow me into danger, but I was afraid at the same time. If anything happened to him, I'd never forgive myself.

"I should go too," said Ash, but her heart wasn't in it. I could see the fear of what almost happened to her the other night in her eyes.

"We need someone to stay here," I said. "If you don't hear back from us, call the cops." Remembering Elaine Cross River's card, I pulled it out of my pocket and handed it to her. "Call Elaine directly. She's not like the others."

Ash tried to hide how relieved she looked, but I couldn't blame her for not coming along. In fact, I felt better that one of us was doing the smart thing.

"Come on," Hector said, "we can take my parents' car."

We ran to his house. Luckily, he already had a copy of the car keys, so we didn't have to make up some sort of excuse. We climbed into the Flores family minivan and drove off.

"I'm sorry for dragging you into this," I said.

"I'm not letting you face this alone," he said, flashing me his best imitation of a confident smile. I could see right through it to the same fear I felt beneath, but I appreciated the effort. I put a hand on his shoulder while I gave him directions to the Redmarch mansion. The sun was setting behind us as we wound our way up the rocky path around the lake.

As the mansion came into view, I saw the setting sun illuminate the broken-tooth pillar on the lake's lone island,

and I remembered Zoe's note. I felt a deep sense of unease for whatever was coming. Hector pulled to a stop next to Keith's Jeep.

"Wait here," I said. "I don't know what I'm going to find inside, and if we have to go quickly, I'll need you to be ready to drive. I'll text you if I need help."

Hector looked unsure, and for a moment I thought he was going to argue, but instead he nodded.

"Clara, be careful. I don't know what I'd do if—"

I didn't want him to finish that sentence.

"What did you want to tell me back in the café?"

He didn't answer. Instead he reached out, pulled me close, and gave me a kiss on the lips. It was sudden, and our mouths didn't meet right at first, but it still sent a shiver through me, and I kissed him back harder, my body moving on its own accord. All the fear and frenzy of that moment vanished in the warmth of his lips. I didn't want to stop, but I had to. This wasn't the time.

Hector's eyes said he was thinking the same thing, and he squeezed my hand once before letting me go to whatever waited inside.

The heavy oak door groaned as I pushed it inward, and the last light of day pierced a few feet into the darkness of the interior. Again I was struck by the wall of gilt-framed portraits; the dark blessing that had benefitted the Redmarch family for generations was easy to see in the beautiful but cruel features of everyone who shared their blood.

"Miss Morris? Excellent, we're in the dining room."

Jonathan Redmarch's sonorous voice came from the other room.

"Clara, you shouldn't have come here."

That was my father. I hurried into the dining room. Mr. Redmarch sat at the head of the heavy oak table. On his left and right were Keith and my father. They each had a glass of wine, and another had been poured for me. The black shape of a pistol sat in front of Mr. Redmarch. He acted as if it wasn't there, but it was within easy reach and its message was clear.

"I'm glad we can sit down and talk like civilized people," said Mr. Redmarch. "There are some disagreements we need to clear up, but really, we should be celebrating. Today is midsummer's eve, and tonight is the full moon. We could not ask for a better time. My son and your daughter are of age, and I think it's well past time we honor the bonds of blood that tie us to this place."

I looked first at Keith, then my father. Both wore expressions of confusion and pure, animal terror. Mr. Redmarch seemed to tower over all of us without even getting up from the table. I looked at the wall where the setting sun threw our shadows into sharp relief. Mr. Redmarch had two distinct shadows, one much larger and darker than the other.

"This isn't happening," said my father. "You'll have to kill me first if you think you're involving my daughter in your sick family."

"Tom, you're my oldest friend, and I have no intention of harming your daughter, unless you do anything stupid." Those last words echoed with a cold fury I'd never heard from Mr. Redmarch before. "You're very lucky I haven't made you pay for leaving us years ago. You have founders' blood, and yet you seem to relish flaunting our laws. The Clyburns forgot their place, seeking to rise beyond their station. Do not repeat their mistake. I know all about your little book, and it's very good that you haven't decided to show it to anyone. I'm going to trust you'll destroy it once this is all over. You'll see I am quite merciful—not only will I forgive your many betrayals, I will give your daughter the honor of joining our family."

My father only stared back at him, face set with a stony defiance I'd never seen him use with me or my mother. He poured years of pain and rage into that stare, but his childhood friend only seemed to drink it in, savoring it like the wine in front of him. The sun was taking forever to set—I guess it really was midsummer's eve. I had no idea what was coming, but those last rays of sunlight were like my last faint hopes fading away.

"I doubt your father has told you the whole truth about this place, Miss Morris," Mr. Redmarch said.

"He told me enough. I know all about your bloodline."

"Did he tell you about yours, as well? Your family shares deep roots in this place. Did you know?"

"My daughter knows not to listen to your lies," my father said.

"Tell me, is it a lie that you brought her back to this town as an infant?"

"We took a trip here to see the place I grew up. My wife had never been."

"Oh yes, I remember, even though you didn't pay your oldest friend the courtesy of a visit. I did arrange for a bottle of wine to be waiting in your room, though. And I made sure what was in it would keep you sleeping deeply for the whole night."

My father was dead silent, his face contorted with rage and disbelief.

"What the hell did you do?"

"Only what you should have done. What your parents did with you and mine with me, all the way back to the founding. I immersed your daughter in the lake, so that she may know her home and it may know her, so that she would always feel her roots calling to her, and so that she would be a fitting bride for my son when he came of age."

I watched my father, hoping he would dismiss any of this, or reveal it to be the lie I desperately hoped it was, but he only looked more and more horrified. I imagined being dunked in that unearthly lake, and I was glad I had no memory of it. Outside, the sun was almost gone at the horizon.

"Dad, what does that mean?"

"Nothing, sweetheart. It's just an old superstition. I didn't want you raised the backward way I was, but it doesn't mean anything."

Mr. Redmarch turned to me. "I beg to differ. Traditions are important, and they must be honored, even when they seem strange and pointless to us now. In truth, they are almost never pointless. Wasn't your father pulled back to this town after trying to leave? Weren't you called here, as well? There is power in our blood, power you are scarcely aware of, and the union of two founding families will take that power to new heights. My parents already added the Clyburn blood to our own—with all the bloodlines united, my grandchildren will be the strongest generation yet."

"That won't happen," my father said through clenched teeth.

Mr. Redmarch ignored my father.

"I'm sorry to say I found only you there that night, Clara. I don't know where your sister was." He flashed me a wicked grin, and I shuddered. "I suspect she wasn't your sister yet. In fact, I believe you tried to steal from me. I have no mercy for thieves, but I'm prepared to forgive all for the sake of the bloodline."

I had no idea what he meant. What could I have stolen from him, and what did it have to do with Zoe?

The sun finally slipped below the hills on the other side of the lake, and Mr. Redmarch's second shadow seemed to stretch as it set, growing taller and darker against the wall. Once dusk had fully descended, he rose from his seat, sweeping up the pistol in one graceful motion.

"Now, if you'd be so kind as to follow me outside."

XVIII.

"What the hell is happening?" I whispered to Keith as we walked.

"I'm sorry, Clara. I'm so sorry. I wish I never met you, or Danny or anyone."

Keith moved like someone in a daze. His whole personality seemed to fade away in his father's presence—the years of fear and abuse that implied made me shudder. My father was also numb with fear. This was something they had both dreaded for a long time, a nightmare coming true. It was that for me, as well, I just had no idea what would happen next.

Mr. Redmarch threw open the front door, revealing a startled Hector, fist raised in mid-knock. In another time, it might have been funny, but nothing was funny now. Hector's eyes went wide when he saw the pistol, now raised to point at his head.

"Coming here was brave of you, if stupid," Mr. Redmarch said.

Hector's eyes were focused on the gun, his muscles tense. *Don't move*, I pleaded silently, *don't move or he'll kill you.*

"I'm afraid you'll have to join us," said Mr. Redmarch. "Outsiders shouldn't taint a night like tonight, but I'll make an exception in your case. You may yet serve a purpose."

We marched in a grim line through the darkening vineyard to the lake shore, where Mr. Redmarch ushered us into the rowboat at the little dock. I stepped gingerly into the boat, which shifted beneath my feet. I'd never been on a boat, besides one trip on the Staten Island Ferry, and for a second, I was afraid I'd tip the whole thing over. Hector stepped in beside me, his weight steadying the boat. Mr. Redmarch gestured to Keith and my father to each take an oar.

"What the hell is happening?" Hector whispered to me.

"Something really bad."

Slowly, Keith and my father began rowing us out to the island. The barrel of Mr. Redmarch's pistol wandered back and forth from my father to Hector to me. He seemed totally relaxed, but his eyes tracked the slightest twitch of a muscle from any of us. He was like a viper, loose and ready to strike.

I thought of twisting and capsizing the boat, or diving into the water. One glance at Hector showed me he was thinking the same thing. We could both see it was a bad idea.

We drifted along the smooth, mirrored surface of the lake as purple evening shadows lengthened to night. This was the first time I'd been out on the lake, and thinking about it started to fill me with an anxious nausea, a twist in the stomach just like I felt looking at those Two Shadows artifacts. This place was wrong. I couldn't tell if I was seeing things or not, but as it grew darker, Mr. Redmarch's eyes seemed to glow, two burning points of light like embers in a dying fire.

There was no dock on the island. The rowboat ran aground on muddy shallows before we reached the bank, and we had to wade a few feet through the cold, clammy lake water before we reached shore. The trees that grew here were twisted and half-dead, green leaves sprouting from their gnarled branches in small patches. Mr. Redmarch urged us onward, and we followed a faint path up from the shore to the mound of earth at the island's center, crowned with its single broken column.

As we got nearer, I saw there was another circle of columns around the mound, sunken into the earth and nearly overgrown with thorny vines. The mound itself was a ring of bare earth where nothing grew. The column at its center was covered in intricate symbols, worked into a whorled pattern like a carved ivory tusk. Imagining it as a giant tooth didn't make me feel any more at ease. The carvings didn't look Native American, or European, or like any other earthly culture—the only thing they resembled were the statues on display at the Clyburn, and the script carved on Danny's flesh. I was glad I had no idea what they meant. Still, I couldn't shake the feeling that the column was somehow watching me, that the carvings were malevolent eyes looking greedily on this place from somewhere beyond.

I hadn't seen it from land, but in the shadow of the pillar, there was a low stone table, a bare, gray slab of slate. My first thought was that it was a massive old grave, but there were no markings on it. Mr. Redmarch led us to that exact spot. This whole place made me sick to my stomach, and it was getting worse by the minute.

"As blood and bone nourish the soil, so too loss and pain nourish the spirit," Mr. Redmarch's voice was low and solemn. "Our lives are brief and worthless, but they nourish those on the other side, who strengthen us in return."

The moon shone out above us, low and huge, trailing a wisp of cloud lit up with silver light. Its reflection shone back just as bright on the surface of the lake, a single disc of bone white in a yawning gulf of black. That night, we could see the true face of the lake. What we saw every day was a mask—even what I'd seen from shore two nights ago barely did it justice. Glimpsed from that island, the lake was a howling, fathomless void. I couldn't look at it long without feeling it would swallow me whole.

"Our two peoples have dwelt side by side for over two hundred years. You have done your duty, nourished the land with suffering and blood. The people of the lake have obeyed their king, as have those on the other side. Now let the worthy bear witness."

Then Mr. Redmarch said something in a language I didn't know. I couldn't even guess the syllables, they were so strange. It was halfway between speech and a guttural snarl. From the forest on the edges of the lake came a chorus of ear-piercing howls. I could see pale ghostly lights in the depths of the lake—lights I knew weren't reflections of the stars. I huddled close to Hector, and to my father.

"Clara, sweetheart, we'll get out of this, I promise," my father whispered.

"But there is discord and betrayal at every corner." Mr. Redmarch looked first to my father, and then to me. "And those who should be loyal are full of plots and schemes. Tonight, it ends. Tonight, my heir takes his rightful place, and the first step toward his inheritance."

Mr. Redmarch gestured to Keith, who reluctantly came forward.

"Dad? Why are you talking like that? Please, I don't want to do this—"

"Don't pretend ignorance, you know more than you admit even to yourself about what I am, and what you are."

"I'm not like you." He trembled as he said this.

For a second, Mr. Redmarch looked at him with something resembling pity. He seemed diminished, a normal man, staring at the frightened boy that was his son.

"I know . . . I am sorry, if you can believe it. We must all do things we don't like. The blood demands it, and it is far older and stronger than you or I."

"You don't have to do anything, Keith," my father said. "Neither do you, Jonathan. Whatever . . . whatever is with you in there—you don't have to listen to it."

Then the look of cold command was back in Mr. Redmarch's eyes, and he seemed to loom over all of us like a giant. His shadow rose dark against the central column, though there was no light to cast it. He gave my father a disdainful look, as if he were an irritating fly.

"You don't understand," he said. "It isn't in me. It *is* me. The King is alive in our blood, passed from parent to child since the founding, that we may share our strength across

254

the worlds. Soon it will pass to my son, as well. And when it passes to my grandchildren, I will be able to enter this world more fully than ever before."

Then, suddenly, he shot my father in the stomach. It rang out like a clap of thunder, and I pressed my ears without thinking. Then Dad crumpled to his knees. I rushed to his side, pressing my sleeve to his wound. It came away soaked with blood. He pushed me away, clutching his stomach.

"No . . . Clara, stay back."

"You needn't worry, Tom, I won't harm her unless you make me. I'm sorry I had to do that, as well, but I can't have you getting in the way."

Mr. Redmarch beckoned for Keith to come forward again. Then he turned the gun on Hector and me, motioning each of us to join Keith at the altar. I glanced back at my father, worried sick. He had propped himself against one of the pillars, using his shirt to stop the bleeding. His eyes said *be strong*.

"One of the founders' blood stands before us—Clara Morris, whose forefathers lie in this soil. She will be joined to the heir, and add the strength of her blood to our own."

Mr. Redmarch regarded me with a piercing stare. The glow was back in his eyes—they caught the light like a wolf's. I tried my hardest to meet his gaze, to stare back my defiance to whatever he had planned.

"You're a monster," I said. "I won't let what happened to you happen to Keith."

Mr. Redmarch only smiled.

"I am a king," he said. "And you're a thief. Tell me, do you know where your sister comes from? You must have suspected. She belonged to me long before she met you. She and the others kept us fed through the long famine, and we will have her back."

I fell back, speechless. What did he know about Zoe? Just hearing him mention her made me feel sick.

"You leave her out of this."

"Oh, she has already involved herself, but soon she will be back where she belongs."

He chuckled at my distress, then turned his gaze on Hector.

"An outsider is among us, treading on our sacred ground, hearing our names and our secrets. His life is forfeit. His blood will nourish the land, and his last breath will be swallowed by the lake. His torment will be a feast for the hounds."

The bone-chilling howls rose again all around the lake, followed by wild yips and barks. Eerie, radiant motes of light like luminescent jellyfish shone out from the depths of the lake, bathing the island in a sinister glow.

"My son, step forward."

Mr. Redmarch beckoned to Keith, who stayed rooted to the spot.

"Step forward."

Mr. Redmarch did not yell, but his voice was full of a terrible force of will. Keith walked forward as if each word were a chain dragging him. Mr. Redmarch pulled a long, gleaming knife from his belt. It was old, and curved out and back into a cruel hook, almost like a sickle. He handed it to Keith, who held it in a trembling hand.

"The Morris girl will be your bride. You must mark her as is our custom."

Keith walked toward me. The knife shook in his hand. Fear and exertion had bled his handsome face milk white. I could see the power his father's voice held over him. He was fighting it with every ounce of strength.

"Clara . . . I won't do this!"

He held up his hands.

"You will, or I will end her father and the outsider now."

The steel edge of command was back in Mr. Redmarch's voice, and something beneath it, a low animal growl. His form seemed to flicker and change when I wasn't looking directly at him. Keith's whole body shook. He raised the knife.

"What the hell is happening?" I said.

"I-I have to cut you, to shed your blood. Oh god, I'm sorry."

Mr. Redmarch watched his son approach me, knife in hand. He smiled.

"When you have received your full inheritance, my son, you will no longer need the knife."

Keith looked paralyzed with fear. If he did nothing, his father would kill mine. I held my hand out.

"Do it," I said. "If it will keep the others alive a little longer . . . whatever it takes."

Keith brought the knife down. He barely grazed my palm, but the blade was razor sharp. I felt nothing at first, then a searing pain and warmth as I began to bleed. I clutched my hand to my chest, determined not to scream or cry. I could feel the wound throbbing, each pulse a new agony. Mr. Redmarch seemed to be weighing his son's effort, to see if it was enough. Finally, he nodded.

"You aren't finished yet. Now you must taste her blood, as her bloodline will be added to our own."

Keith stiffened, a look of horror frozen on his face. I held my injured hand tighter.

"You must do it, boy, or I will tear her father limb from limb."

Had Jonathan Redmarch had to do this, too, years ago? Hurt the girl he'd loved for years, and then keep hurting her, until the thing that stood before us now owned him completely? His eyes flickered with inhuman malice, and I had no doubt he really would tear my father, his childhood best friend, apart. Trembling, I stretched my hand out to Keith, blood running down my palm as I slowly opened my fingers. I gritted my teeth against the pain.

"I'm–I'm sorry," Keith mumbled.

"Do it," I said, "just do it."

He fumbled for my hand, and I shuddered as I felt his mouth on the wound. Then it was over, and I clutched my injured hand tight again.

"Good boy. Tom, my son has saved your life. You should be grateful. Now, we spill the outsider's blood. Bring him to the table."

Keith didn't move. He just stood there, trembling.

"Son, you will bring him to the table."

Keith remained still. Whatever power his father held over him, it had limits.

"How disappointing."

Mr. Redmarch had had enough. He leaped over the altar, moving so quickly he was a dark blur. He shoved Keith out of the way, sending him sprawling to the ground. Hector tried to dive out or reach, but Mr. Redmarch was too fast. He punched him hard in the face, nearly knocking him to the floor, then seized him by the arm, dragging him savagely toward the altar. The wild chorus of howling rose up around the lake again, but now there was another sound cutting through it, a mechanical buzz that seemed to come from another, saner world. A motorboat.

Hector managed a thin smile through bloody lips.

"What is this?" Mr. Redmarch said.

"You called the sheriff?" I said. "When?" I could barely allow myself to hope this was true.

"They've been on speaker-phone since you left the house."

XIX.

Mr. Redmarch snarled, a guttural, vicious sound. He twisted Hector's arm until I heard a snap, then threw him to the ground, backing away. The motor was getting closer, and we could see the boat's headlight standing out from the eerie radiance of the lake. Elaine Cross River was driving, Deputies Bill and Harry sat next to her, flashlights in hand.

"Drop your weapon and put your hands up!" Elaine shouted through a bullhorn. They landed the boat in the muddy shallows, leaping out with their guns drawn and scrambling up toward the mound. I didn't like that Harry was with them—I didn't know whose side he was really on. I hoped more deputies were on their way, along with an ambulance for my father and Hector.

Elaine looked completely shocked by what she saw, as if nothing like it could still exist in the twenty-first century, but Bill's face was a mask of animal terror. Like my father, like Keith—on some level, the residents of Redmarch Lake knew what this was, and it filled them with dread. Even Harry looked pale and ready to bolt into the woods.

Mr. Redmarch let his pistol fall to the ground like it was a common rock.

"This is all a misunderstanding," he said. "Surely we can work something out. Deputy Chief Cross River, you are an outsider, but they must have briefed you on my family and our ties to this community. I was a donor to your superior's campaign."

"Keep your mouth shut and your hands up!" Elaine shouted.

Mr. Redmarch slowly raised his hands in the air, as if he were only humoring her. He said something else in the language he'd used before—less like a word and more like an animal snarl. The eerie radiance of the lake suddenly faded away, and a thick fog rose from the water, engulfing the island in darkness. Mr. Redmarch stepped back from the mound and was gone, his guttural words dissolving into a mocking laugh.

The fog was so thick, I could barely see my own hands. I stretched my arms out, calling out for Hector, for Keith or my father. I stumbled, encountering no one where I had been sure Hector had fallen.

"Dad! Elaine!" I shouted out into the darkness. There was no response.

"They cannot help you."

With a shock, I felt cold, gnarled fingers close around my neck from behind. They were hard and gray-black, like dead branches, and they ended in long, cruel claws. I knew who they belonged to, though I couldn't imagine what he looked like now, with his human form cast aside. His strength was terrible, holding me up by my neck so that my feet could barely touch the ground as if I weighed next to nothing. I was shivering with fear, barely able to breathe with his grip on my throat.

"You should be honored at what I'm giving you, but you have polluted the night with outsiders," I felt his snarling voice at my ear. There was still something of Jonathan Redmarch's baritone, mixed with that otherworldly growl. "Now you will have to witness all I do here, before you are joined to my son."

I tried to tell him no, I would never let it happen, but I could barely open my mouth to breathe.

"The part of me that is still human thought he could spare your father by wounding him, but now I will flay the life from him slowly, as I will from your little outsider friend. You think you know who and what I am, but you have no idea. You would weep if I told you. I am older than stars and colder than the space between. I have tasted the sweetness of your world, and I will have all of it I crave, and you will not stop me. Now watch what comes next, and don't count yourself fortunate that I spare you. You know the life of suffering that awaits you."

Suddenly, the hand released its grip, and I fell to the ground. I took a deep, rasping breath, gasping for air. I felt my neck with my good hand, the flesh there bruised and raw. I looked over and saw Hector lying nearby. I crawled over to him, taking his good hand in mine, and we helped each other stand.

Hector's arm was badly broken, I could tell he was in terrible pain, and my hand was still bleeding. I looked for my father, unable to see him in the gloom.

"The King . . ." Keith muttered, "The King of the Wood . . ."

"Clara!" I heard my father cry out from somewhere in the fog.

I ran to him, Hector and Keith following as quickly as they could manage. He was still propped against the pillar. His face was pale and his teeth were clenched against the pain.

"It'll be all right, Dad," I said. "The sheriff is here, which means the ambulance isn't far behind." Even as I said these words, I couldn't believe them. I could still feel those hands on my neck. Any minute now, the King would make good on his threats. My father took no comfort in my words—he knew what we were facing better than I did.

"No," he said through gritted teeth. "No, they don't stand a chance."

Elaine and the deputies were fanning out, searching the island for any sign of Mr. Redmarch. The island was small, but the fog made it impossible to see more than a foot in front of you. He could be lurking anywhere. I could only see the three of them because of the frail glow of their flashlights.

"Jonathan Redmarch, you're under arrest," said Elaine. "If you resist arrest, we will have no choice but to respond with force."

"Show yourself!" Bill said, his voice quavering.

I could hear Bill walking, not far from where we stood. The beam of his flashlight swung frantic through the fog, little more than a glimmer. Then he screamed, a raw cry of shock and pain that was cut off as soon as it began. His gun fired wildly into the air, hitting nothing. The next thing we heard was the wet thud of his body hitting the ground.

"Bill! Oh God," my father said.

"What the hell are you?" Elaine called out into the fog. So far, she had faced this nightmare with a level head, but even she was beginning to crack. We all were, if we weren't cracked already.

Then we heard another voice from out of the fog. It was Deputy Harry, his lips trembling. His gun was pointed at Elaine.

"We should not have come here. This is not for us to see. You're an outsider. The King will spare me if I give him your life."

He raised his pistol, trying to aim through the dense fog. Elaine turned toward him.

"Harry, that's insane! Let's talk about this."

"Don't move!" Harry shouted.

A shot rang out in the darkness, and for a terrifying second, I didn't know who'd been hit. Then Deputy Harry fell to the ground, a red stain on his chest. Elaine hadn't had time to raise her gun. I looked over at my father. He had dragged his wounded body to Jonathan Redmarch's discarded pistol.

We didn't have time for a sigh of relief. Suddenly, a grim, haunting laugh echoed all around us.

"The first to die are lucky. I will take my time with those who remain."

I scanned the mound, hoping to spot a trace of Mr. Redmarch, or whatever the hell he was. He would be shrouded in darkness, like he had been when he'd come for Ash. In this fog, he was all but invisible.

Elaine was getting frantic, spinning around to cover every direction. She spun to her right at a sudden noise, pistol raised, only to scream when an unseen force knocked her to the ground from behind. Slowly she hobbled to her feet, her left leg was slick with blood.

"You are in my place of strength," Mr. Redmarch's voice seemed to come from everywhere. "I have all night."

As his grim laughter echoed through the darkness, I looked from Hector to my father to Keith, the same look of despair on all our faces. How could we have any hope against something we couldn't see, or even understand? It would tear all of us apart, one piece at a time.

I had only one place left to turn. *Zoe,* I thought, *you've been trying to help me all this time, trying to keep me safe. Zoe, if you can, help me now.*

For an awful moment, no one made a sound. We just stood there, waiting for death.

Then I saw something move from the corner of my eye, but it wasn't Mr. Redmarch. A figure stepped from behind the broken column, and all my breath left me. Standing ten feet from me was a girl that could have been my mirror image— anyone who saw us would think we were the same person, except the two of us. I was looking at Zoe. I wanted to run to her, throw my arms around her, I wanted to tell her all the ways I missed her, but those words died in my throat. She was trembling, pointing at something behind me. I looked, following her finger, and all of a sudden I saw it, a patch of darkness denser than the fog, moving toward Elaine. It raised a tendril of shadow like an arm, ending in long, wicked claws.

"Elaine!" I shouted, "There!"

In one motion, she turned and fired at the spot I pointed to, emptying her clip into the darkness. The staccato burst of the gunshots echoed off the ring of stones. Then there was another sound, a cry of unimaginable pain and rage. Slowly, the fog began to lift. We looked in horror to see Jonathan Redmarch standing in front of Elaine, his face contorted into an expression of unearthly malice, his outstretched arm like a gnarled black branch, ending in long, wicked claws. Dark, barbed growths protruded from his skin, warping and twisting his form. With a hideous bellow of rage, he took a step toward Elaine, clawed fingers raised. She drew back in fear. He took another step, before he stumbled, and finally collapsed to the ground.

I turned back to where Zoe was, running to the spot I'd seen her. There was nothing there. Not even a trace.

As the fog cleared, I saw Keith and Hector helping my father to his feet. Bill's corpse lay mangled on the ground, his stomach torn open. I couldn't stand to look for long.

Elaine was breathing heavy, both hands still on her gun. Jonathan Redmarch lay dead at her feet. He looked older in death, his hair streaked with gray and his face still creased with pain and fury, but now he was human again—not the thing we had seen when the mists parted. Then, as we stood transfixed with fear, something started to rise from his wounds. It was like black, oily smoke; like pure night, and it rose from every bullet hole in his chest.

Somewhere on shore, a high, keening howl began. It was soon joined by others, until we were surrounded by an unearthly dirge.

"My God, what . . ."

Elaine backed away, stumbling on her injured leg. We all fell back. Jonathan Redmarch's corpse was deflating like an old balloon, collapsing until it was just a withered husk, like an ancient mummy. The dark cloud that rose out of him hovered there for a second, a mass of pure malevolence. Staring into it, I felt a stomach-churning tide of hate, of fear; it wanted all of us to suffer. It needed it. I felt the same nausea I'd felt seeing the Two Shadows figures, but a thousand times stronger. Beside me I heard Hector retching. Lights shone within the cloud, a thousand baleful eyes watching us. But it was weakening, parts of it evaporating by the second. I could almost see the lake through it on the other side.

Suddenly, the cloud surged forward, rushing like a flood wave directly toward Keith. He didn't have time to run, or even move. It drove itself toward him, into him, coiling itself around him like a snake.

"No, Keith! Fight it!" I shouted.

It was too late. When Keith looked up, there was a familiar smolder in his eyes, like two burning embers. My father and Hector both saw, their eyes going wide with fear. They tried to hold him, but he savagely punched my father right in his gut wound. He collapsed, howling in pain.

Hector couldn't do much with one good arm, but he tried, swinging wildly at Keith. He connected once, a solid blow right to the jaw, but Keith just shrugged it off and hit Hector across the face with a brutal backhand.

"Stop!" I shouted. "You don't have to do this."

"Oh, he does,"

The voice that came out of Keith's mouth was partly his, but with the same animal snarl I'd heard in his father's. Behind me, Elaine raised her gun.

"Don't!" I shouted, putting myself between her and Keith.

Keith reached down, picking up the curved knife he'd used to cut my hand. He gave me a single, hateful glare before he launched himself toward Hector, knife raised for the kill.

I raced toward them, watching in horror as Keith plunged the knife into Hector's abdomen. For a second, everything seemed frozen, as Keith snarled, giving the knife a cruel twist. Hector screamed, and with strength I could scarcely believe, Keith threw him to the floor.

I raced toward him, praying he wasn't dead, wishing I could somehow reverse what had just happened. Keith turned to me. I couldn't bear to see the horrible grin on his face. He lunged at me.

I acted without thinking, twisting my body as he came at me. Even without the creature inside him, he was much bigger and stronger than me, but he expected me to be easy prey. His hands grabbed for my neck and missed, but then his body collided with mine, sending both of us tumbling head over heels. His hands snaked out, frightfully strong, grasping for my throat as we rolled.

Then we plunged off the edge of the island, and our bodies broke the black surface of the lake.

XX.

I fell into darkness, darker than deep space.

I sensed things moving around me, shapes I could barely imagine. Strange lights appeared in the depths. I shut my eyes, thrashing in the frigid water, fighting to find the surface. I realized with horror that I no longer knew which way was up.

Once again, I felt the terrible weight of drowning as the water tried to consume me. I had never been so cold or so lost. Things brushed past me in the darkness. The lake whispered in my ears, words I was grateful I could not understand.

I saw a light above me, what I thought was above, and I swam for it furiously. My lungs were burning, and I fought to keep from picturing them filling with that black lake water, dragging me down to the bottom. I swam harder, panicked that I'd pass out before I made it. There was something strange about the light, something I couldn't place, but I swam for it frantically anyway. I could feel pressure building in my ears, like I was swimming deeper into the water, but the light was all I could see now, a pale, eerie glow, and I swam for it with all the strength I had left.

Just as I thought my burning lungs would give out, I felt a hand take mine and pull me up.

I broke the surface with a gasp. It was harder than it should have been, like the lake was trying to keep me down or pull me back. Rising up out of that water felt like being turned inside out, and when I opened my eyes, I couldn't believe where I was.

At first it seemed like I was back at the shore of the lake, near where we had boarded the boat, but something was very wrong. Everything felt hazy and indistinct. There was no moon. Instead, a pale, ghostly glow that seemed to come from nowhere infused the entire sky with dim, pearlescent light. I looked at the hand that held mine, seeing with a shock that it was identical to my own. I looked up to see my sister staring back at me, a mix of love and desperate fear on a face that was a mirror of mine.

"They . . . they told me you weren't real," I said.

"I'm real."

I felt such an incredible surge of joy at seeing Zoe in front of me again that I couldn't think of anything else. She seemed to share it at first, but her eyes were filled with terror and sadness.

"You shouldn't be here," she said. "He won't let you leave."

Before I could embrace her, or even speak, a single, ferocious howl shattered the moment, answered by a chorus of others all around us. A dark shape suddenly loomed above Zoe, and her eyes went wide in a silent scream as her hand was wrenched out of mine. Faster than I could blink, she was dragged back toward the forest, whatever held her pulling faster than anything should have been able to.

I thrashed onto the shore, heaving myself up onto the bank. I could hear her screaming ahead of me—whatever had her was crashing through the underbrush. I followed as fast as I could, my chest heaving after my near-drowning in the lake. As I ran, the landscape shifted around me, hazy and half formed like in a dream. I lost sight of Zoe ahead of me, but I could hear her cry out in a voice identical to mine, and see the trail the thing that held her left.

I couldn't explain it, but somehow I knew I'd come through the lake to the other side, where the King was from. I thought with panic of Hector and my father back on our side—praying they were still alive and help would get to them in time, if that was even possible. No one could help me here, and I was running straight toward a living nightmare, but I couldn't let that horrible thing have my sister. I raced after it, knowing it could mean death or something worse for both of us.

Around me, I heard other howls from the forest, saw dark shapes running after me, and I ran harder. On the other side, I'd only known these creatures by their burning eyes, their forms half-glimpsed in darkness—barely able to enter our world. Now I could see pale, fearsome things coming toward me in the forest as I ran after Zoe. At first I thought they were wolves, but their legs were too long, and they moved wrong, sometimes on four limbs and sometimes on two. There was no path to keep them at bay. The only advantage I had was my small size, darting between trees and through the underbrush, hoping it would slow them down. My heart was hammering in my chest.

Then I realized where the King was taking Zoe.

We had been running uphill for a while now, and every moment I was afraid I'd collapse, and the creatures chasing me would tear me apart. Then, suddenly, I burst out of the forest and into the vineyard by the Redmarch manor. I darted between the rows of grapevines—hazy and indistinct as the trees, more like the idea of grapevines glimpsed in a dream. I could hear the creatures following behind me.

When I saw the house, I almost couldn't believe it. Every straight line was somehow bent or skewed, so the old colonial manse looked more like a half-formed ruin, a twisted child's drawing brought to life. The door hung open, swinging in the wind. Behind me, I heard the creatures chasing me come to a stop and join together in an eerie chorus of howls. I realized they'd done what they intended all along—drive me right to the King.

They didn't follow me inside, but I could hear them outside the door, pacing and howling. I had no way back.

I ran deeper into the house—or was it just a reflection of the house in this weird mirror world?—only to find an empty hall. There wasn't even furniture in this shadow of the Redmarch manor, only the portraits of the Redmarch ancestors lining the walls. The pictures of their poor wives and husbands seemed to be screaming in pain, but every Redmarch descendent had their face blotted out by an oily black stain.

I raced through the empty rooms, looking for Zoe, but I found no trace. The upstairs was just as empty as the first floor. I ran to the back of the house, only to hear the creatures stalking at the back door, as well. Then I heard Zoe scream again, from somewhere deeper within. I retraced my steps, hoping to find something I missed. She screamed again, a horrible, keening wail, and a shudder passed through my whole body. I had to find her soon! I remembered Lyman Redmarch and the chamber of horrors they'd found under the mansion. And then, as if that thought were a key, I looked behind me to see an alcove I swore I'd never passed before, though I'd been up and down the same hallway several times. I opened the door and saw an old stone staircase leading down.

Zoe cried out once more, and I raced down the stairs, which kept going flight after flight, much longer than basement stairs had any right to. I couldn't believe how deep I was going into the earth. The air got cold and clammy, and I could smell the fetid odor of the lake.

Finally, the stairwell ended in an old stone archway, etched with the same markings I'd seen on the column, and the Two Shadows artifacts. I hurried through, into a chamber dimly lit by flickering candles.

"Come in," said the King, "You're just in time."

His voice had shed everything human about it; it was creaking branches and the rasp of falling rocks. Hunched over, his form scraped the low ceiling of the chamber. I could see him in full now, without the darkness obscuring him, and I wished I couldn't. His limbs were long and thin, but gnarled with knotty muscle, the gray black of burnt trees. His fingers ended in claws like scythes. His head was something like a wolf, or a crocodile, but refracted through a nightmare lens, so that everything came out wrong. His head was crowned with thorny black antlers, which also sprouted from his spine and the bones of his shoulders. I could barely stand to look at him directly—the wrongness of it twisted up my stomach and filled me with an acrid, animal panic.

He towered over a rough stone slab, where Zoe lay, her face a mask of pain and fear. When she saw me, she shook her head slowly. She didn't have to speak to tell me how she felt—*I'm sorry, I wish you hadn't come here.* Below the slab, between them and me, was a black pool, as still and mirror smooth as the lake. I had no doubt that was where the water came from. I thought of my father and Hector, still on the other side of the lake, and wondered if I'd ever make it back.

The King brushed a cruel claw along Zoe's cheek, drawing a thin line of blood. Zoe bit her lip but did not scream again.

"You know she lied to you," he growled. "She isn't your sister. She has been with me longer than your short life, always plotting to get away. You were just a means to her escape. But she has done me one service. She has brought you here to me. If I must lose your world for now, at least you will suffer for it."

The King pinned Zoe down with one immense hand, while with the other he cut a spiral pattern into her arm, a whorled glyph like we'd seen cut into poor Danny. This time Zoe did scream.

I couldn't bear to see that thing hurt my sister. It didn't matter that she wasn't really my sister—she was in every way that counted, and I couldn't let this happen.

"Stop!" I shouted.

The King looked up at me and laughed, a horrible sound like rocks scraping together.

"What will you do, little bird? When I am finished, you will no longer look alike, at least until I start on you. You will not die here, unless I wish it. Your suffering will sustain me until I return to your world."

I shook with fury as much as fear as he carved another letter on Zoe's arm. What could I do against this living nightmare? His shadowy form filled half the chamber. I had never felt so small. Then I remembered something, something so desperate and crazy I could barely believe it—I had something he wanted.

"Wait! If-if you stop and let her go, I'll—"

"Yes?"

The King raised his awful red eyes to me. I could not meet them.

"If you let her go, I'll be your vessel. You can come back into my world through me."

"Clara, no!" Zoe shouted, "you can't!"

The King's hand closed around her neck, silencing her.

"I come from an old bloodline. I was bathed in the lake as an infant. You must need a host to agree, or you would just take one. So, I agree—take me, but you have to let her go."

I could only imagine what this would mean, but I'd seen enough with Keith and his father. I'd have to go far,

far away from anyone I cared about, or I'd make their life a living hell. I'd have to endure as it brought out everything cruel and hateful in me. I already felt despair settling in my chest, but I felt a kind of grim joy as well, knowing Zoe would be free.

The King glared at me a moment longer, his clawed fingers flexing, and for a moment, I thought he would tear me in half for daring to bargain with him. Then he bared his fangs in what I could only guess was a smile.

"Very well. I grant you your wish."

He took his hand off Zoe, who curled into a ball on the stone altar, shivering. The look she gave me was pure horror. She knew better than me what I just agreed to.

"Step closer," the King said, "into the pool."

I took steps into the cold, clammy lake water, wincing where it touched my skin. The pool was shallow, fed by a source I couldn't see.

"Give me your hand."

I knew he meant the one that Keith had marked, the cut that had barely stopped bleeding. Grimacing, I opened my hand and held it out to him. With a swift flick of his claw, he opened the cut again. I tried to pull my hand away, but his grip was too strong. I wasn't prepared for what came next. He plunged his hand into the open wound—it was more painful than anything I'd ever felt. I screamed, expecting to see a bloody ruin instead of my palm when I looked down. Instead, the King was melting. . . . That was the only way I could describe it. His hand, and now his arm, was flowing into mine, seeping slowly into my body. Every moment of it was agony. And worse than the pain, I could feel the King seeping into my thoughts, sifting through my memories. He dragged all of them out, showing me the very worst in each one. Everything and everyone in my life was tainted somehow, I could see that now as never before. I hated my father for leaving, for not being strong enough to fix things, for almost letting me drown; I hated my mother for her need to control me, and for fawning over an idiot like Chuck; I hated Keith for obeying his father, and accepting all the privilege it brought, even as he claimed to hate it; I hated Ash for her cowardice, and her acceptance of a rotten life; I hated Hector for his farce of smug detachment; most of all I hated Zoe . . . Zoe . . .

She just lay there shivering, watching me with fear, or was it disgust?

She had lied to me my whole life, made me a freak and an outcast. She had kept me from having real friends, or a normal childhood. She . . .

She had saved my life, twice.

I didn't hate Zoe. I loved her. She had been everything to me for so long, and she was finally here with me. I told myself it was the King who hated her, who hated all the people I loved, not me. I tried to resist, to clear my memories of his infection and see them the way I used to. I couldn't. I could only remind myself this wasn't true. I needed help. The King was halfway into me by now, his horrible predator's face drawing closer to mine.

Desperate, flailing, I reached my other hand out to Zoe. Somehow, her fingers found mine, and held on tight.

In an instant, another memory came to me—a dim recollection of being bathed in the lake long ago, at the beginning of my life. Zoe had found me then, a kindred spirit in that darkness. I knew then that before being Zoe, she had been someone else, someone as lost as me. I saw her long ago, a different person, laying down her life for her family, enduring pain and death so they could live. I knew she had seen my pain and tried to save me, as well.

Together we were stronger than we ever could be alone. Just holding her hand in mine, I could see us together, playing in the park that for us was an enchanted forest, speaking the language only we understood. We had a bond no one could break, not even the King.

I focused on those memories, running down the wooded path with Zoe, telling each other stories until we fell asleep, and I felt the darkness recede. I heard the King roar as his form began to flow back out of my hand.

His other hand closed around my neck, choking the life from me, but I clung tight to Zoe and felt him recede even further.

"No! I'll tear you to shreds! I'll bleed everything you love!" He howled, but we held on tight, and finally I felt the darkness leave me. The King staggered, roaring in pain and rage.

"Now, hurry!"

Zoe grabbed me, pulling me down with her into the black pool of lake water.

I braced to hit the shallow bottom, but somehow we just kept falling through the darkness, swimming through the black depths of the lake. Zoe led me, swimming until little glowing lights appeared out of the darkness, swirling around us and rising toward what I could only hope was the surface.

Then Zoe began to rise. I felt her, lifting me, pulling me upward. She smiled then, her face breaking into the sly grin I'd missed for so long. Just by looking in her eyes, I could see it had hurt her as much as me to be apart. There was so much to say, but we needed to say none of it—we looked at each other and we understood.

All around me, pale lights were rising in the darkness of the lake, rising with me and Zoe toward the sky. With a shock, I broke through the surface of the water, air rushing into my lungs. I held tight to Zoe's hand, but she kept rising, slipping through my fingers.

I cried out to her, but I felt the exhaustive weight of everything I just survived catching up with me, and my body could take no more. The last thing I saw before consciousness left me was her face looking back, giving me that mischievous smile she always did when she was the first to run down a dark forest path or dive into the deep end of the pool. The last thing I heard was her voice saying, *Ah lora soo, sosa—I love you, sister.*

XXI.

I woke up to see my mother's face above me. As soon as she saw me open my eyes, she held me tight.

"Oh, Clara. I came as soon as I heard."

I was in a stiff, uncomfortable bed which propped me up at an angle. An IV drip was connected to my arm. It was obvious, but it still took me a minute to realize I was in a hospital.

"They found you in the lake, barely breathing. They had to beat that awful water out of your lungs. Then after that, you wouldn't wake up, and they didn't know why . . . and after almost losing you twice, I told them I wouldn't move until your eyes were open."

She squeezed me to her again. I coughed a little, doing my best to hug her back.

"Dad . . . and my friends . . ."

My throat was scraped raw; it hurt to talk.

"Your father lost part of his intestine, and it'll take time to mend, but he'll be okay. The Redmarch boy was in some kind of shock, but he's doing better. Poor kid, to see his father do something so awful."

"A–and Hector?"

My mother frowned, and all of a sudden I felt like I was back at the bottom of the lake. If Hector was gone, I wasn't sure I wanted to be back here.

"He's alive. . . . His condition is still critical."

It was hard for me to focus on anything without knowing Hector was okay. I let the nurse poke and prod me a while longer, badgering her for news she didn't have. Finally, she decided I was well enough to take a walk and stretch my muscles. I made straight for my father's room, rolling the IV bag on its stand with me like an old man's cane.

Dad was napping when I came in, but his eyes snapped open as soon as he heard me, and when he saw who it was, his face lit up with joy and relief.

"Clara, sweetheart, I'm . . . I—"

The relief was plain in his face, his wound and the enormity of everything we'd just lived through made it too hard to say more. He was pale, drowsy from the pain meds, and still fighting through what must have been serious agony, but he seemed happy in a way I hadn't seen him in a long time. There was a cloth covering his wound, and whatever apparatus they'd rigged to help with bodily functions, which he said was too disgusting for words.

"Really, though, I'm lucky," he said. "That was everything I'd dreaded my whole life, and I can't believe we're alive—"

He saw my worried look, my eyes drifting off toward whatever wing of the hospital Hector lay unconscious, probably wired to a battery of bleeping machines. Even now, I could imagine him making some sort of joke about being too attached to his technology.

"I'm sorry, sweetheart. I think Hector will be all right—we just have to give him time. We were really worried about you, too. I'm sorry, you never should have been anywhere near this place."

"Don't," I said. "This was bigger than either of us knew, and it wasn't your fault."

"Now I know how it feels to have a million questions," he said. "Maybe someday you can tell me what I missed."

I nodded and gave him a kiss on the cheek, letting him get back to resting.

As I was about to go, he called me back, his voice as hoarse as mine from not talking.

"Clara, there's something I have to tell you."

I came back to his bedside. The strain was evident in his face.

"Dad, you need to rest."

"I'll rest, but you need to hear this. I should have thought of it sooner. The twin you almost had in your mother's womb. Maybe you were supposed to have a twin, somehow, and when she wasn't born . . . maybe when Jonathan bathed you in the lake," my father shuddered at the thought of this, "somehow some-someone came through, and took the place of the sister you were supposed to have."

I nodded. I'd been wondering nonstop about those last moments in the lake, but to have my father say the same thing I'd been thinking out loud made me shiver.

"She saved my life," I said. "That night, eight years ago. I think she used up whatever power she had in this world to do it, which would have sent her back to the lake." My heart ached, imagining Zoe doing this for me. "She saved me again last night."

"I wish I could thank her," my father said.

"I think-I think she's free now. I think all the souls they'd trapped are free."

I remembered the lights rising around me. I hoped she was free, though I wondered if that meant I'd never see her again.

I squeezed my father's hand. There were tears forming in the corners of my eyes.

"Sweetheart, I'm sorry. I spent so long trying to disbelieve the place I came from. I should have known. . . . I should have believed you. . . ."

"No, Dad. It'll take time, but it'll be all right." I could barely talk, afraid the tears would start flowing. Just a short while ago, I had hated both my parents, but when I thought of all my father came from, and how hard he tried to protect me, I couldn't do it anymore. It would take me a long time to get over the lies, but I loved my parents, and after everything I'd seen in Redmarch Lake, I felt like I finally knew my father.

"You need to rest now," I said.

They had a few more tests for me, and then the nurse removed my IV. I had been out for more than a day—I had no idea how time passed where I was. I could barely bring myself to think it, let alone say it. Zoe had saved me again, and at least this time, I returned the favor.

When it was just Mom and me again, I knew I had to tell her Dad had revealed what they'd been keeping from me.

"Mom, Dad told me about Zoe."

She nodded.

"He was afraid you'd hate him, he still is. I'm sorry, dear, it's . . . well, I can't even imagine how hard that is. We had no idea what we were doing; we just wanted to do whatever would make it better, but I guess we made it worse. When we almost lost you at the beach, and then after, when you wouldn't respond to anything, I didn't know what to do. I hope you can forgive us."

"I love you guys, but I'm still processing it. I guess it will take a while."

She held me close again. After everything I just lived through, it was good to see her, good to know my parents were both okay. Sorting out all our drama could come later. Right now, I felt like I'd just put down a burden I'd been carrying a long time, and only now realized how heavy it was. I just wanted to rest—as much as I could rest while not knowing about Hector.

"Mom?"

"Yes, honey?"

"Thanks for not bringing the Woodchuck."

I expected my mother to give me another disappointed frown, but she actually laughed a little.

"He found out you call him that. He actually thinks it's hilarious. He said no one ever thought of it, even in high school. Clara, I'm sorry about all this, I know it's hard. But you have to admit he has a great sense of humor."

I had to admit nothing, but I did kind of like that he found the whole Woodchuck thing funny. I couldn't picture myself ever liking Charlie Woods, but I didn't feel like dealing with it now. It could wait, just like everything else.

A little while later, my mother said I had several visitors. The first to come back was Elaine Cross River, limping slightly on a bandaged leg. She gave me a firm handshake when she saw me.

"You saved my life back there, kid. I won't forget a thing like that. I'd give you a medal if we had one for that sort of thing."

"Being alive feels good enough for me," I said.

"Well said. I'm afraid my visit isn't only social. Ms. Morris—"

"DiStefano," my mother said.

"Right, Ms. DiStefano, could you leave us alone for a moment?"

My mother hesitated, but she ultimately walked out. Elaine's face turned serious.

"We have to be very careful about this incident," she said. "The statements we've taken so far all name Jonathan Redmarch as the perpetrator, possibly by reason of insanity, now deceased in a firefight with sheriff's deputies. Is that your recollection of the night in question?"

She gave me a meaningful look as she said this, subtly nodding her head.

"Y-yes," I said.

"Good." She looked relieved but not happy. I could see this would gnaw at her for a long time. It would do that to all of us.

"Stay strong, Clara. I have a feeling you'll get into more trouble in your life. You seem to have a real talent for it. Maybe someday you can tell me what really happened."

She shook my hand again, put her hat back on, and headed out the door, giving me a final wave as she left.

Next they finally let Ash and Keith in to see me. The two of them overwhelmed me with hugs. It was almost too much to see them both right after what we'd all been though—I was overjoyed, but we were all still scared to death about Hector.

I had to take a deep breath when I first saw Keith— the memory of his eyes glowing with that awful fire came rushing back to me, but it took only a moment to see that was gone, and he was my friend again.

I couldn't tell if it was lack of sleep or something more mysterious, but he didn't seem quite as tall or as roguishly handsome as he once had. He was still incredibly good looking, but there was an extra something he no longer possessed, and based on where it came from, I think he was all the better for it.

"I'm so sorry I wasn't there to help," said Ash. "I called the cops when I saw lights on the island, but they were already on their way thanks to Hector."

"And we wouldn't have made it if not for Clara's sharp eyes," said Keith.

As I'd suspected, I was the only one who'd seen Zoe. I guess that was how it used to happen back when I was a kid. I could see Keith wince at Hector's name. I couldn't be angry at him—I knew what was in him when he stabbed Hector, since it had been in me, too. But I knew if Hector didn't make it, Keith would never stop punishing himself.

Ash had brought me a bouquet of black roses, which matched her lipstick and eye shadow. From anyone else, it would have been too morbid for a hospital, but from her it was perfect. She'd also smuggled me a box of cookies from the café, courtesy of Lady Daphne. After a while, Ash said her goodbyes to go start her shift, and Keith stayed behind, a haunted look on his face.

"You okay?" I said.

Keith only nodded. I couldn't imagine what he was going through right now, to lose a parent in such a horrible way, and to almost lose himself. He winced when he looked at my bandaged hand.

"Clara, I want you to know how sorry I am, for you and for . . . for . . ."

"Don't," I said. "You have nothing to be sorry for. You can't decide who your parents are, and . . . other things . . ."

He leaned in toward me, barely able to whisper what came next.

"It was only inside me for a moment, before we hit the water," Keith said. "But it was . . . it was sickening. In those few moments, everything I loved, I could have destroyed. I wanted to destroy it. That was the worst part. It wasn't like *The Exorcist*, or anything like that. It knew me. It didn't control my actions, it . . . it made me *want* to hurt everyone I cared about."

"I know," I said. "Don't ask me how, but I know. And I think we don't have to worry anymore. For now, anyway."

He nodded, slightly relieved. Anything more would take time.

We shared one final hug. When everyone was gone, my mother told me they wanted to keep me in the hospital one more night for observation..

"I got a room at a motel near the hospital," she said. "After tonight, you can stay there with me until your father gets out."

I knew it took an epic force of will for her not to ship me back to the city this instant, so I thanked her for it. We said goodbye for the night, and a little while later, they brought me dinner, which I only ate a bit of. The whole time I was worried about Hector. Then, just when I thought I would go crazy flipping channels on the stupid hospital TV, the nurse walked in.

"I just wanted to let you know, your friend is stable. He's out of the worst of it."

Joy flooded me, along with worry. I wanted to see for myself, to hold him tight and make sure.

"Can I—"

"He's resting," she said. "Maybe tomorrow he can see people."

She turned off the light in my room. I should have been exhausted after all I'd been through. I should have been able to sleep for a week, but I couldn't even close my eyes. I was thinking of Hector, and Dad, and of the King on the other side of the lake. Would he find a way back? I wasn't much of a prayer, but I prayed that wouldn't happen anyway. I thought of Zoe, free now, I hoped, but far away from me. I'd lost her as soon as I'd found her again, but I wouldn't take back anything I did.

I knew I wouldn't sleep a wink lying here, with the strip of bright antiseptic hospital light shining beneath the door. I slipped out of bed, feeling silly in my slippers and paper gown. This hospital wasn't that big, serving a rural area like this. It wasn't that hard to follow the signs and find the intensive care ward. I waited until the two nurses at the station were in the depths of conversation before I walked quickly by, like I knew exactly where I was going. I peered in room after room, until I finally saw a familiar mop of jet black hair and slipped into his room.

Somehow he looked older and younger at the same time, asleep like that. I wanted to wrap my arms around him, but his midsection was swaddled in bandages, and his arm was in an elevated cast. I reached out and touched his cheek, gentle as I could. His eyes fluttered open.

"Clara?"

"Shh—they'll catch us," I said. "I was so worried about you. Never do that again."

"They said an inch lower or higher and I would have been done," he said. His voice was weak, but his cocky smirk was still there. He glanced over at his arm in its heavy cast. "This is going to put a dent in my productivity."

"I'm serious. Do something like this again, and I'll finish you off myself."

He smiled, then he seemed to realize something, and he gave me a hard look.

"What do you care, you're leaving soon."

"Not yet, I'll be here while my dad gets better. Besides, I like it here."

His eyebrows shot up.

"Are you crazy? You do remember what we've been though over the past few days, right?"

"I like it here because of the people."

His smirk was back.

"Which people?"

I didn't say anything. Instead, I leaned in and kissed him. Our lips met just right this time, and I kissed him deeply, his tongue gently circling mine. His skin was hot, and I could feel the downy stubble on his chin.

"I'll come visit you," he said between kisses. "I don't care what excuse I have to make up."

"We can do this," I said. "I'll use any stupid chat app if it lets me see or hear you."

"I'll graduate early," he said. "I'll go to college in the city."

We went on kissing and making grandiose future plans until our mouths were sore. We only stopped when I realized it was only a matter of time before someone caught us. When we slowly pulled apart, he whispered "I love you" in my ear, and I felt my whole body tingle.

"I love you, too," I said.

We promised to talk later, to not stop talking, and I snuck back to my room like I was floating on the breeze.

Before I went back to bed, I stopped in the bathroom.

I stared at my reflection in the mirror, hoping it would stop being me, hoping I would catch a glimpse of Zoe's mischievous face, but all I saw was how bloodshot and haunted my eyes were. Wherever Zoe was, she wasn't here.

I was surprised at how that made me feel. I missed her—I would always miss her—but for the first time in my life, I felt whole. For so long, I had felt guilty for surviving when she was gone, like I couldn't exist without that half of myself. Now I knew the truth, and though it was stranger than I could imagine, it brought me more peace than I'd ever dared to hope for. I treasured those years I had with Zoe, and all she had done for me, but now I could move forward like never before. I reached out and touched the face in the mirror, content for the first time to see only me.

ACKNOWLEDGMENTS

There are so many people who made this possible, and nothing I say could express the depth of gratitude I feel—this is a dream come true. Thanks to my amazing agent, Jason Anthony of Massie & McQuilkin Literary Agents, and editor Nicole Frail, and huge thanks also to Alison Weiss and Amanda Panitch. This would not have been possible without any of them. Thanks to Tiffany Morris for an insightful sensitivity read. Thanks to Kate Gartner for the incredible cover, and everyone else at Skyhorse for making this book a reality.

Thanks to my teachers Justin Cronin, Erin McGraw, Lee K. Abbot, Michelle Herman, Lee Martin, and Kathy Fagan, and to the wonderful writers I was honored to work alongside at Ohio State. Thanks to Nicole Guijarro for believing in and encouraging my writing. Thanks to dear friends Mike Jeffries and Beverly Wang, Eric and Katka Leong, Doug Watson and Michelle Burke, Dave and Meg Levine, Maureen Traverse and Zack Leven, and Erin Ferencik, and to so many others.

Thanks to Neila Douglas for her energetic support. Thanks to my parents, Ed Scorza and Patricia Barth, and my brother, Andrew, for years of putting up with my writing and all the help they offered along the way, and of course special thanks to Melanie Douglas for far more than I could ever put into words.